Also by Shaun Sinclair

Blood Ties

The Crescent Crew Series
Street Rap
King Reece
Dirty Music

DIRTY MUSIC

WITHDRAWN

SHAUN SINCLAIR

Dafina
BOOKS

KENSINGTON BOOKS

www.kensingtonbooks.com

DAFINA BOOKS are published by

Kensington Publishing Corp.
119 West 40th Street
New York, NY 10018

ISBN-13: 978-1-4967-2865-4
ISBN-10: 1-4967-2865-3
First Kensington Trade Paperback Printing: October 2020

ISBN-13: 978-1-4967-2867-8 (ebook)
ISBN-10: 1-4967-2867-X (ebook)
First Kensington Electronic Edition: October 2020

10 9 8 7 6 5 4 3 2 1

Printed in the United States of America

Prologue

September 11, 2010

The Crown Coliseum was packed with mourners as the whole city turned out to pay their respects to the man who had ruled the Southeast with an iron fist. In life, he was both feared and respected as he was both ruthless and fair. In death, his status had been elevated to near sainthood in the same manner of Jesús Malverde—a patron saint to the trap lords of the street.

He had dug his way out of the trenches and clawed his way to the top of the underworld. Then, like a ghetto Robin Hood, he had blessed the city with his riches, providing shelter for single mothers, employing wayward fathers in his various enterprises, and turning young, broke men into rich *streetpreneurs*. The man had grown from a peasant to a king the hard way, then escaped into the world of legit enterprise like all true bosses do. Like many other gangsters seeking refuge in the business world, he had chosen the lucrative music business to reinvent himself.

In the music business, his reign had been short but impactful, shifting the course of the culture forever. He had brought the tactics learned in the streets into the boardroom, and his whole team had excelled. Then, at the height of his legitimate power, just when it seemed as if he had turned the corner, his life and legacy had been snatched away violently.

King Reece had been a man of diverse taste and relationships, and his mourning party reflected that. In attendance to pay their respects to their fallen comrade and business associates were a mixture of legendary street figures from all over the U.S. and entertainment moguls from the music and television industries. Of course, when a man of this stature was laid to rest, the requisite authorities were present as well. Among the mourners, everyone had their own agenda for attending the farewell service to the late King Reece.

For some of the street figures, they were there to pay their respects because they had done good business with the Crescent Crew, and their hearts were genuinely weeping for the organization. Other street figures were there to gauge the temperature of the room to see who their competition would be to take over and seize power in the vacuum created by King Reece's demise. The early word was that a foreign entity had killed King Reece, so there presumably wouldn't be a retaliatory domestic drug war. This meant that as soon as the ceremony was over it would be business as usual, and every up-and-coming crew would be scrambling for position.

For some of the mourners attending from the entertainment industry, they were there to be seen by the cameras; of course, as all press was good press. However, they were also there to confirm his demise. He had been in the industry for a short time, but he was already instilling terror in the hard-bottom shoes of the squares with his aggressive street tactics. It was alleged that he had given the order to strong-arm an artist from her contract and bring her over to his label. The move had shaken the industry up and planted fear in the hearts of executives. Although some of them admired his moxie, no one wanted that moxie aimed at them. For these executives, they were paying their respects to their fear.

Other executives and artists came out of respect to the fallen man's comrade and brother, Qwess. When news broke of King Reece's demise, it was reported that the brother of the multi-platinum, Grammy-winning rapper and mogul, Qwess, had been brutally murdered by a Mexican drug cartel. The news shook the industry and sent people scurrying. So close on the heels of Qwess being shot himself, the incident reignited suspicion that the Crescent Crew—the notoriously violent crime cartel that Qwess had co-founded with King Reece—was embroiled in a war for control of the East Coast's narcotics trade.

The last Crescent Crew war had been ignited when some rivals murdered Qwess's pregnant fiancée, Shauntay, on the night of Qwess's album release party. Rumor held that it was King Reece who had exacted retribution on the perpetrators and allowed Qwess to escape into the music industry and become a legend. Years later, King Reece had plead guilty to a five-year federal bid to save Qwess from harm once again. From behind the wall, King Reece exerted his considerable influence to keep the wolves of the music industry at bay.

At every juncture, King Reece had put his life on the line to make sure Qwess would win. Now, King Reece had run out of lives to give. He had made the ultimate sacrifice and paid the ultimate price, and Qwess was left to pick up the pieces. He was devastated. Broken. The last batch of industry insiders was there to help pick him up.

Qwess sat in the front row of the mourners with his head slightly bowed as the god, Born, summed up his eulogy. He was attempting to appear stoic, but his pain was etched on his face like a buck-fifty scar.

"Baby, are you okay?" Lisa Ivory whispered. She nudged

him gently and took his hand into hers. "I'm here for you. You don't have to go through this alone. Matter of fact, if you want to leave right now, we can."

Qwess offered a weak smile. "Nah, I have to do this. There is no one else to do it," he reminded her.

It was true. Qwess was the only family that King Reece had besides his Crescent Crew family and associates, who occupied the whole right side of the coliseum. There were nearly 500 soldiers and associates in the building to see their leader away, and they wouldn't accept anyone eulogizing their god except Qwess.

"I know, baby, but all these people here . . . they didn't know Reece like that," Lisa pointed out as she craned her slender neck to look around the room. "I mean, they're vultures and opportunists."

"For sure," Qwess agreed. He shrugged. "That's what they're here for, but I have to do me regardless, so here goes."

Qwess rose and adjusted his Cartier glasses. Slowly, methodically, he ascended to the podium and surveyed the room before him. There were easily more than 2,000 people in attendance, a mini concert. These days Qwess would get upward of $100,000 to entertain a crowd this size. But today he wasn't here to entertain. He was here to celebrate a life.

To the back of Qwess was a huge screen stretching the length of the wall. On the screen was a montage of Reece's life playing on repeat. Qwess turned and watched the screen as he gathered his thoughts. Each slide evoked a different memory of his brother. There were pictures of Reece in the early days of the Crew, posing in front of his very first slant-nose Porsche 911. Qwess chuckled to himself as he recalled chastising Reece about his flamboyant ways. Of course Reece hadn't listened, and the rest of the slides proved this as each image grew more and more outlandish.

The final slide marinated on the screen for a few moments,

and this was the slide that encapsulated King Reece's life the most. It was a picture of King Reece posing poolside at his mansion draped in gold and diamonds. His arm was draped around the neck of his lion cub.

The king of the concrete with the king of the jungle.

Qwess stepped to the podium, opened his mouth, and eulogized his comrade with the things that had made him a very rich man.

His words.

As Qwess gave a speech reminiscent of a hip-hop Martin Luther King, he couldn't keep his eyes off the twin caskets below him. In the glass-topped caskets lay King Reece and his woman, Katrina Destiny Hill.

Destiny, the woman who had been the Achilles heel in King Reece's life, was being buried with him. The decision to share the funerals nearly birthed a civil war among the Crescent Crew because the other members weren't as forgiving as King Reece. However, Qwess and Born had flexed their power and issued an edict for them to stand down. It was an O.G. call that only one man could've made. The call wasn't liked, but it was respected.

Qwess kept it simple and paid homage to the good man that King Reece was. He spoke about the good things, like how he single-handedly stimulated the economy with his generous spending and his multiple businesses. He left out the part about how he simultaneously pumped his powerful poison through the streets with his monopolization of the drug trade. He highlighted how King Reece had taken on the task of uplifting single mothers. He left out the part about his torture chamber in the country where he disciplined his adversaries. For nearly an hour, Qwess waxed poetic about his comrade, repainting the narrative of a sociopath. When he was done, he had whipped the room up into a perfect mixture of sorrow and joy. He had achieved his goal.

What Qwess couldn't possibly have known is that King Reece's death was the impetus for an impending mutiny that would tear down everything he had built with the Crescent Crew.

Things were about to get dirty.

Chapter 1

May 26, 2012
I-40 West, Oklahoma

Qwess downshifted to third gear and the V12 behind him roared like a lion attacking its prey. He floored the accelerator, and the Pagani Zonda R rocketed forward in the left lane of I-40, as he whizzed by other cars doing over 120 miles an hour! He was on the second to last leg of the Gumball 3000, and he was having the time of his life.

The Gumball 3000 was an annual race (disguised as a rally) that globe-trotted to different countries every year. Each year the rally grew bigger and bigger, and the locations more distant. Qwess was a regular staple on the circuit, and he especially loved the routes in Europe as they allowed him to thrash out his stable of exotic cars. Back in the day, he would bring members of his Crew along and allow them to run his cars in the rally along with him. Imagine, wild youngsters barreling through exotic locations in funny-shaped cars. However, over the years, his circle had grown considerably smaller the more successful he became.

This year the rally was being run in the good ole U.S. of A., and Qwess was rolling dolo in the Zonda. Times like this were what Qwess craved the most. His superstar status had relegated him to becoming a prisoner to fame, so whipping his supercar out in the boonies was his definition of time away from it all. He had always been a car nut, so running the rally was his idea of heaven on earth. The Gumball had stopping points along the route. At each stopping point the participants would park their cars for the night and attend lavish parties thrown by the event organizers. The stopping point for this night was in Vegas.

Qwess spotted a Mercedes SLR McLaren in his rearview challenging him. The car was bright silver and resembled a shiny bullet barreling toward his rear. Qwess pushed the Zonda into fourth gear and floored it. The engine wailed like only a V-twizzy could and the car leaped from 130 to 160 in a millisecond. But the SLR was right there with him every step of the way.

Suddenly, the SLR pulled up beside him at 160 miles per hour, and the tinted window glided down. Qwess's eyes darted from the road to the window easing down. He tried to make out the driver of the half-million-dollar machine, but all he could see was long blond hair whipping in the wind. Her jeweled hand waved at him, and that was all he could see before his superior machine pulled away, leaving the SLR in the dust.

In his rearview Qwess saw a bloodred Lamborghini Aventador catching up to him. The car was moving so fast it was nearly invisible as it drew up beside him. Qwess's top was peeled back in the Zonda, so the occupants of the Lambo could see him clearly. However, the Lambo was tinted out as black as midnight. Qwess figured it was probably a sheikh from the Middle East or one of their heirs starstruck from seeing a bona fide mogul in the flesh. Qwess decided to put on for the spectator. He cranked the audio up to the max and allowed an unreleased track to bleed out into the air as he revved the engine on the Zonda. The Aventador revved its engine and matched Qwess bar for bar, and the two V12s made a beautiful melody out on the road.

Suddenly, the Aventador swerved into Qwess's lane, nearly sideswiping him. He stomped on the brake and recovered just in time to read the license plate of the Aventador.

It read: *Diamante!*

Qwess fumed as he readjusted the Zonda along with his mood. However, this was his time and he wasn't going to allow anything to dampen his mood. He retrieved a freshly rolled joint and slowed down to fire it up. The wind whipping through the luxury confines of the car was making his task difficult. (Because Qwess wasn't really a smoker it took him a while to learn he had to cup the flame, but he eventually got it.) Once his mission was complete, he dropped the throttle and sped off into the desert.

Destination: Las Vegas.

The MGM Grand was Ground Zero for the most lavish party of the Gumball. Over 10,000 people from all over the world packed into one large building was turning into a movie. Texas oil tycoons mingled with Middle Eastern oil barons. Athletes partied with rock stars. Models partied with gold diggers—well, *they* were actually one and the same.

With entry into the Gumball costing nearly $100,000, it was more than just a rally. It was actually a worldwide networking event for the ultra-rich. The parties in each city every night after the conclusion of the day's events were full of wheeling and dealing, lewd, lascivious acts, and overall fun. The Gumball was the next level of the game.

Qwess was escorted into the party with only his right-hand man and personal protector, Hulk, leading the way. Hulk was one of the few remaining members of the Crescent Crew. He had been Qwess's bodyguard when Qwess ruled the streets at the helm of the Crescent Crew and he had clung to his side as Qwess forayed into the music industry. Hulk's loyalty was unparalleled and without question. He lived for Qwess and would quickly die for him too. In fact, Hulk's twin brother, Samson, was pulling time for Qwess at the moment.

"Damn, this party is all that," Hulk yelled over the Pharrell track quaking the room, as he escorted Qwess to their perch high above everyone so they could have a bird's eye view of everything.

Qwess was sauced up on his walk up. He was rich-casual and cool in ripped, distressed denim jeans, Giuseppe Zanotti sneakers and a white satin button up with the top flayed open. He flicked the Richard Mille on his wrist as he nodded to his comrade.

"Absolutely, my brother. Absolutely. This is what it's about, working hard and playing harder."

"Damn right!" Hulk agreed.

Qwess took a spot at the tabletop and bobbed his head to the music. He was allowing himself to get lost in the vibe. Losing his best friend, King Reece, forced him to put things in perspective. He had the world and never paused enough to enjoy it. Since King Reece's untimely death he made a vow to himself to do better.

Qwess scanned the room, and something caught his attention on one of the dance floors. A woman with a blond streak of hair was bobbing up and down, flinging wildly, having a grand time. Qwess's eyes followed south past the mane of hair and drank in all of her curves, stuffed tastefully inside a peach bodysuit. Her light skin glowed beneath the kaleidoscope of lights streaming through the room. As if she felt him observing her, she spun around and locked eyes with Qwess. They smiled in unison, and she began teasing him, writhing her body seductively, rubbing her curves, arching her back like a cat in heat.

Qwess licked his lips and sipped his drink as he enjoyed

the tease. He tapped Hulk to allow him to share in the show. After all, it wasn't no fun if the homies can't have none. Hulk shook his head and grimaced as if her beauty was so pure it hurt him to view it. Meanwhile, the beauty continued her show.

As Qwess and Hulk watched the woman put on her show, a huge commotion erupted by the entrance. They tore their eyes away from the woman and saw a mob of people pushing their way through the crowd. As the crowd parted, a sea of men wearing all red materialized. There were no less than twenty of them in all, following lockstep behind a behemoth of a man leading the way. The man cut an intimidating presence, all height, muscle, and jewelry, the highlight of his ensemble being an impressive twenty-carat charm in the shape of a diamond draped across his chest.

The man bogarted his way through the crowd until he pulled right up on the beauty that was tantalizing Qwess and Hulk. He saw her and followed her gaze right up to Qwess. Qwess returned the man's stare with a smirk, and the giant saluted him. Qwess snubbed the salute and turned his back to that crowd. Waiting for him in his area was a tall man with a nose so big he resembled an eagle.

Hulk tensed up and stood in front of Qwess.

The tall man raised his palms in surrender. "Calm down, big guy. I come in peace."

Qwess peeked his head around Hulk. "Well, you better speak fast then. State your name and your business."

The man smiled. "Qwess, I can assure you no one in this building means you any harm. This is Gumball—we're all wealthy!"

The man had a point. Qwess relaxed a bit. "You got a point there."

"Sure I do! I'm Liam Cohen; I always make the right point. Sit down, let's have a drink and talk some business."

Qwess obliged the man. They sat down and popped a couple bottles of Krug Rosé champagne. Meanwhile, Hulk stood guard over Qwess's shoulder.

"So, I hear you're quite the car collector," Liam noted. "That's your Zonda outside, and I hear you have a Huayra on order too. Then, of course your cherished LaFerrari, and fleet of Lambos."

Qwess nodded. "My Huayra is actually done. I couldn't get it shipped here in time for the rally," he corrected, referring to the new model by Pagani, of which only a hundred were made. The car was valued at over $2 million.

Liam chuckled and kicked his right leg over his left knee. "Impressive indeed. A man that has it all."

Qwess took a swig of his champagne and shrugged. "Eh, I do all right."

Liam chuckled. "This guy," he said to no one in particular. "Well, let's toast to success!"

The men clanged their glasses, and Qwess spoke next. "So, Liam, you say your name is? You seem to know so much about me, but I don't know you at all."

"And that's normally how I prefer to keep things. I like to stay behind the scenes and let the guys like you peacock and hog the spotlight. I don't like to come out much, unless I need to."

"I can relate."

"Yeah, I know. You like to stay in the shadows yourself these days. A lot has been going on in your life. Lots of tragedy and misfortune."

As Liam spoke Qwess was beginning to see this wasn't just a casual visit among Gumballers. Liam seemed to have come over with intent. With all that Qwess had been going through lately, he had yet to discern if Liam was friend or foe.

"Again, Liam, you seem to know so much about me. Why don't you tell me who you are?"

Liam sighed and waved his hand dismissively as if his identity was not of importance. "I *used* to be a very big figure in the entertainment industry."

"Used to be?" Qwess fished his mental Rolodex for a name. He knew of all the major players in the entertainment industry, and this man's name was foreign to him. "I don't recall hearing your name in my circles, and I've done it all. Music, film, books."

"Well, someone like you wouldn't know of someone like me—no disrespect intended."

"Ahhh, you definitely sound like you turning on Disrespect Street to me," Qwess pointed out.

"Not intentional, my friend. I can assure you."

"Okay . . ." Qwess spread his hands, waiting for him to go on. "I'm listening."

"So, I'm in the entertainment industry, on the distribution and delivery side. Well, I was a partner in the largest music distribution network in the world, but the climate of the music world is changing, so recently I cashed out."

"You cashed out?"

"Yeah, I sold my stake in the company."

Qwess nodded and stroked his chin. At his level, when people managed to get close to him, they always had a ploy or an idea to separate him from his money.

"Why on earth would you do that?" Qwess asked.

"Because I'm a visionary. I see things before others do, and sometimes that forces you to be the only man in the room. You understand that, I'm sure."

"Yeah, I do, but let's stop talking in riddles. I thought you said you wanted to talk business. I'm actually on vacation, but I obliged you because you seem to be an interesting man. But my patience is getting short."

Liam sighed heavily. "Fair enough. I'll get right to it."

"Good."

"Qwess, simply put, trouble is coming your way. The Linda Swansen incident? It's not going anywhere."

Upon hearing Linda Swansen's name, Qwess perked up. Linda Swansen was a music executive who had hired someone to kill him in retaliation for him enacting "Crew Business" to finagle his vice president's wife out of a bad contract.

"People in high places have blackballed you. Everyone in the industry has deemed you persona non grata. They have all joined forces to break you."

Qwess was amused. With the money he and his wife had amassed, combined with the fortune King Reece had left behind, he was *alllllll* the way up.

Liam knew that smirk all too well. "I know you're a very wealthy man, but there is more than one meaning to 'breaking a man.' Business is not about money; it's about relationships. Money is just the reward."

"Touché."

"Fortunately for you, I have burned some profitable relationships, and I'm ready to forge new ones."

"Well, I'm sure you're not an altruist, so what does this have to do with me?"

"Qwess, if you are willing to embrace technology, I can make you the first hip-hop billionaire."

Qwess smiled. "Now you're talking my language."

Chapter 2

Fayetteville, North Carolina

The man slid through the door of the lounge off Bragg Boulevard with his chest poked out and looked up at the moon. He was a bit tipsy from the alcohol he consumed, but he was absolutely drunk off power.

The man looped his arm around the tall Latina to his left and motioned for the big man in front of him to lead the way to the Toyota Tundra sitting tall on a customized lift kit. As he followed his escort he stumped his pointy, ostrich-skinned boot on the pavement. The blunder elicited a giggle from the beauty under his arm.

They made it to the truck, and the man helped the lady get into the back. Excited about diving between the hot young woman's thighs, he turned to rush to the passenger side of the truck so they could leave.

He never saw the black-on-black Durango truck creeping up alongside him.

The passenger side window of the Durango eased down,

and a long, silenced barrel extended out past the tinted window.

"Psst, yo, my man . . ." someone whispered.

The man turned around just in time to see the barrel of the automatic weapon light up. A split second later bullets flipped from the AK-47 and ripped into his upper torso. His body slammed against the door of the truck, pinning his bodyguard inside. More shots lifted him up in the air before his body crumpled to the pavement on the driver's side of the Tundra. As he lay on the ground shaking and convulsing, four men poured from the Durango and surrounded the Tundra. In unison, they opened fire with silenced automatic weapons, killing the beautiful woman inside. The bodyguard attempted to even things up, but before he could palm the pistol underneath his arm, two bullets slammed into his forehead and exited out the back of his skull, leaving golf ball–sized holes.

The shooters scanned the area for more enemies and smiled when they saw that they had eliminated all opps. They stood guard on each side of the Tundra while the front passenger door of the Durango slowly opened.

Bone stepped from the Durango and stood tall over the Latino man writhing in pain on the pavement. Bone aimed the AK-47 at the man's head.

"Ole badass, Chabo. You really thought we wouldn't catch up with yo' ass?" Bone taunted. "It took us a while, but I swore to god that I wouldn't rest until you do."

It was true. Bone had vowed to King Reece to track down his killers. Although he had learned that Chabo *and* Gil had fired the fatal shots that eventually took King Reece out, Gil had been confirmed dead at the scene of the crime inside the bunker that day.

Chabo, however, had managed to escape death. He survived a chest shot at point-blank range inflicted by King Reece. Instead of laying low, he had worn his wound like a badge of honor and turned all the way up. His superstitious comrades believed that he had been protected by Santa Muerte (the patron saint of death) that day, and surviving an attack by the infamous King Reece had elevated him to don status. He quickly used the new reputation to pad his riches, traveling in and out of the States building a new team on both sides of the border. Little did he know that half of the Black criminal world was looking for him. King Reece was beloved and re-spected by all. The irony of the streets' code of honor was that if a Black gang had killed King Reece, it would have been tragic, but not deemed disrespectful. The fact that a Mexican gang had murdered him was like a smack in the face to every hustler in the hood. So hustlers from state to state were more than eager to collect the bounty placed on Chabo's head by the Crescent Crew. It had taken nearly two years, but now Chabo's luck had run out.

Bone kicked Chabo in the ass with his heavy Timberland boot. "Turn yo' punk ass over, motherfucker!"

Chabo clutched one of his wounds in his chest and grunted, "¡Mierda! ¿Quién eres tú?"

Bone smiled, pleased that he understood Chabo. In his quest to track Chabo down, he had even learned a little bit of Spanish.

"I'm your death angel, nigga! The last fucking thing you will see in this life," Bone snarled. Suddenly, something around Chabo's neck caught Bone's eye. "Wait, hold up, I know that's not what I think it is?"

Bone leaned down and gripped the medallion hanging on the end of the necklace around Chabo's neck. He inspected it and, sure enough, it was a gold-and-diamond emblem of the coat of arms for the Crescent Crew. However, a crude slash of red rubies was etched over the middle of the medallion. The implication was clear and full of disrespect.

Bone was livid!

"You disrespectful wetback motherfucker!!!" Bone roared. He crashed his boot into Chabo's head and chest repeatedly.

That's when he felt the bulletproof vest Chabo wore. "Oh, you a slick-ass, huh? Bet a few of them rounds from that chopper still lit that ass up, though."

Bone kicked Chabo in his mouth, and blood poured onto the pavement. He smiled a sinister smile. "You know what? I actually prefer it this way. You gonna pay for what you did, motherfucker. Aye, pop that hatch in the back," Bone called out to one of his shooters. "Once again, it's on!"

Chapter 3

Miami, Florida

The first time Flame laid eyes on Sasha Beaufont he knew she was going to be his. He just didn't know that getting her would cost so much.

The first time he actually met her was down in Miami for the SoBe Fashion Show. He was scheduled to perform his new ballad with Saigon. *Yes, ballad!* Flame was about to drop an R&B album.

He had done the rap game to death and needed something else to challenge him. No one could have guessed that singing would be his new thang. Nevertheless, here he was about to explode on some thugged-out R&B shit!

So far, the industry had embraced his new foray, so he was given carte blanche while in Miami. Even though his net worth was estimated to be around $10 million, the sponsors of the show still provided everything free. His suite at the Delano, exotic transportation, food, liquor, drugs . . . name it and he had it laid at his feet in spades. This was the next level of the game—superstar status. Li'l Joey had come a long way from shooting craps on Bunce Road.

Flame hadn't rolled with a large entourage since back in the day when his homies had accompanied him to Myrtle Beach for Bike Week. They had run a train on some white girls and caught a statutory rape charge for their heroics. The incident had nearly cost Flame his freedom *and* his career. He learned from that day about the importance of having the right circle around him. For the Miami trip, he was only rolling with his personal assistant, Freeman, his bodyguard and best friend, 8-Ball, and one of the models he had personally selected to debut his fall clothing collection. Her name was Anetral and she was bad as fuck! Six feet even, smooth caramel skin, cheeks sharp enough to cut diamonds, and long, wavy hair like a black Rapunzel, the chick was baaaad.

For Flame, the only bad thing about her was she was vegetarian, as in no meat, as in carpet-muncher. Other words: pure lesbian.

Flame's crew was checking into the hotel when a big, chromed-out SUV rolled up, obstructing his view from where he sat in the back of a white Rolls-Royce Ghost. 8-Ball reached for his piece just in case some funny shit was about to go down, but the arrival was harmless. Two big black dudes popped out the back of the SUV and guided a black Bentley limo into an illegal parking space right in front of the hotel. Behind the Bentley was another truck identical to the first one. When the vehicles drifted to a stop, Kim Rawls, Monica Wilson, and Sasha Beaufont slid from the back of the car looking like the supergroup they were.

Collectively, they were known as the chart-topping girl group Kismet, the heir apparent to DC. Kismet had been killing the game for the past two years and weren't showing any signs of slowing down, and they were just as fine as they were talented.

As their hired muscle hustled them inside the hotel, the

women strutted right past Flame's open window. Perfumed tits and ass soothed his nostrils as Kim and Monica breezed past in short shorts and thin tank tops. He watched as Sasha lingered behind them a bit. As the lead singer and undisputed star of the group, she possessed a little more clout than the other members. It showed in her confident stride and high fashion that she knew she was the shit. Where the others wore sandals, Sasha rocked silver stiletto heels. Her jean shorts were even fitting a little tighter, showcasing that famous banging body. Flame's eyes zoomed right between Sasha's legs where her fat camel toe was poking out.

Flame shook his head and called out her name just as she walked past his open window. "Sasha!" Sasha whirled around and looked right into his A/X sunglasses. Flame lowered his shades, licked his lips like LL, and said, "Wassup, gurl."

She squinted her light brown eyes to get a closer look at him while her security mugged him like he had done something wrong, like he was a commoner, like he wasn't a star himself.

Recognition flashed in Sasha's eyes and she spoke—sang really. "Heeey, Flame."

Flame smiled when Sasha cooed his name. It felt like it belonged on her lips. Like it was natural. Like he was the only man that existed in her world.

Then just like that, she was gone, disappearing inside the hotel, leaving him with the smell of her scent and the vision of her perfectly round ass popping out the bottom of those jean shorts.

He made up his mind right then that he was going to fuck Sasha Beaufont.

Later that night, Flame tore shit up on stage, ripping through his extensive catalog of rap hits while models prowled the catwalk around him showcasing dark denim and fur jean suits from his fall collection. A few buff, bald-headed cats with

that I'll-take-something or I-just-got-outta-jail-for-taking-
something look modeled the pieces for the fellas, while Anetral featured fits for the ladies.

When the time came for Flame to debut his new R&B
single, all the lights in the house dropped completely. Seconds
later, the spotlight shone on him standing in the middle of the
catwalk, head down, shirtless, exposing the huge "Fayettenam" tattoo that stretched the entire length of his upper back.
A long iced-out A. B. P. chain dangled all the way down past
his ripped abdomen to where his hands held the mic over his
erection.

The house full of ladies went berserk!

Flame loved this shit! Performing was like sex for him,
their praise the ultimate orgasm. It was as if he was having sex
with every lady in the crowd simultaneously, and just as always happened when he was performing, tremors slithered
through his body, and *that* feeling consumed him.

The deep-bass beat (produced by Qwess) thumped from
the speakers as Anetral came out in a red chain-mail shorts
jumper with a plunging neckline and no sleeves. Her beautiful
hair was hidden beneath the hood. Like a panther, she stalked
the stage in black leather stiletto boots that caressed her thighs.
A red satin flame snaked from her knee down to the heel of
the boots. Anetral seduced the audience with her sexy sashay
until she reached Flame, still standing center stage with his
head bowed as if he was in prayer.

Anetral embraced Flame from behind. He spread his arms
wide and tilted his head back like he was being crucified. The
crowd snapped to silence and gave Flame their full attention.
It was moments like this he lived for. These were the high-
lights of his stardom. Not the foreign cars, the exotic trips, or
high five-figure concert bookings. It was this, touching the
people, that gave Flame purpose.

Flame gripped the gold mic and belted out the first single
from his new album, an up-tempo R&B cut about getting

freaky any place the feeling inspired him to. It was pretty much similar content from his rap hits, but he was singing it this time—and singing it well. His song was a mixture of Too Short and Jodeci, but his performance was all vintage Flame.

By the time he sang the last line about sliding his tongue through the crack of a woman's ass, three chicks in the front row threw their wet panties on the stage. One pair hit Flame right in the face while he was singing. He calmly moved the mic aside and took a good whiff of the panties. Then he held them high in the air for everyone to see and slid his tongue all inside the seat of the panties, tasting her juices that she'd left for him.

The crowd went insane!

He had them then. His voice could've been as weak as Ashanti's and they would have still supported him.

Anetral released Flame and began trotting seductively across the stage, while tossing alluring looks over her shoulder. Flame trailed Anetral's footsteps, continuing to rock the house.

Flame finished his song just as Anetral disappeared behind the curtains, leaving Flame alone on the stage. The music screeched to a halt and was instantly replaced by a keyed-up piano loop. A steady snare drum laid underneath the piano marking tempo as Flame glided back to the center of the cat-walk as smooth as Mike in his prime.

Suddenly, the energy from the audience shifted a bit. The vibe from the crowd let him know this was the moment everyone had been anticipating, to see if the boy Flame could really blow. Flame took a deep breath and addressed his audience.

"Thank you all for coming out tonight to witness my re-birth. Ya know, I got a lot of things to get off my chest . . ." He paused and closed his eyes to absorb the crowd's essence. He took a second to let his words penetrate their minds before he continued. "Like love . . . Anybody ever been in love?" Screams from the crowd greeted him. "I mean really in love?"

More screams.

"Well, maybe you can relate to this song, then. I'ma break it down like this . . ."

Flame dug down deep in his diaphragm and found a note that killed any doubts about him being official. He held the note, a real crisp tenor, for about ten seconds, then blessed them with a ballad about reciprocity in love. He hadn't written this song, because he didn't know shit about no reciprocity in love. In his life, women were used as objects of conquest or tools of pleasure, nothing more. The hottest songwriting duo in the industry, a down-low gay couple, had penned this hit, and Flame was killing it!

Words couldn't describe the reaction of the crowd. Words couldn't describe how he felt from the reaction of the crowd. The adoration felt so good his dick went brick.

As Flame continued to woo the crowd, working his way across the stage, catching eye contact with the ladies, and popping his hips, he saw her. Sasha Beaufont. Sitting in the front row with her *amigas*, Kim Rawls and Monica Wilson.

Flame quickly made his way over to their side of the stage, still pouring honey from his lips. He hesitated at the end of the stage for a second, and then stepped down into the front row, right in Kim's face, his crotch at eye level. She couldn't miss his hard meat pressing against his linen drawstring pants threatening to escape and spew venom everywhere as he grinded his hips to the slow beat. In his peripheral vision he saw Sasha cutting her eyes at him, blushing, and knew his plan was working.

Once Flame was satisfied that his quest for Sasha's attention was in effect, he returned to the stage to complete his set. As he completed his performance, every now and then he spared a glance in Sasha's direction to ensure she was still enthralled. Sure enough, Sasha couldn't tear her eyes away from Flame's sweaty body. He saw her squirming in her seat, losing the battle of attempting to be uninterested.

Flame's performance carried him back over to Sasha and

her crew. He couldn't keep his eyes off her, and the more he stared, the more he was in awe of Sasha. Her brown hair was hanging long and straight, and her juicy lips were shining harder than the chrome on his Aston Martin. Her titties exploded from her tight white tank top, and he could clearly see she wasn't wearing a bra. She was just his type of chick, divaed-out, but still hood enough to bob her head to his dirty cuts. Flame decided right then that she was too fly to be with anybody else but him.

Just as Flame was completing his set, he saw the crowd part like someone had pulled out a gun. He braced himself for a stampede, but it was a false alarm. Turned out, it was none other than the six-foot, four-inch, 285-pound Tyshawn "Diamond" Barker making his grand entrance. Diamond was CEO of Diamond World Music Group, aka the most popular music executive in the world. He also pulled double duty as Sasha Beaufont's boyfriend of five years, and rumored fiancé.

From the stage, Flame watched Diamond kindly remove Monica from her seat and sit down next to Sasha. Sasha said something slick to him, but Diamond pulled her into his lap and planted a wet one right on her lips. Monica quickly took Sasha's abandoned seat and continued to watch Flame get busy.

Flame was a little pissed that Diamond had swept some of Flame's shine in his direction so he was determined to finish off in a grand fashion to remind him, and everyone else, this was his show.

Flame signaled for the DJ to mute the music, then he locked eyes with a thick Latina in the front row. While all eyes were on him—sweaty body, jewels glistening, fresh Caesar, hard dick—he pointed right at the Selena lookalike and wailed out the last line of the song. He held the last note 'til he was damn near out of breath. Just when he felt like he was going to pass out, he stopped singing and blew a kiss at Selena. She fainted, and everybody screamed.

His mission was accomplished.

Flame retreated backstage, applause and cheers at his back.

As he waded through the throng of scantily clad models and gay stylists backstage, he ran right into Freeman. Freeman passed Flame a handful of invitations to an after-party being held at a mansion on Star Island. This was the way invitations were extended in the big leagues. No rowdy radio promos, no ads in magazines; just a predetermined list of who's who, and a method to reach those people. Flame was in the upper echelon of the music business now. He was the epitome of the Who's Who and he loved every bit of his stardom.

He greeted a few more people (and eyed a few more models) then gathered 8-Ball and Anetral. They dipped back to the Delano to prepare for the party.

Little did he know that party would change his life forever.

Chapter 4

Atlanta, Georgia, Midtown

Qwess swiped through Instagram's explorer page and saw that Flame was trending. He went over to Twitter and saw the same thing. His performance in Miami was trending on all the platforms. Qwess smiled. *The li'l nigga made good on his promise*, he thought.

For years, Flame had been pleading to Qwess to drop an R&B album. Qwess had to admit that Flame could blow, but singing was not what made the dough for Flame. Flame had amassed millions for ABP with his brash delivery, and Qwess was reluctant to divert the gravy train, but when a Canadian artist flipped the whole game on its head, he gave Flame the go-ahead. Judging from the response of social media—the new barometer for success—his gamble had paid off.

Qwess placed his phone face down on his desk and shuffled some papers. The conversation he had had with Liam a few weeks ago in Vegas was still reverberating in his head like a pinball machine. The numbers he was talking were astounding! He had even sent some papers to validate his estimates. For sure, the game was changing with the rise of digital streaming, but Qwess didn't see it affecting things this much.

Qwess flipped his television on CNN to see the latest news, and the top story hit close to home:

> *"Early this morning, authorities discovered the severed head of the alleged leader of a burgeoning Mexican drug cartel, Chabo "El Rey" Guzman. Guzman is reputed to be the leader of the violent Reyes Cartel, which operated between Fayetteville, North Carolina, and Michoacán, Mexico. According to reports, the Reyes Cartel seized control of the Southeastern drug trade after they wrested power from the hands of the Crescent Crew, led by its deceased leader, King Reece. After King Reece's death, El Rey allegedly opened a drug pipeline from the Carolinas directly to Mexico, which shifted the balance of power in the United States. Now, with the death of El Rey confirmed, authorities fear we may be in the midst of a violent drug war . . ."*

Photos of King Reece's mugshot flashed on the screen, followed by video footage of his funeral. Next, they showed a photo of Chabo. Seeing the photo of Chabo filled Qwess with mixed emotions. On the one hand, knowing the men that killed his brother were now resting in the afterlife gave him a sense of relief. On the other hand, he knew this murder would inevitably bring more heat to his door. In the court of public opinion—and the legal courts—he would forever be inextricably entwined with the Crescent Crew. No matter how high he climbed the ladder in the entertainment world, he just couldn't live down his past.

On cue, Qwess's personal cell phone rang with a 910 area code. He closed the door to his office and answered the call.

"*As salaam alayka!*"

"*Wa alaykum salaam*, Akhi. *Qisas* has been carried out by my hands. Our comrade can rest now. Stay tuned."

The line went dead. Qwess shook his head at the audacity of it all. That was Bone on the other end, personally claiming responsibility for Chabo. *Qisas* meant "an eye for an eye" in Islam. Carrying out retribution had become Bone's thing in the Crew. He had made his bones in the Crescent Crew by murdering a cop in cold blood for killing one of their members, Jersey Ali. Now, with King Reece dead and Samson incarcerated, Bone had become the acting leader of the Crescent Crew. He could have had any of them carry out revenge, but he chose to do it himself. Years ago, Qwess would have welcomed and commended this type of ambition and loyalty. Now, he was disgusted by it. Years of good living had softened him up and taken him out of touch with the harsh realities of life in the streets.

Qwess sighed, leaned back in his chair, and massaged his temples. Life was coming at him fast. His number one act was cutting up, his wife was clamoring for more of his time, and he was still reeling from the fallout of his incident with Linda Swansen. Liam wasn't lying about him being blackballed in the industry. It was like once he learned of the plot, he immediately felt the effects of it. People whom he had been doing business with for years were not returning his calls.

A soft knock at the door awakened Qwess from his thoughts.

"Yeah, come in," he said.

His administrative assistant peeked her head in the door and whispered, "There is someone here to see you."

"Who?"

"I don't know. Looks like police. Well, he doesn't look like a police officer, but he's persistent like one."

Qwess sighed. He was used to the routine by now. Every time someone from the Crew performed a heinous act, the authorities came to pay him a visit to shake him up.

"Let him in," Qwess said.

A few seconds later a slim black man in a tailored suit walked through the door with a briefcase under his arm.

"Qwess?"

"You know who I am, otherwise, you wouldn't be here, right?"

The man chuckled. "You have a point there," he said, checking out the digs in Qwess's office. He walked over to the glass wall overlooking the city. "This is a nice office here."

Qwess huffed. "Yeah, but whoever you are, I'm sure you didn't come all the way here to compliment my taste. What's your business here?"

"Ahhh . . ." The man turned to Qwess and fished for something in his briefcase. He retrieved a stack of papers and slapped them on Qwess's desk. He stood tall and issued Qwess a stern look. "You've been served."

"Served? Served with what?"

The man turned to walk out. "Read it; it's all there."

The man closed the door, and Qwess shuffled through the papers. Apparently, it was a lawsuit of some sort. Qwess read the caption and saw his name. *He* was being sued by AMG Recording and Distribution for "tortious interference." They were asking for a whopping $75 million!

Qwess couldn't believe this shit. He opened his phone and dialed his super attorney, Malik Shabazz.

The theme was Greek Bacchanalian, Flame learned. Flame never claimed to be the smartest man in the world, but he had been to Greece so he could personally attest that the Greeks were some of the freakiest bastards in the world. Therefore he wasn't too thrilled about attending a Greek-themed event. In Miami too? There was bound to be trouble.

However, Flame didn't want to be a spoiler for the remainder of his staff he'd flown in earlier that day to attend the event. A lot of them were interns and low-wage salary workers he had recruited to do grunt work for the launch of his fashion line. He wanted them to get the total industry experience just like his mentor, Qwess, had done for him years ago. That experience had whetted Flame's appetite more than ever and motivated him to be all that he could be. He was hoping this would motivate his staff to hump for him the same way.

In the theme of the Greeks, all attendees were required to wear a toga to gain entry to the party. Flame wasn't having it. He tried really hard to swallow his pride and don the toga required for entry to the party, but it just didn't fit a man of his stature. He was FLAME, gotdammit! He represented one of the hardest towns in the South: Fayettenam. He wouldn't be able to go back to the block if a pic of him in one of those things was posted on the Internet. He decided the toga was out. Instead, he freaked some white linen slacks and a hoe-beater with some all-white 1's and rolled out like that.

Waiting outside for Flame and his crew were two white Rolls-Royce Ghosts. His young staff climbed in one, and he slid in the other with his vets.

As the luxury land yachts glided to Star Island, the sights of Miami were captivating. They must have passed a dozen drop-top Lambos—real Lambos with scissor-style doors, not that budget shit. They saw just as many dropped Ferraris too, and a couple of Enzos. Of course, the lovely Latinas were there as well. 8-Ball was so gassed on the lovely Latinas teetering around in heels and dental floss with all their beautiful curves jiggling around like warm Jell-O he nearly lost his mind. Flame couldn't believe it. He was disgusted. All the pussy 8–Ball had gotten over the years, and he was still a cum-freak. But hey, beautiful women never got old, even for the rich and famous.

Attempting to steal 8-Ball's mind from the gutter, Flame tapped him.

"You see how ya boy Diamond tried to hog my shine?" Flame asked.

"Hell yeah! My nigga came in and everybody started taking pictures of him like he was performing an' shit," 8-Ball agreed. "And did you see his broad? Dayum! She baaad, fam. Word!"

"Yeah, she is," Flame admitted. He wanted to tell his friend how she was checking for him on the low, but he knew that 8-Ball felt all women wanted him. Most of 'em did, in his mind.

"That nigga Diamond lucky, falling up in that pussy every night. Bet it's pretty too," 8-Ball wondered aloud. "Monica straight too, though. You know she checking for me, right?"

"Yeah?"

"Yeeeeah!"

"Get you, fam. Get you," Flame said, encouraging him to go for it. 8-Ball wasn't the most handsome dude, but being next to Flame had upgraded his confidence.

Up front, Anetral was chirping away on her cell like a bird, oblivious to Flame sizing up the smooth skin seeping from beneath her toga. Flame was plotting on the gay beauty. He was praying that she would relapse on her diet. If she did, he would plug her ass like a dam. He just knew that she had a good shot between all that thickness, and he had been pulling out all the tricks for her to let him find out, but she refused to budge.

Soon, they arrived at the bridge to cross over to the island. They showed their tickets, then breezed through, following a convoy of exotic cars to the mansion.

When they arrived, all sorts of people were milling about on the spacious lawn. No sooner had the cars stopped, than the valet appeared to relieve them of their vehicles. The valet took one look at Flame and 8-Ball and scrunched his swarthy nose up as if they stank or some shit.

"No, you can't come in," he informed them, shaking his head like he was disappointed with them for rebelling against the dress code.

"What? I got an invitation," Flame insisted, thrusting his papers in his face. He jerked his thumb toward the valet. "This fuckin' Mexican tripping."

The valet pointed to their clothes. "This is a toga party. To-ga. Strictly enforced."

"What, nigga? You know who I am?" Flame barked, ready to blank out. "You wasting my damn time!"

Fortunately Flame was rescued. "I know who you are."

The soothing female voice came from behind him. He stepped aside and saw Kim Rawls, standing with her hands on her slender hips. She wore a cream toga cinched at the waist by a gold buckle. Her toga didn't pass her knees. Her toned, chocolate legs were on full display, as were her sculpted shoulders. Kim rocked that toga like it came fresh from a runway in Paris. From the bright lights shining down, she appeared to be glowing.

Immediately, Flame changed his mind about resisting. If Kim was looking this good in her toga, he would've walked through fire asshole-naked with gasoline hanging from his balls to see what Sasha looked like in her toga.

"Come on, Flame," Kim said. "Follow me, I'll take care of you. I'd hate for you to miss this party." She winked at Flame.

The entourage followed Kim into the mansion. They walked past the raucous party going on in the front room and entered a side room filled with new togas still wrapped inside expensive packaging. Kim and an assistant rifled through the pile searching for a toga big enough to fit 8-Ball. They eventually found something that looked like an elaborate sheet and tossed it to 8-Ball to try it on. Once they were sure it fit, they both left the room, leaving Kim and Flame alone in the small room.

Kim waved her tiny hands at Flame. "Come on, take it off," she ordered. "Gotta find out what size you are."

Flame smiled. "Shit, you ain't saying nothing but a word."

He stripped down to his boxers and Kim's eyes went straight to his bulge in his briefs. "Hmmm . . . look like you full of promises," she mumbled.

"Damn right."

Kim found something that fit Flame and helped him put it on while he complained.

"Yo, I've been to Greece and I ain't have to wear a toga there," he grumbled as Kim fastened fabric around his waist.

"Actually, this whole thing is of Roman origin, not Greek," she corrected. "But since the two societies were so closely related, it's not a big deal."

Flame was pleasantly surprised. "Ahh, a well-read woman. I'm shocked."

She smiled prettily. "Not all of us are dumb, shallow women, ya know?"

Flame knew the girl wasn't dumb. Most women from the South were low-key bookworms, but he thought the Bible was more her speed. He'd read in the tabloids that her whole group were strong church girls, born and bred in Southeast Texas. He heard they gripped that Bible like rigor mortis had kicked in.

"You have a nice body, Flame," Kim complimented out of the blue. "I hope you don't mind me saying so."

"Nah, not at all. You're good yourself."

"Good?" She struck a pose. "Just good?"

Flame laughed, and his eyes roamed over her body lasciviously. "Nah, you're bad as hell, actually. Just didn't want you to take it the wrong way."

Suggestively, she raised her eyebrows. "Is there any other way to take it?" Before Flame could answer, she spun and walked away.

Flame followed Kim through the party watching her shake her hips harder than Shakira. He saw a few video models that he had slutted out in the past doing their thing on the dance floor. They were so wrapped up plotting on their next sucker, or high on molly, they didn't even notice him, which was cool with Flame. Flame was the king of the one-night stand. He didn't want them to ask questions about how he ghosted them.

They entered another room with marble floors, marble walls, gold chandeliers—pure opulence. A full moon shone down on them through the glass ceiling. Granite gargoyles held sentry on the walls. Beneath those gargoyles, people lined the walls lining their noses with drugs. In fact, drugs were everywhere. Cocaine, molly, lean, so much weed that it didn't even register as a drug. Hollywood starlets, music executives, and R&B singers—past and present—were passing plates of the white girl around like hors d'oeuvres. A couple of them were nodded out riding that white horse too. Flame wanted no part of that scene. Weed and a li'l X every now and then was his fix. Anything else was out of his league.

Kim guided them from the room of beautiful ugly people and out by the pool. The scene looked familiar. More beautiful ugly people showcasing their insecurities. Topless women crowded the pool, spilling goblets of champagne into the aqua-blue water.

"Chill here, Flame. I'll be back," Kim instructed.

As soon as Kim left, Flame searched for 8-Ball. He knew he couldn't be far. As he looked around the room, steam rising from the pool carried the aroma of stale pussy and weed far into the air, and he could easily imagine all the pills rolling around like tiny wheels. The most stunning thing to Flame was the architecture of the pool. It was multi-leveled, and all the layers were shaped like diamonds. Shit was fire, but he was growing tired of the scene fast. During his first few years in the industry he had done the party thing to death. Plus, being a tagalong of the Crescent Crew, he had been a part of the most lavish parties ever thrown, so this type of scene was old hat to him.

Suddenly, Flame felt a hand tap him on his shoulder.

"Take a walk with me," a voice said. "I know you tired of this scene. Pro'ly seen it a thousand times, yo."

Flame turned around and looked up at Tyshawn "Diamond" Barker. The dude was huge, almost to the point of being intimidating. Almost.

"No doubt," Flame uttered uneasily. He craned his neck to see if Ball's big ass was around, but he was ghost.

"Looking for your man?" Diamond asked, when he noticed Flame looking around. "He wit' me. Come on."

Flame had finally put it together and realized the mansion belonged to Diamond. He followed him to his massive master bedroom. In the center of the white marble floor was a wide Jacuzzi. Inside the Jacuzzi sat one-third of Kismet and Flame's delinquent security, 8-Ball.

"Yo, my dude, what's up?" Ball called out from the bubbly water. Monica Wilson sat beside him, snuggled up beneath his rolls of fat. They passed a gold bottle of champagne between them.

"Man, I've been looking for you," Flame told 8-Ball. "How you supposed to watch my back way up here?"

This was a recurring argument between them. The line between friend and bodyguard often blurred.

"Whoa," Diamond interrupted. "You safe here. This is *my* spot. Ain't shit gonna happen to you up in here. Trust that. So relax, jump in. Let's talk."

Diamond shucked his toga, and to everyone's surprise he wore Speedos, the ones that look like panties. His family jewels were crammed all inside the tight fabric and bulged out like a battering ram. He owned no shame, standing there looking like a pro wrestling porn star. He jumped right in the water like nothing was wrong with a near 300-pound diesel black man sporting Speedos.

What the fuck? Flame frowned, totally disgusted. He hesitated on getting in the pool until Kim and Sasha walked into the room.

Kim slid out of her toga real sexy-like, revealing a bikini in Brazilian colors with the hot-yellow string crammed in the crevices of her pretty chocolate-dipped ass. Flame eyed every part of her show. She was finer than Flame thought. She flexed a six-pack tighter than his, but she was still feminine with it. Her breasts were a lot juicer than he imagined too. He imagined all types of freaky episodes with Kim, and for a second he got lost in his daydream.

Until Sasha stepped out of her toga.

Wow! Everything Flame imagined was true, and he drank all of her in, taking mental notes as if he was writing a song about her. From head to toe, her light skin was flawless. She had ass for days . . . literally . . . days! Her waist couldn't have been bigger than a size two, and her camel toe was bunched up like knuckles down there. Her stomach was flat but it wasn't as chiseled as Kim's, and even without makeup on her face she still radiated with beauty. Kim and Sasha both hopped in the Jacuzzi, and Flame followed right behind them.

Kim cozied up next to Flame while Diamond wrapped Sasha in a tight embrace.

"Yo, Flame, allow me to reintroduce myself," Diamond said. He stuck his hand out. "I'm Diamond. I know you've heard of me, right?"

Was he kidding? Flame knew all about Tyshawn "Diamond" Barker.

Born and raised in East New York, he had run with a crew of crazed-out extortionists from the time he was twelve years old. It was said that Diamond was riding a Maserati when other kids his age were riding the bus. He was cutting out of town to get money when other kids were cutting school. His crew had Brownsville on smash and by the time he was sixteen years old he was rumored to have a few bodies under his belt too. It was said that Diamond was playing with seven figures at seventeen years old. Legend had it that Diamond once chopped up an adversary's girlfriend because she refused to give up his whereabouts. As the story goes, he fed her to her pit bull limb by limb while she was still alive until she eventually broke down and told him what he wanted to know.

Then, right before the feds swooped in, Diamond made a ceremonious exit from the game and started a record label with one of his cronies.

On wax, Diamond boasted about their exploits in the streets. Because his street cred was verified, the hood loved his music. He blew up overnight, it seemed. Then all of a sudden, five million albums later, his crony, his partner in crime and business, went missing.

"Yeah. I know of you," Flame told him nonchalantly, as he eased his head back and lay on the heated marble slab surrounding the pool. Meanwhile Kim rubbed his leg under the water.

"Guess you had to, huh?" Diamond replied arrogantly. "Tell the truth, B, I've been smashing the game for the last five summers, huh?" Flame frowned, and Diamond quickly switched his tone. "Aiight, aiight, your ABP fam been eating too—but I've been killing it! Music, movies, jewelry, restaurants." He ticked off each of his accomplishment on his fingers. "Name it, I done it to death."

Flame had enough of his boasting. "Yo, Diamond, you did your thing, but I hope you didn't call me up here to stroke you; especially when you have such a beautiful lady to do it for you," he replied and gave Sasha what could only be described as a flirtatious smirk.

Everybody got so quiet if a gnat farted it would sound like a cannon exploding. Even the Jacuzzi seemed to stop bubbling. *Nobody* dared question the great Diamond.

Diamond eyed Flame through slits, then laughed. "Ha, ha, you're right, B. I can get carried away sometimes. I ain't call you up here for all that. I called you in here to discuss business with you."

"What kind of business?"

Diamond sipped from the gold bottle. "Fashion. I saw your work, man, and it's . . . it's . . ." Diamond looked to Sasha. "How you say it, babe?"

"Everything you envisioned but couldn't articulate," Sasha mocked in an English accent.

"Yeah, yeah, what she said."

They all laughed, easing the tension.

"Anyway, I wanna go in business with you," Diamond said. "I want to be your partner, man. You got an eye. I want to collab with you."

Never in a million years did Flame think his clothes were that hot. He knew he had done magic to make them work with the type of budget he had to work with. Still, he knew they weren't world-class. However, it felt good to know that Diamond felt they were hot enough to invest in. Flame was excited by the possibilities, but he knew he had to be careful with Diamond. He had a reputation of being the type of man to tell you to go to hell and make you look forward to the trip.

"What kind of collab, though?" Flame asked cautiously.

"Sheeeeit, however you need it! Money, resources, distribution, whatever you need, I'm here for you." Diamond shrugged his broad shoulders. "Fifty-fifty. We split the profits."

"Word?"

"Hell yeah! I know a star when I see one, B, and I would be a fool not to get in early before this star takes off to the next galaxy."

Diamond's words were like silk to Flame's ears. It felt good to finally be appreciated. He had been trying to tell Qwess that he was bigger and greater than just a freaky rapper. He was a budding mogul! But Qwess always laughed him off. Now, here was a stranger—a boss in his own right—singing his praises.

Flame looked at his surroundings. The lavish pool, the R&B starlets, and decided this was where he needed to be. Not so fast, though.

"Sounds good so far, but ah, let me check with my people and get back with you," Flame said.

"Wouldn't expect nothing less," Diamond replied with a cheeky smile. He raised his hefty frame from the water and beckoned for Sasha. Sasha raised up and made a show of looking at the water rolling off her hard nipples.

So did Flame.

"Get at me when you get back to the city, Flame. You based in the A, right?"

"Yeah."

"Aiight, cool. I got a spot there too. Enjoy the night." He nodded to Kim. "If things go right, we'll be spending a lot of time together. Come on, babe."

Sasha grabbed Diamond's hand. She turned to Flame and melted her brown eyes into his. "Bye, Flaaame," she cooed.

Flame could've sworn he saw a twinkle in Sasha's eye. It appeared she was choosing right in front of Diamond. That was bold. For a brief second, he forgot all about Kim stroking his leg beneath the water. He forgot about Diamond and his reputation as a killer too. He forgot about everything that a sane man should think about. He was in predator mode.

And Sasha Beaufont was the prey.

Chapter 5

Fayetteville, North Carolina

Qwess sat across the table from famed attorney Malik Shabazz. Malik was riding high on the heels of his victory of getting an accused contract killer, Justus Moore, off on gruesome multiple murder charges. His appearances on CNN had bolstered his name into the legal stratosphere, and Qwess needed that star power on his side right now. He had flown to North Carolina the previous morning to meet with Malik Shabazz in person.

"So, what is all this shit they're trying to say, Akhi?" Qwess asked as he shuffled through his copy of the lawsuit.

Malik Shabazz stroked his long red goatee. "Well, brother, they're alleging that you strong-armed an artist from their roster by carrying out a violent assault. That's considered a tort. Then they're saying that you interfered with their business practices by this act, and that interference caused them to lose out on an estimated seventy-five million dollars."

"That's bullshit! I barely even made five million dollars off her catalog."

Malik Shabazz raised his bushy eyebrows. "So are you saying you did this act, but you didn't get nearly the amount off it? Is that what you're admitting to?"

"Of course not! I'm not admitting to anything."

"Okay, well, you need to be mindful of what you say."

"I'm just saying this whole lawsuit is bullshit," Qwess clarified.

Malik Shabazz smiled. "That's better. Remember, game face, all the time." Qwess nodded. "Now what I want to know is where are they getting their info from?"

Qwess shrugged. "I have no idea."

"Mmm hmm . . . what about the fella in prison for the beating? You think he talking?"

Qwess thought about Samson in prison. He still had nine more calendars to go before he would see the streets again. Yet the fifteen years he received for the assault paled in comparison to what he was really facing if they discovered his true identity.

Qwess shook his head vehemently. "Nah, he would never snitch."

"You sure? 'Cause, brother, I have seen sons tell on mothers, fathers tell on sons, and husbands tell on wives. You never know what kind of weight a person can't hold."

Again, Qwess thought about Samson and came up with the same thing. "Nah, he's solid."

Malik Shabazz shrugged. "Okay, if you say so. What about the other two men in here? Are they solid too?"

Qwess couldn't hold back his smirk. "I can *assure* you those guys are not telling anything on anybody anywhere."

Malik Shabazz had defended enough gangsters to know what that statement meant. "Fair enough. So that means they are getting this info from somewhere else."

"Yeah."

"By the way, I never got to extend my personal condolences on the passing of your brother, Reece. You were so busy at the memorial that I didn't get a chance to speak with you. Then, you went MIA. Look, not only was he my best client, we had also established a bond. He was special, and he will be missed."

"Thank you for that. Reece is probably in this room right now talking shit, telling us not to let them win."

Malik Shabazz looked around his spacious office and laughed. "Probably so. Well, Reece, if you in here, you know that this will be our next victory."

Qwess smiled. "That's what I like to hear."

For the next hour, Malik Shabazz and Qwess pored over the lawsuit, breaking everything down. Malik Shabazz volleyed questions, and Qwess returned answers. At the end of the hour, the picture became clearer. Qwess had a fight on his hands. The lawsuit had some strong points.

"So, what am I looking at?" Qwess asked Malik Shabazz. "Worst case scenario?"

Malik Shabazz frowned. "Worst case, they hit you for the seventy-five million and you have to pay it. Of course, you can always file for bankruptcy and save a number of your assets, but then they could possibly go after your wife's assets also. Not to mention, a loss here can potentially open you up to more civil penalties and"—Malik Shabazz raised a finger—"criminal penalties as well. If they get a favorable verdict here, then they will probably press criminal charges against you."

"Are you serious?"

"As cancer, AIDS, and heart attacks combined. We have to find out the source of the leak. The details in the suit are too spot on for it to be coincidence."

Qwess sighed. "Fuck. My. Life."

Qwess had all the keys to life. Money. Power. Respect. Now he was at risk of losing it all behind some nigga shit.

Flame arrived in New York about two weeks after meeting Diamond in Miami. He and Diamond had met briefly in

Atlanta the week before, and it was obvious Diamond was pulling out all the stops to recruit Flame to his team. In Atlanta, he openly invited Flame to partake in his luxurious lifestyle.

Diamond was balling on another level. He had Rolls (plural), Ferrari Enzos, a Bugatti Veyron, Maybach, and a Pagani Huayra. He owned homes, condos, townhouses, mansions, and estates in various states. And he had influence in the city. They were touting him as the king of New York City and he was extending his long arm to Flame.

Diamond had arranged for Flame to use his Maybach while he was in the city. Although Flame had a small apartment in Harlem and a Bentley GT to cruise the city in, being under Diamond's wing was a lot better. If he wanted to let Flame skate around the city on a half mil, Flame was not going to refuse.

Diamond's Maybach met Flame at JFK and shot him to his apartment in Manhattan. He had copped the big-boy apartment in New York because most of his fashion interests were centered there. Oh, he still had his homes in Carolina, but since his fashion headquarters was there, he decided to boss-up and rent something befitting a man of his stature.

Flame had a full day lined up. He had to meet with his business manager, Amin, to discuss Diamond's proposal in detail. Then he was supposed to meet with Diamond. Next, it was on to ABP's New York office to meet with Qwess.

At noon, Flame opened his door for Amin. He took a seat in the front room while Flame finished getting ready. Amin was actually the financial guru for ABP, but since he'd served Flame so well over the years, he enlisted him to help pursue his other ventures also.

"Yo, I can't believe Diamond want to fuck with you," Amin yelled from the front. Ever since Flame told him about the offer he had been acting like a straight groupie. He was riding Diamond's dick harder than Sasha.

"Why wouldn't he? Our shit hot."

"I know, but I'm saying . . ."

Just like a hater, Flame thought. He wasn't expecting Amin to be all in on his new allegiance to Diamond, he just needed him to advise him on the details. Fuck what he thought.

Flame stepped out his room in a blue pinstriped suit with a red tie, ready to show his business side. The world knew him as a raunchy rapper. He knew that in order for him to be taken seriously he had to dress the part.

Flame tapped Amin on the shoulder. "Let's go. Our ride is waiting."

A few minutes later Flame and Amin glided through the clean streets of New York in Diamond's Maybach. Amin was giddy like a kid, peering up at the tall buildings through the panoramic roof like he hadn't been living there for half a decade. Flame initially was disgusted at Amin's open display of groupie-ism, but he could sympathize with him. The world just looked better when you looked at it from behind the glass of a nice automobile.

The shock-and-awe campaign continued as they stepped foot in Diamond's office building. It was like the nigga was determined to show the world he was the shit. Everything was super-sized. All glass, brass, marble, and gold. Diamond's receptionist ushered them into Diamond's personal office where they enjoyed a view of the city from forty floors up while they waited for Diamond to materialize. After allowing enough time for the leather conference chairs to form to their bodies, in walked Diamond wearing expensive carpenter pants, retro Jordans, and a hot white t-shirt with a hologram logo on it. A short, balding, obviously Jewish man was at his side.

"Flame, what up, my nigga." Diamond greased Flame's palm and took a seat beside him. To the Jewish dude he said, "This the guy I was talking about."

Flame introduced Amin as his business manager, and they

got down to business. A Jew, a Muslim, a Christian, and a thug.

Only in New York City.

Diamond threw his pitch like he played for the league. He spit words, facts, and figures quicker than Russell Simmons on speed. He whipped out a chart to show projected figures for the first two quarters of the year. The following year. Things were moving so swiftly Flame attempted to look to Amin for clarity, but he was just giddy to be at the table.

From what Flame saw in the papers, what Diamond was proposing was a dream come true. He was basically gifting Flame a chance to finance all his dreams on Diamond's dime. All Flame had to do was design the patterns with his team and promote the line on his public appearances. That was it. The profit, again, would be split fifty-fifty.

The deal almost sounded too good to be true, so Flame was skeptical. He knew all about bad contracts. Hell, he still owed ABP millions from his first contract. Millions sold, and he still owed.

However, that did teach Flame to prepare for the future. There was no guarantee he would be hot tomorrow. With what Diamond was suggesting he could use it as his backup plan. There was no way he could lose in the long run.

So despite the warning alarms ringing in his head, he signed some papers and made it official. He was now in business with Diamond Barker.

Then the other shoe dropped.

"Word, son. That's what's up. Check it, I already got, like, a hunnid-thou made up just like this shirt," Diamond relayed. He pulled his t-shirt down to expose the logo.

For the first time, Flame realized what the logo on the shirt was. The hologram was actually a diamond on fire.

"Flaming Diamond, that's what this line will be called," Diamond explained as if he could read Flame's mind. "After the t-shirts, we'll drop the denim, then the leather jump-offs. Since it's official, I'll get on the horn and tell my man to put the shirts in the street. Then, tomorrow we can go on Wendy and hype shit up."

"Whoa. What now?" Flame said.

"You look worried, fam," Diamond said. "No need to worry. I got this under control."

"It ain't nothin'," Flame lied. "I was just tripping on how fast everything happening."

"Yo, I'm saying, fam, the early bird gets the worm," Diamond reasoned. "I had a few printed up by my peoples to get the word out. Way I see it, the initial run of the t-shirts will pay for everything else. We break profit in a few months."

Flame looked at Amin. Amin nodded and smiled. Flame grimaced.

He was officially in business with Diamond.

Qwess stared at the murals on the walls with a heavy heart. The images were a testament to the duality of the man that had occupied the space. To understand King Reece, you had to understand dichotomy. On the one hand, he destroyed his community. On the other, he helped his community. He raped, but he also saved.

Qwess rubbed his hands over the marble walls, and it was as if the coarse material transported him back in time. They made so much money together . . . caused so much pain, death, and destruction . . . but their bond was unbreakable—even in death. Every time Qwess came home, he came to the mausoleum to pay his respects. Inside these walls he found peace.

As irony would have it, Qwess wasn't the only person to come pay his respects. King Reece had grown larger in life than in death. Hustlers from all over the country came to the mausoleum in Raeford to pay their respects and present offerings at his feet. Some would make the trek to pray as if it was the dope boy's version of the *Ka'ba,* as if the ground was hallowed and could confer special powers on them. Some of them left stacks of money and jewelry at the entrance to the mausoleum in tribute. Some would even camp out. In the little town of Raeford, so much traffic upset the locals. It became so much of an issue that security eventually had to be hired. Qwess was here to honor his comrade, but he also was here for other reasons as well.

Qwess heard a car outside. He said his goodbyes and saluted to the entombed body of Reece, then he walked outside.

A cream-colored Maybach had pulled up outside the mausoleum right beside Qwess's red F12 Berlinetta. Green flags flapped on the front corners of the half-million-dollar vehicle, and the chrome grill gleamed in the sunlight. Qwess had to squint just to see the whole car. The driver's door opened, and a large man crawled out. He saluted Qwess then reached out to open the rear door for him. Qwess returned the salute and climbed in the back of the Maybach.

"*As salaam alayka*, good brother," Bone greeted.

Qwess almost didn't recognize Bone. He wore a red-and-white-checkered *keffiyeh* on his head and a long white collared *jellabiya*. His beard was thick and trimmed and hung down on his chest.

"*Wa alaykum as salaam!*" Qwess replied proudly. "How have you been? Shit, from the looks of things, life is good," he said, looking around the luxurious Maybach. "The *deen* looks good on you."

Bone smiled and bowed his head slightly. "*Ma shallah.* Allah blesses the believers."

Qwess was trying hard not to be surprised by this new Bone. He knew Bone had dedicated his life to Islam, but he also knew that Bone was still heavy in the streets. Again, dichotomy.

"Indeed, indeed," Qwess replied, nodding. "So what's

going on? You said you needed to holla at me while I was here, and I definitely need to holla at you about something."

Bone perked up. "Word? What's up, OG?"

Qwess pumped his hands. "Nah, nah, it's on you first. I came here to see you."

Bone chuckled. "That's peace. So check this out," he said. "Hold up a second."

Bone touched a button, and the tinted partition bisecting the front and back of the car slid up. As soon as the partition was closed Bone pulled out his phone and plugged it into the screen on the back of the front seat.

"Hold up, you might want a drink for this," Bone said. He pulled down the middle compartment and retrieved a bottle of Ace of Spades champagne and two flutes. He poured up while the video loaded on the screen. He grabbed the remote and started the video.

On the screen was a grainy video that cleared up and revealed an image of Chabo gagged and bound to a chair in a room. He was badly beaten, and his left eye was dangling from his face. He was groaning and spitting gibberish in Spanish. The surround sound in the Maybach made it seem as if he was in the car with them. Bone appeared in the frame holding a long, curved *saif*. That's when things really got interesting.

"Watch this," Bone said with glee. Between sips, he began mouthing the words along with his image on the screen as he tortured Chabo mercilessly.

"You the king, huh? El Rey, right? Look at me, KING!"

Bone slapped Chabo with the face of the sword, and a loud cracking sound echoed throughout the leather and wood of the Maybach.

Qwess squirmed in his seat. He already knew where this was going. He croaked, "Yo . . ."

Bone pointed at the screen. "You gonna miss the best part."

On the screen Bone slowly fastened a necklace around

Chabo's neck. It was the same necklace he had taken from him earlier outside the lounge.

"You want to wear this around your neck and disrespect my family, KING? Well, heavy is the head that wears the crown, so let me help you with that."

Bone stood behind Chabo and snatched his head back by his hair. He held it and placed the *saif* beneath Chabo's sweaty neck. Bone paused a brief second before he screamed, "Allahu Akbar!" and dug in with the blade.

Blood spurted high into the air from Chabo's neck as the oddly-shaped sword sliced a gaping wound in his neck. Chabo tried to scream but instead he gurgled then wheezed as nothing was connected to create sound. Bone dug the blade in deeper and moved the sword back and forth over Chabo's neck until his head was hanging on to his neck by a thin string of meaty flesh. Bone dropped the blade and twisted and yanked Chabo's head until he detached it from his body. Chabo's headless body fell over onto the dirty ground, convulsing and shaking.

Bone held Chabo's decapitated head in his hands. He spun it around and looked directly into the eyes that were, surprisingly, still open. Chabo's detached head blinked at Bone. Bone didn't even flinch. Instead, he smiled and placed a kiss on his bloody forehead. Then the screen went blank.

Qwess was spooked. He looked around outside the car as if the authorities were going to rush in at any moment. He was speechless, but he eventually found the words to articulate what he was feeling.

"Yo, what the fuck did I just witness?" Qwess asked, shaking his head in disbelief.

Bone smiled like a proud child trying to please his father. "That was Crew business—new and improved. This is the final chapter in King Reece's story. This is the last guy that was there when the god was killed."

"Yeah, I figured as much when you first told me."

"What's wrong, OG? You don't look too good over there. I didn't do too much, did I?"

Qwess shook his head. "Nah, you did what you felt you had to do. I wouldn't have had it any other way. It's just . . ."

"Gruesome, huh?" Bone finished his thought for him. "Yeah, you been away awhile. Living too good will make you forget what it's like when a wolf is *hangry*."

"Hangry?"

"Yeah—hungry *and* angry." Bone chuckled lightly. "But, yeah, you been away from this scene for a while, living the high life and shit."

Qwess raised his eyebrows and gestured around the May-bach. "*I'm* living the high life?"

Bone smiled mischievously. "I mean, this is street shit, street money. It's all dirty. I have to move a certain way, keep things low and stay in touch with the streets or else I lose it. You up in lofty offices and I'm down in the trenches, so it's easy for you to lose your edge. No disrespect intended, OG."

"None taken."

Qwess wasn't offended by Bone's words, he was offended that his actions didn't match up. He claimed to move "low" but probably owned one of only a few Maybachs in the whole city. He definitely had the only Maybach with flags flapping on the fenders. Then he was traipsing around town like the damn Taliban in expensive robes. Qwess followed him on In-stagram, and Bone regularly flexed with mountains of cash and jewelry. He was of this new era, the era of what Qwess called the "Missouri" hustlers—they had a show-me mentality.

However, Bone did have a throwback quality that was immeasurable: He was loyal to the bone and just as deadly as Reece had been. That's the real reason why Qwess had sum-moned him.

Qwess leaned over and whispered directly in Bone's ear. "I need something from you, though."

The move caught Bone off guard, but he understood.

Qwess was old-school; he had seen his whole family dismantled by listening devices. Even if he knew his line was thorough, that didn't exempt them from the watchful eye of the law.

Bone nodded for Qwess to go on.

"I need all the info on that AMG raid from a few years back," Qwess whispered. "Names of who was there and who knew about it. You know the one, right?"

Again, Bone nodded.

"I need that, like, yesterday."

Bone nodded and whispered. "Say no more, OG. I got you."

Qwess thought about something else. "Aye, when the last time you spoke with the big homie? You know who."

Bone adjusted his headdress and scratched his temple. The diamonds in his Rolex flashed like paparazzi. "Ahh, I heard from him a few weeks ago. He in the box right now. Had to serve some Mexican niggas in there. Ever since this war out here started, it's been making things hard for him in there."

Qwess shook his head. "Damn, he supposed to be laying low in there. If any of that other shit come out . . ."

Bone nodded vigorously. He frowned. "Yeah, you right, but he gotta do what he gotta do."

"You haven't heard anything else about that other thing, though, have you? Nothing came up?"

Bone understood now. Qwess was fishing. Something had him spooked. "Not that I know of," he replied. "He holding it down, and you know he gonna stay ten toes down to the end."

That was all Qwess needed to hear. But if Samson wasn't going soft and leaking, then who was?

"Yeah, find out that other thing for me ASAP," Qwess insisted.

"I got you."

Qwess reached in his pocket and peeled a stack of hundreds from his roll. "See to it that the big homie get this for me, and make sure he know it came from me."

"No doubt."

Qwess dapped Bone up and tapped on the window to exit. As he waited on the soldier to open the door, he turned to Bone. "Yo, I'm proud of you, man. You holding this shit together and repping that flag like you supposed to. You holding our line together and making it stronger than ever. That's what's up."

Bone bumped his chest. "It's Crescent Crew to the death with me, homie. You already know. Death before dishonor. Stay up."

"I'm up."

Qwess exited the Maybach with his mind a little at ease. His line was still intact, and even though he wasn't active, he still felt good that what he'd built so many years ago was still standing.

Chapter 6

Atlanta, Georgia

Flame stepped into Atlantic Beach Productions' reception area with Amin in tow and an extra bop in his step. Getting new money on his own felt good. Showing Qwess that he didn't need him felt even better.

As soon as the receptionist, Khadijah, saw them she extended an Islamic greeting to Amin, scoffed at Flame, and then whipped her scarf around her face like a ninja.

She muttered, "Khafir." Then she hit a button on the phone. Seconds later, Qwess's wife, Lisa Ivory, peeked out from behind the oak office door.

Lisa was a star in her own right. She used to be an R&B star and child prodigy on the piano. Her first two albums went multi-platinum, but rumors of her sexuality began affecting her record sales. She married Qwess in a desperate attempt to salvage her career, but the damage was already done. She and Qwess had a child, and now her career was as cold as the ice on Flame's watch.

Flame and Amin strolled toward Qwess's office door feeling like a billion bucks, but Lisa stopped Amin with a frown. "This is a private meeting," she told him.

Here come the bullshit, Flame thought. He felt Qwess had been holding him up for too long, and he was ready to strike out on his own.

Flame stepped inside the office, and his camel colored Ferragamos melted into the cream carpet. Qwess sat behind his large, shiny, green desk looking like a boss. He was dressed comfortably in a tailored pinstriped business suit without a tie while his wife stood behind him with her left hand on his right shoulder. On the wall behind his desk was a huge oil painting of their family.

Qwess motioned to the leather chair in front of his desk. "Take a seat, let's talk."

Flame remained standing.

Qwess shrugged, "Aiight. Look, you know you got to do the Breakfast Club tomorrow and then in a couple of weeks we got to do the BET Awards in Cali?"

Flame scoffed, "Of course I know."

"Yeah, I know you know. Just making sure you don't get, uhh, sidetracked."

"What's that supposed to mean?"

"Look, Joey, what's up with you and ole boy?" Qwess asked. He knew Flame hated to be called by his government name. Even his mama called him Flame now. Qwess purposely did it to pull rank, piss him off. He had been hearing rumors about Diamond and Flame gallivanting all around town.

"Who?" Flame asked innocently.

"Diamond," Qwess slid through gritted teeth.

Diamond was the northern counterpart to Qwess. What Qwess was to the Southern hip-hop scene, Diamond was to the Northern hip-hop scene. He had been a splinter in Qwess's side for a while now, pulling stunts to get his attention, showing up at industry functions trying to hog the spotlight, and taking digs at Qwess on social media. Then, Diamond repeatedly tried to one-up Qwess. Everything Qwess did, Diamond followed. Qwess came out of retirement to rap, Diamond came out of retirement to rap. Qwess shot movies, Diamond shot movies. Qwess opened restaurants, Diamond opened eateries. Qwess bagged an R&B chick, Diamond bagged one. Qwess came out with a jewelry line . . . you get the drift. Qwess tried his hardest to ignore him, but that splinter was turning into a thorn.

"Oh, that's just business," Flame replied nonchalantly. He knew he was digging into Qwess's skin.

Qwess's eyes narrowed. "Business, huh?"

"Yup."

"Okay, just be careful, man. Dude ain't right. Word. He into some shit you don't know nothing about. I'd hate to see you crossed up on a humbug."

Flame scoffed. Who was he kidding? Flame felt that all Qwess cared about was leeching off his talents. Besides, he and Diamond were cut from the same cloth. When Flame joined ABP, Qwess was still an active member of the Crescent Crew, the infamous cocaine cartel that had the Southeast in a stranglehold when he was younger. Then, just like Diamond, Qwess got his money, squared up, then started writing positive rhymes. Then he quit rapping altogether, saying the industry was evil. Flame felt being broke was evil, and Diamond was about to help him get money.

"Well, I've already been in a situation like that before," Flame said, alluding to his own past. "I think I can handle it."

"All right, if you say so." Qwess glanced up at his wife with a smug look on his face, then returned his attention to Flame. "Well, don't you forget you're obligated to Atlantic Beach Productions, first and foremost. Your little hobby comes second."

Hobby?! Hobby? Flame was seething.

"Now let's go over this itinerary for the award show," Qwess said calmly, as if he didn't just smack Flame in the face with an insult.

The whole while Qwess droned on about the schedule, Flame's mind was on one thing. He was going to prove to Qwess he didn't need him anymore. He had screwed him with a bad contract years ago to keep him dependent on him. Now, with his adversary's help, he was going to prove to him his worth. Prove this was the real deal. Prove that the world didn't revolve around Qwess.

The following morning Flame appeared on the Breakfast Club. Everyone was still shocked that he could actually blow. They compared him to Tyrese, although Flame felt the comparison was an insult. He was thinking he was more along the lines of Ginuwine as far as raw talent, but more than anything he was just pleased that they were accepting of him and his new mode of expression. Bringing something new to the table was always a gamble, especially with someone as popular as Flame. In this case, it appeared his gamble was paying off.

Halfway through the interview it dawned on Flame what all the hosts were wearing. No sooner the realization hit him, the hosts went in.

"So you see we wearing these dope-ass Flaming Diamond shirts," the dark-skinned host said in his raspy voice. "Salute to my guy, Diamond, but what's up with you guys? The skreets is going crazy about a partnership!"

"Yeah, Flame, what's up with that? Isn't Diamond and Qwess beefing?"

Flame was totally caught off guard. The way he felt Qwess had played him the previous day was still fresh in his head, so it gave him extra incentive to get some revenge in front of the world.

"Who is Qwess?" Flame asked.

"Ooooooh!!!! He said, who is Qwess? Damn, that's harsh!"

The third of their trio piped in with his usual spiel, but this time it was necessary. "For those that don't know, Flame is signed to ABP, which is owned by Qwess. Flame, you guys got a lot of money together; what's up with that?"

"Yeah, Flame, I thought you guys were homeboys too?" the female host reminded him.

Flame offered an awkward smile, and rubbed his hand over his 360 waves. "Yeah, well, homeboys are those who have your best interest in mind," he said, low-key throwing a direct shot at Qwess. Those were the exact words Qwess had uttered so many years ago when Flame's homeboy, J.D., had exposed him to a case. "Homie hasn't had that for me in a long time."

"Daaaaaamn! I gotta call my peoples down in the Cack and see what is going on," the other host said.

"Nah, everything is love, man. We just do business together, and that's it. We just have to iron some business issues out, you know?"

"I can understand that," the light-skinned member of the trio said.

"So, Flame, you don't care about Diamond's reputation out here in these skreets? They say Diamond into some *other* other shit," the host said cryptically.

"You know, someone just asked me that recently," Flame said. "As if they didn't know how I came in this game. Yo, don't let this singing shit fuck y'all head up; I'm still from Fayettenam. Ain't shit sweet about me."

"Knock it off, Flame. You been eating good for years, man. You don't have that skreet shit in you no more. What you worth, 'bout ten mil?"

Flame smirked. "Not even close. Just know, I'm good over here, and me and Diamond about to shock the world."

The hosts chopped it up for a few more minutes, trying to throw shots every now and then, but Flame was an expert. He handled it well.

Toward the end of the interview, the hard questions eased up. When Flame walked into the hallway, he saw why. Diamond was waiting on him.

"Flame! My nigga, what's good, B!" Diamond greeted.

"What up, homie?" Flame returned with excitement.

"You know I had to come and check my li'l homie out. I got a few spots for us to hit," Diamond said. "We going over to Wendy."

"Word?"

"Word, nigga! You think it's a game? I'ma make you a believer."

Flame followed Diamond's large frame out the building. Downstairs a red Lamborghini was parked illegally right in front of the building with the scissor-style doors wide open.

"Yo, Flame, ride with me!" Diamond ordered, gesturing to the Lamborghini.

"Damn, this you too?" Flame asked.

"What you think?" Diamond said, pointing to the license plate. The tag read "Diamante."

"Yeeeeah, this shit nice."

"Nothing but the best, baby."

Flame climbed into the passenger seat, and Diamond ripped through the city in the Lambo like he owned the streets, zipping in and out of traffic. By the time they arrived at Wendy's show, Flame's knuckles were white.

Outside the building, a huge crowd was assembled as if they were awaiting their arrival. Flame hopped out the Lambo and waded through the crowd, stopping to sign a few autographs before stepping inside. As always, he stopped at the most attractive women in the crowd to leave his signature with, and this time was no different. A beautiful Latina asked him to sign her shirt right over her breast. It was then that he noticed it. She was wearing a Flaming Diamond shirt also. Flame inspected the crowd a bit closer and realized over half of the crowd were wearing the same shirt. Shocked, he looked at Diamond for an explanation. Diamond simply smiled.

Just before they went into the entrance, a red Ferrari California sped up to the curb in front of the crowd and screeched to a halt. The top was peeled back, allowing everyone to see the occupants. It was Sasha Beaufont and Kim Rawls.

The crowd went berserk.

They quickly rushed the car, screaming at the top of their lungs.

"Sasha!"

"Sasha!"

"Sasha!"

It was total pandemonium. Throngs of fans screaming Sasha's name, snapping pictures with their smartphones, and flailing their arms like fish out of water. A few young girls even passed out. Seemingly out of nowhere, Sasha's security rushed the car and created a barrier between Sasha and the fans.

While all the commotion was going on, Flame stood transfixed in place with his muscular arms crossed and an arrogant smirk on his face. He lived for moments like this. He had been popping for nearly a decade, but this type of hype was different. He was a part of hip-hop royalty now, and he loved every minute of it.

Before a full riot broke out, Sasha snapped the roof shut on the Ferrari, put the windows up, and drove off into traffic, burning rubber. She was a rock star and she took every opportunity to remind the world of who she was.

Flame and Diamond went inside and waited in Wendy's pink room until it was time to come out. Flame took the time to ask Diamond about the shirts he saw in the crowd.

Diamond laughed it off. "Thought it was a game? I'm a businessmaaan."

Wendy sent for them, and they took a seat opposite her on the leopard-print couch. After the ambush at the radio show, Flame was prepared for the worst. Of course, Wendy didn't disappoint.

"Before we start," Wendy said. She was wearing big heels and bigger hair. "I have a blind item. See if you can help me."

She shuffled some papers and read: "This popular rapper just changed his destiny and has been rumored to be seeing a new starlet unlike any of his previous conquests. Hint: He is known for keeping the fire burning in the bedroom but hasn't blazed this one yet. Is this you, Flame?"

Flame was speechless. Luckily, Diamond was a seasoned vet. He spoke up and steered the conversation right toward the clothing line. He pitched it perfectly, touting the durability of the t-shirts, the fine fabric of the denim, and the genius of their partnership.

Hearing Diamond gush about their partnership piqued Wendy's interest. She dived in.

"Wait, so how does this work?" she asked. "Everyone knows you are signed to ABP, and Qwess doesn't get along with Diamond. Hear the streets tell it and they're enemies." Her eyes bulged like they were going to burst. Her diamond necklace almost blinded them.

Flame repeated the same spiel he gave at the radio station. "First of all, I'm my own man. And I have to do things to secure my future, just like everyone else."

She leaned back. "Oooh, do tell. Is there trouble in paradise? Flame? Flame, is there trouble in paradise?" Wendy cooed.

"Nah, it's nothing like that. I just gotta do me, ya know?"

"All right."

Diamond interjected and directed the conversation back to Flaming Diamond. He was truly a pro. After Wendy saw there wasn't much more info to pump out of Flame, she detoured and swung back around to put the focus back on Diamond. The two of them shared a tumultuous history, and she was glad to be able to assist him when he called on her.

They wrapped up the interview, took a few questions, then dipped out.

Outside, the day was still young, so Diamond removed the roof on the Lamborghini and they cruised the streets of Manhattan like the stars they were, soaking in the exhaust fumes and praise simultaneously, bumping Uncle Murda. They ended up at Diamond's soul food restaurant and found a surprise waiting on them at a booth in the back.

Sasha and Kim.

The beautiful starlets greeted them with smiles, and the men took their seats. Flame sat beside Kim, and Diamond sat beneath Sasha.

"Baby, I ordered you some chicken and dumplings," Sasha relayed to Diamond.

He kissed her on the lips. "Thanks."

Kim rubbed Flame's legs under the table and asked, "What do you want, Flame?"

Flame ordered fish and veggies while checking Kim out. She looked good in a green form-fitting flight suit and construction heels with a red bottom. The zipper was pulled down to her waist, showing off her smooth brown skin, six-pack, and nice breasts. Her black hair was pressed down to her neck and flipped up on the end.

But once again, Sasha was crushing her. Sasha's long brown hair looked wet. She wore simple blue jeans and a low-cut V-neck sweater, but it looked extra special on her. Large gold earrings jangled every time she moved, competing with the diamond-encrusted bangles on her arm. Her skin appeared to be glowing.

Flame was relieved when Diamond started talking, because it stopped him from slyly admiring his chick.

"Me and my man gonna do big things together," Diamond said to the ladies. "We got a lot in common. Remind me of myself. Came up scrapping and scraping to earn his bread. Caught a break and ain't never trying to go back to broke, huh?"

Diamond looked at Flame for a co-sign, but the story he was weaving wasn't exactly true. Truth was, Flame's story was nothing like Diamond's. Flame used to be a low-level jack-boy and compulsive gambler until Qwess gave him a shot at the music game. Hell, if it wasn't for Qwess, he'd probably have been dead or in jail. Before rap, Flame feared people like who Diamond was before rap. But he wasn't going to admit it. If Diamond wanted to big him up in front of the ladies, he wasn't going to stop him.

"Pretty much," Flame lied with a straight face.

"Word!" Diamond barked. "I ain't neva going back to broke! Top of the world, baby!" He raised his glass in the air then downed it and belched. "Check it, Flame. You want to vacay with us next week?"

"Huh?"

Diamond cut his eyes at Kim sternly. "You ain't ask him?"

"I didn't have time to ask—"

"Yo, Flame, you want to go to France with us next week? It'll be fun. Me, you, Sasha, Kim, and your man 8-Ball and Monica. They kicking it kind of strong from what I hear, been spending time together."

This was news to Flame.

"Well, I have the BET awards in a couple weeks," Flame told him.

"Sheeeit, we do too. We can fly out from the same place to the awards. Trust me, B."

Flame thought quick and hard. He thought about chilling in the sun with Kim. Thought about seeing Sasha in a bikini again. Thought about his obligations in Cali prior to the actual awards show. A few radio stops and parties.

Then he thought about Qwess.

He thought about how Qwess would feel when he heard he was out of the country with Diamond. He thought about himself posting pics on Instagram for the world to see and how it would affect Qwess to see him living his best life without him.

Flame emitted a sinister chuckle. "Yeeeeah, I'm game," he said.

"Yes!" Kim screamed and surprised Flame with a kiss on the lips. "It'll be fun."

Flame cut his eyes across the table at Sasha, who was staring right back at him. *I bet it will be fun,* he thought.

The trip couldn't come fast enough.

Chapter 7

Charlotte, North Carolina

Bone sat inside the blacked-out Dodge Charger in the parking lot of the tall office building in Center City. It was just after five p.m., and the streets were just beginning to crowd with traffic. Bone had been in the same spot since four p.m. waiting for the same person to exit the building. From where he sat, he had a clear view to the entrance of the building. When the man came out, Bone wouldn't miss him.

"Yo, what time he supposed to get off?" Bone's passenger asked. His name was Shaheed, and he was here to make his bones for their de facto leader.

At just nineteen years old, Shaheed had been a part of the Crescent Crew for about six months, and although he had proven to be a good earner, flipping kilos of raw cocaine and the popular Percocet pills all through the Carolinas, his ultimate loyalty was still in question. With the low prices the Crew let their work go for, anybody affiliated with them could easily make money. That was nothing. To be a card-carrying member of the Crescent Crew, they had to be willing to go above and beyond hustling. They maintained their power by being willing to do what others wouldn't do in pursuit of power, so they were blood-in, blood-out. Every member of the Crescent Crew had a body under their belt. The more brazen the hit, the higher their standing within the Crew, so when Bone came to Shaheed with the proposition that he needed something personal handled, Shaheed jumped at the chance.

Bone looked at his plain-Jane Richard Mille. "He was supposed to come out since five thirty," Bone answered.

"What if he left through another exit?" Shaheed suggested.

"Nah, that muthafucka in there," Bone whispered, staring at the entrance. "He never leave out another way. That motherfucker is predictable as a grandfather clock. Trust me."

Bone knew because he had been tracking the man since Qwess had asked him about the incident that day. Although Qwess asked about the members of the Crew, Bone devised a plan to kill two birds with one stone. Instead of looking inside his ranks, he decided to go straight to the top to eliminate the threat.

Bone tapped Shaheed on his arm. "Yo, you might have to go in there and flush him out," Bone said.

This was another reason he had chosen Shaheed to accompany him on the mission, just in case he had to go in. Shaheed was still young and inexperienced compared to the other members of the Crew. His soul hadn't been completely corrupted yet, so he could still blend in with the regular folk. Hardened criminals had this . . . *thing* about them, like the aura of the "streets" just leaped off them. Other members of the Crew would've stuck out like a hard dick in a monastery for this mission. Shaheed's smooth baby face, charming good looks, and uppity dress code would serve him well this time. No one would ever expect him to be a ruthless killer.

"You want me to go *in*?" Shaheed asked.

"You might have to."

"What about the cameras?"

"Fuck those cameras! We have to take care of this today," Bone insisted. "Hold up, hold up . . . there he go right there."

Sure enough, John Meyers, executive VP of AMG, was walking out the front entrance with a briefcase in his hand. He walked with a slight limp, courtesy of his beatdown at the hands of the Crescent Crew.

"What you want me to do?" Shaheed asked.

"Just like we talked about. I want you to walk up to him, put the gun under his chin, and blow his brains out. Then, I want you to hit his ass six more times in the chest—seven shots in all."

Shaheed went silent.

"You good, brother?" Bone asked.

"Yeah, I'm good. Seven shots, right?"

"Seven shots."

Shaheed eased out of the Charger holding his silenced pistol on his leg, his eyes locked on John Meyers's back. He walked quickly until he fell in step just a few feet away from John Meyers.

Bone watched Shaheed in anticipation of what was next to come. He pulled out his phone, started a video, and placed the phone on the dash to record the hit.

John Meyers was just a few feet away from his Maserati, and Shaheed was right on his heels. A jolt of excitement slithered through Bone's veins as he watched the action unfold. He saw John Meyers turn around, and he imagined Shaheed had called the music executive to get his attention. Bone smiled. Shaheed wanted to give it to him up close and personal. Bone watched Shaheed ease his pistol up from beside his leg and . . . tuck it in his back.

What the fuck?

Bone watched with disappointment as Shaheed walked

right past John Meyers and disappeared around the corner. John Meyers fired up his Maserati and sped out of the parking lot.

Bone was livid!

A few minutes later, Shaheed tapped on the window of the Charger. Bone unlocked the door and tore into Shaheed.

"Yo, what the fuck happened?! You had a clean shot!"

Shaheed frowned and shook his head. "Nah, man, you didn't see that woman get out her car a few doors down. She was in a white Lexus."

"I don't give a fuck! You shoulda popped her ass too! She was collateral damage."

"Plus, man, it's still daylight outside," Shaheed protested.

"That's the fucking point!" Bone roared, as he pushed the start button and brought the SRT Charger to life. He slowly pulled from the parking lot chewing on his inner jaw. "Man! We had that nigga," Bone said to himself.

"Aye, ain't that the dude that run the record label?" Shaheed asked. "I just saw him at some music conference, and he was in XXL as executive of the year. This got something to do with Qwess?"

Bone cut his eyes at Shaheed but he didn't offer a response. Finally, he said, "Don't worry about all that. We'll get him next time."

Bone maneuvered the Charger through traffic exiting the city. A song from Flame quaked through the factory Beats speakers in the car as Shaheed rolled up a blunt.

"This that shit," Shaheed said, licking the blunt closed. He fired up the weed and nodded his head to the music as Bone piloted the Charger onto Highway 74 headed back to Fayetteville.

They rode in silence for about thirty minutes when suddenly Bone pulled the car to the side of the road.

"Aye, let's put these burners in the trunk just in case popo fuck around and stop us," Bone decided. "As long as they in the trunk we good 'cause they can't search the trunk without a warrant."

"Hell, yeah." High out of his mind, Shaheed thought that was a good idea.

The men exited the car and walked to the back of the Charger together. Shaheed pushed the button beneath the rear spoiler, and the trunk lid raised slowly.

Bone pointed inside the trunk. "Lift that gray thing up so we can put them down there beside the tire," he said as he looked both ways to see if traffic was coming.

As soon as Shaheed ducked his head in the trunk to move the "gray thing," Bone fired two shots from his silenced .45 right in the back of Shaheed's wavy head. Shaheed actually saw his blood splatter on the carpet in the trunk, but he collapsed in the trunk, dead, before it registered that it was his blood.

Bone flipped the rest of Shaheed's body into the trunk and slammed it shut. Then he called Qwess.

"OG, I got some news for you . . ."

Lake Lanier, Georgia

"What's good, li'l homie?" Qwess said into the phone as he piloted his 103-foot yacht. Costing a little over $5 million, the ship came equipped with autopilot, but Qwess fancied himself a renaissance man so he took joy in doing the honors himself.

"I tried to cut that hit for you, but my engineer wasn't ready to put the hours in the studio, so I had to get rid of him," Bone said, speaking in code.

Qwess was confused. Oh, he understood Bone's lingo, but

he hadn't issued a hit on anyone. "Which song you talking about?" he asked.

"You know, the one with the guy from back in the day singing on it."

"Ohhhhh, that song. Was the artist in-house?" Qwess asked. *Was he a member of the Crew?*

"Sheeeit, I was going to the original source. I wasn't even getting the sample cleared."

Qwess paused to decipher what Bone was telling him. When it became clear, Qwess nearly panicked. "Whoa, hold off on that. Matter fact, pull up."

"Say no more. I'll be in touch."

Qwess ended the call and replayed the conversation in his head. It sounded like Bone was telling him he was about to take out Linda Swansen or John Meyers. That move would be suicide! With a $75 million dollar lawsuit hanging on his head, he would be suspect number one.

Qwess exhaled a ball of stress and peered out of the cabin to the deck where Doe and Prince were fishing. Soon-to-be-eight-year-old Prince was struggling with his fishing pole while Doe tried to guide him. This trip was supposed to be about relaxation, a quick unwind session before the team left for L.A. to attend the BET Awards. However, it seemed Qwess was wearing stress and trouble like a blanket lately, more like a straitjacket.

"Yooo! Come on out here, man," Doe called to Qwess. "These fish biting."

Qwess joined Doe and Prince on the deck and found his pole.

"What was that about?" Doe asked. With his fisherman bucket hat pulled low, he resembled a mix between EPMD and Gilligan. His bare face was supposed to make him look younger, but with his light skin and long hair, he looked just like the rapper Ice-T—now.

Qwess waved his hand. "That ain't about nothing."

He said it nonchalantly, but the lie didn't settle in his gut. He actually felt as if the walls were closing in on him. Grief, lawsuits, his frequent trips back to the streets, his renegade superstar riding with his nemesis . . . all of it was weighing on him, and wisdom taught him things would probably get worse before things got better.

He just didn't know how right he was.

Chapter 8

South of France

Diamond was balling on another level. How else could Flame explain laying up on a yacht big enough to rival a battleship?

Diamond's yacht was named *Bertha*, after his late mother. It boasted enough bedrooms to sleep twelve (outside of the eighteen-man crew), a full-scale kitchen, a dining area, movie theater, pool, spa, basketball/tennis court, dance room, and three full bars. A helicopter rested on the upper deck, four jet skis and a speedboat lay in the bowels of the ship. Six hundred five feet of floating luxury.

The first night they all had dinner on the aft bridge deck and watched the sunset. Beautiful! By the time the last drop of champagne dripped into Flame's mouth, he and Kim were alone together. They spent the entire night together, fondling each other like teenagers, but Kim refused to let Flame go any further. It was like she had a force field around her vagina. She allowed him to smell it, feel it, and even see it. But she would not let him fuck her.

The following few days were a whirlwind of drinking, smoking, and eating. They spent the majority of the time coupled off, and Flame learned a lot about Kim.

Kim told Flame all about her growing up in Houston, Texas. Her parents were well off and supported her music aspirations early on. She and Sasha were like sisters. They grew up a mere house away from each other, while Monica was from the Southside. Just as their careers began to take off it was revealed that Sasha's father had an illegitimate child. The news shattered Sasha's family, and she delved into music to keep herself distracted. Their fledgling group needed a den mother to assist them as they traveled, so they chose Sasha's mother to keep her away from home. From then on, Sasha's family was virtually nonexistent. She moved in with Kim full-time, where she remained until they blew up.

Flame was digging Kim's vibe. She was cool people, but he made a note to never confide in her. She spilled her "sister's" business like she was subpoenaed at a deposition.

On the third day they found a cove tucked deep in the Mediterranean and dropped an anchor. Kim and Flame jumped on separate jet skis and ran them out like they were competing in the water Olympics. The European women gawked at Flame as if he was an exotic fish. Maybe they recognized him. Maybe they didn't. Flame wasn't concerned about those women. He was focused on Kim. She had hijacked all his attention. She hadn't packed anything other than string bikinis for the whole trip, and she wore them often and well. Yellow ones. Reds. Zebra prints. Brazilian colors. The whole fuckin' rainbow! Taunting and teasing Flame. After shutting Flame down the previous night, the way she was flaunting her curves in his face should have been a crime.

Flame heard Kim was a virgin, and if she planned on maintaining that V-card she was messing with the wrong dude.

Flame finally cornered Kim on the beach. After playing tag, he snatched her up, and she fell on top of him in the soft sand. They kissed slowly and passionately with lots of tongue and saliva.

Flame dug inside her treasure. She was so wet, fish could've swum inside her walls. He deftly slipped a finger inside her G-string and started strumming like a guitar.

"Stop, Flame," Kim moaned. But she kept grinding on his stiff dick. Flame was ready to roll her over and beat sparks from her pussy right there in front of everybody.

"Come on, Kim," Flame begged.

"There are people out here," Kim whined between kisses.

"And?"

She was hot. So wet. So ready.

"*And?*"

"I'm saying, just let me put the head in. Ain't nobody thinking 'bout us. Come on, Kim. You scared?"

She was moaning and bucking so hard they might as well have been fuckin'. Flame reached inside his trunks to pull his man out. He was harder than granite and primed like a cannon. Kim saw it, and her eyes grew large, then small, as she fell into the moment.

Flame slid her yellow G-string aside, and the heat from her center rushed on Flame. Then . . .

SPLASH!

A tidal wave crashed over them. Soaked them to the bone. Flame peeked around Kim and saw Sasha climbing off a jet ski. As she stormed in their direction Flame saw that scene from James Bond with Halle Berry in his head. Sasha was sporting the same orange bikini, white belt and all. Only thing she was missing was the knife. But her curves cut the air sharper than any blade would. Flame visualized children swimming inside those hips.

Sasha snatched Kim up. "We need to talk."

"What?" Kim asked, confused. But Sasha was already headed back to the jet ski. "Oh, lord, they at it again," Kim huffed. "Look, I have to help Sasha. Her and Diamond at it again."

Flame was standing there with a dick harder than a mountain and she was on some crusade with Sasha? Flame shook his head.

Kim looked back and stared right at Flame's woody. "I got you, Flame. Don't worry," she said. "I'ma take care of you later."

Then she jumped on her jet ski and followed Sasha, the machines spewing water up like a dolphin's blowhole.

Later found Kim and Flame on the bow of the ship finishing what they began earlier. The others were lost in the bowels of the ship where the private quarters were located. The moon shone down on them, illuminating their paths to exploration as Flame kissed Kim long and deep. She pressed her bare back against the railing and thrust her hips forward into Flame. He could feel the heat from her pussy warming his bare stomach. He reached between her legs and slid his finger through the lips of her pussy. Her hot wetness coated his fingers, thick and sticky. He curled them inside her, and she went crazy.

"Ohhh, Flame," she moaned into his ear, grinding against him. "Yessssss," she hissed. She reached down and cupped his dick. Squeezed it. Stroked it. Moaned at the length and girth.

She must didn't know who she was playing with, poor little church girl. He was Flame the Furrier. If skinning women was murder, he'd be Hitler. She wasn't ready for him.

Or so he thought.

Kim dropped to her knees, and with no hesitation, put his erection in her warm mouth. His knees buckled and immediately Kim was in. She became a goddess in his eyes.

See, Flame had this principle. No matter how fine or beautiful a woman was, no matter how successful or rich, no matter how smart she was or how many degrees she hung on the wall, if she couldn't suck a good dick, he had no need for her. Not in the long run.

The way Kim was getting down, he could see himself rocking with her forever. Church girl? Sheeeit! She must have likened herself to Bathsheba.

Kim got into a good rhythm, sucking him off with just the right amount of pressure, saliva, and hands. Flame cocked his head back and enjoyed the moment. This was the life of a superstar, getting good head in a foreign land from an international bitch on a yacht while the moon beamed down on him. This was the life he always envisioned for himself.

Kim continued to do her thing until Flame felt his nut bubbling to the surface. He was ready to squeeze off right in Kim's mouth when suddenly she stopped sucking. She looked up at Flame while holding his stiffness in her hand. Slowly, she licked him up and down with the tip of her tongue, from the head down to his balls. Then she started tea-bagging them, dropping both balls inside her mouth one at a time. She definitely knew how to do more with that mouth than just sing. Flame was in heaven!

But he still wanted to feel that pussy.

Flame pulled Kim up and turned her around. He bent her over the railing. He slipped her G-string to the side and tested her with his finger. She was more than ready. He caught a whiff of her scent as evidence. Flame grabbed his dick and guided it toward her opening. He felt the hot heat from her pussy licking at his head. She was so tight he had a little trouble sliding his thick ten inches past the opening. Just as he was about to penetrate her, someone screamed.

Loud.

Kim spun around. "Ohmygod, that's Sasha!"

Kim pushed Flame away and craned her neck in the air, her hand on her heaving chest.

Again, Sasha screamed.

Flame started in the direction but before he could pull the cape out, Kim stopped him.

"Wait. Don't get involved," Kim urged. "Don't! You don't want to cross Diamond."

Flame was confused. Don't cross Diamond? Her "sister" sounded like she was getting tarred and feathered and she was worried about him crossing Diamond?

A louder scream shot up from the bowels of the ship, and Flame couldn't restrain himself. He tore off in their direction, half sliding, half stumbling down the steps two at a time. He hung a right at the base of the steps and ran right into the master bedroom. The door was half open. He saw Diamond's bare ass hovering over Sasha's naked body like Ali did to Liston in that great fight. Diamond drew his fist back to hit her again, but Flame dashed into the room and grabbed Diamond's arm before it could connect with Sasha's face.

Diamond flung Flame like a rag doll into the mirrored wall. He recovered, then ran and jumped on his broad back. Flame held on for dear life, silently urging Sasha to get light, but she remained sprawled out on the bed like she wanted to get beat or something.

"Fuck off me, son!" Diamond barked, as he slung Flame around the room into a brass lamp. He and the lamp tumbled to the carpeted floor. Diamond hoisted Flame into the air from the floor and pinned him to the wall. Flame thought he heard his back break.

"Chill, dawg! Don't beat your girl!" Flame begged.

"Fuck dat! Bitch get outta line, she get beat!"

There was no way Flame could hold him back any longer. He had to try something, because Sasha still refused to move. The girl must have been a glutton for punishment.

"Yo, dawg, this supposed to be a vacation. Come *onnn!*" Flame urged. "Take it easy."

Thankfully, those words seemed to do the trick. Diamond calmed down. It was as if the words had flipped a switch.

Diamond nodded. "You know, you right, you right, li'l homie. This *is* a vacation. Can't let no bitch fuck dat up."

"Yeah, you know, I'm saying . . ." He was *saying* anything to get him up out of that room.

Diamond stepped into a pair of basketball shorts from the floor and led the way outside. Through the mirror on the wall Flame saw him mouth something to Sasha. She cringed and frowned. Flame decided to follow Diamond before things escalated again, but before he walked through the door after Diamond, he spared a look over his shoulder at Sasha's naked body. Even distressed and disheveled, she was still beautiful as an angel. The image of her red nipples and neatly trimmed vagina seared into Flame's mind forever. He felt it was one of the most beautiful visions he had ever seen. He thought to himself, *What kind of monster would abuse a woman this beautiful?*

Flame and Diamond settled on the stern of the ship, and for the remainder of the night they posted up sipping champagne, blowing weed, and politicking. Of course, Diamond steered the conversation to what he cared about most: himself.

"Yo, the bitch love me, son. She'll never leave me," he stated confidently, referring to Sasha. "Know why?"

Flame eagerly awaited his answer. He wanted to know the secret. How could this rich, uncouth Neanderthal keep such a stunning woman loyal to him? What was the secret he possessed that made a woman that niggas lusted all over the world for stay with his abusive ass?

Diamond allowed Flame to hang on to his words before he answered, "'Cause I treat her like any other bitch."

Flame thought his ears were deceiving him. Was he serious? Clearly, Diamond had clearly flipped his wig. Yet he continued with the fuckery.

"Word, son. Let me tell you something about women," he began. "Women like to be abused, B; I'm telling you! They love drama! Yo, if you don't have drama in your relationship a bitch will create some just to be happy. These bitches don't know what happiness is because a lot of these bitches come from broken homes. They never seen happy before, so they don't want to be it."

Flame thought about what Kim had said about Sasha when
she snitched her out. Surely, that was the low point of Sasha's
life, and here he was using it to exploit her.

Diamond continued, "And Sasha is no different. She
probably worse. If I treated her like she deserved to be treated,
she'd take advantage of me. I treat her like she wants to be
treated, so I'm taking advantage of her." He shrugged. "It's
simple. It's either I lead or I follow, and I'm a boss, so you already know."

Diamond really believed the hype. He believed every
word he uttered. Flame was flabbergasted.

Diamond continued to bash women and brag about how
he abused Sasha. With every word he spoke, Flame was rearranging his motives inside his head. Initially, all he'd wanted
to do was fuck Sasha, but if she was an accomplice to this type
of treatment, then he knew he could easily sweep her off her
feet and make her his. Like he was watching a movie, Flame
saw pictures of himself and Sasha ruling the entertainment
world. The artist in him painted vivid images of him holding
Sasha's hand at some of the same events he'd seen her attend
with Diamond. He simply exchanged Diamond's face for his
own. The sight was so pretty he had to stifle a smile while Diamond ranted and pretty much laid his broad in Flame's lap.

So, as Diamond spoke ill about Sasha all night, Flame sympathized and devised a plan to make her feel better.

Diamond was in his zone, talking about himself. He became really incensed and tapped Flame on the arm.

"Let me tell you a little story about why I treat these
bitches how I do," Diamond said. He took a long pull from
his Kush joint and gazed out into the waters. "Bitch I loved
before, when I was younger, played me for a fool. Man, I gave
that bitch everything! Back when I was getting money too, so

I kept her laced." Diamond pulled deep on the weed and reminisced deeper. He seemed to find images of the memory in the fire of the blunt. "Yep, betrayed me with my right-hand man."

"Damn, that's fucked up," Flame whispered, thinking about how bad he wanted to fuck Sasha right then.

"I suspected these muthafuckas of cheating all the time. Nigga was always in her face, cheesing and grinning and shit, then talking bad about her to me."

"Damn."

"I asked her about the nigga, and she lied. Told me, nah, the nigga ain't never came on to her. Swore on her kids, mama grave . . . hell, she swore on everything that wasn't nailed down. But in the end, the bitch was lying. Caught her fucking the nigga in *my* bed in *my* house."

"Damn, that's fucked up!"

"Nah." Diamond chuckled. "What's fucked up is what happened to them. Let's just say they won't be crossing any-body anymore."

Flame figured that he was referring to the notorious incident that made Diamond a street legend, the incident where he allegedly chopped up his woman and the guy. He never knew the guy was his friend.

Diamond turned to Flame with fire blazing in his eyes. "My nigga, I ain't never told this to nobody outside my circle and if I ever hear it again, I'll know where it came from, but yo . . . when I heard that nigga scream . . ." A sinister smile spread across Diamond's face, and he let his words linger.

Flame quickly steered the conversation in another direction. He wanted no part of a murder confession. Nor did he want to hear about what happened to a man that did the very thing he was fantasizing about at that exact moment.

"Yo, you ever dreamed that you would be this rich?" Flame said.

"Fuuuuck yeah. I always knew I was going to be a money-getting nigga. I always knew I would get rich or die trying. Word."

For the next hour Diamond told war stories about ways he got to the bag in his youth. Flame only half listened. He was just glad that the tension was eased and Diamond was done with his come-to-Jesus moments.

The next morning Flame woke up alone. He searched around the 700-count Egyptian sheets for Kim, but she was nowhere to be found. He looked on the nightstand and found a note: *Gone shopping.*

Flame eased out of bed and ventured upstairs to the kitchen for a bite to eat. His sweaty t-shirt clung to his back while the cool air massaged his morning erection through the thin pajamas he wore. In the kitchen he found a burnt sausage in a frying pan. He palmed it and dipped out of the kitchen.

On his way back downstairs he saw Sasha standing alone on the railing looking far off into the water as if she was searching for her soul. After what he'd witnessed and heard the previous night, he didn't trust himself around her. Although she was now draped in a sheer sarong and bikini top, all he saw when he looked at her were the images burned into his brain of her naked body. He didn't want to invade her space, or tempt himself, so he pretended not to see her and kept walking.

Fat chance.

He wasn't around the corner good before she called his name. "Flame, got a second?"

Flame doubled back and stood beside her chomping on his sausage. "Where's Diamond?" he asked.

"They all went shopping," she told him in her Southern twang. Damn, she was countrier than cornbread and catfish. She pointed to the empty helipad. "They took the chopper."

"Everybody?" Flame asked. Sasha nodded.

Damn, it was just them.

Flame leaned over the railing beside her and stared off into the calm waters with her, content to remain silent, but Sasha had other plans.

"Why, Flame? Why do men fight so hard to get us, then fight to push us away?" she wondered aloud.

Flame couldn't fathom ever fighting or pushing her away. He told her just that.

"That's what they all say," she replied and rolled her eyes.

"I'm not all of them. Or none of them."

She looked at Flame thoughtfully. He looked away. She threw a few more questions his way. He either dodged them or batted them out of the park. Each time she gave him more thoughtful glances.

For close to an hour, Sasha and Flame exchanged light and playful banter while he tried to keep his erection in check (or at least out of sight).

When they heard the chopper approaching in the distance, they fell silent and stole glances at each other as if they both were trying to lock the memory in forever. They remained silent as if they were two criminals stealing something. In a way, they were stealing something: a moment.

The chopper landed on the helipad, and Sasha turned to Flame. "Flame, do you think I'm sexy?"

A lump gathered in Flame's throat. This was Sasha Beaufont. *People*, *Vibe*, *Smooth*, and *Maxim* magazines had all voted her sexiest woman alive at some point. And no one could dispute it.

"Come on, Sasha, you were voted sexiest in the world by everybody," he reminded her.

"But you're not everybody or nobody," she quipped, turning his words against him. "I want to know what *you* think."

Diamond, Ball, Monica, and Kim stepped from the chopper, hands filled with bags. They were headed toward them with Diamond leading the way. Flame instantly felt guilty and wondered if Diamond could intuit that he'd had mind sex with his chick for the majority of the morning. He had polished his crown jewel while he was out collecting more worthless things.

"Flame?" Sasha persisted. "Do you think I'm sexy?"

Diamond was getting closer.

Flame looked at Sasha from head to toe. Did it twice, so she could see him looking. He allowed her to see his eyes rest on her pretty toes and zoom up to her thick bowed legs. He allowed her to watch his eyes sweep across her tight six-pack, up to her brown eyes, and fall to rest on her camel toe that he could see peeking from behind the sheer sarong she wore.

Flame mumbled through clenched teeth, "Sexier than a muthafucka."

Sasha's smile beamed brighter than the sun roasting France. "Thanks," she gushed.

Diamond reached them and hugged Sasha tightly. Flame did the same with Kim. Over Kim's head Flame could see Sasha's face nestled into Diamond's massive chest. She was still smiling, looking at him with dreamy eyes.

Flame's erection pulsated against Kim's thigh, and she smiled. Little did she know it had nothing to do with her. Flame was thinking about all the things he was going to do to Sasha, for he knew right then, he was, indeed, going to fuck Sasha Beaufont.

Chapter 9

Diamond was making it too easy for Flame.

As luck would have it, a last-minute emergency popped up that prevented Sasha from making her flight from Atlanta to Cali with Diamond for the awards show. Being that Flame and his crew were flying private on a Gulfstream, Diamond called and asked if Sasha could tag along on his plane to Cali. He said that Flame was the only one he trusted with his bitch.

Ohhh, the irony!

The entire five-hour flight Sasha and Flame posted up in the back of the plane away from everyone. As the champagne flowed, their lips became looser and looser. Naturally, the conversation turned to France.

"So did you enjoy yourself over there?" Sasha asked. "Seems like Kim was really feeling you," she added.

"Yeah, it was fun. Light fun," Flame answered evasively. It was obvious she was on a fishing expedition.

"Light fun? Come on, I barely saw you guys!"

Flame laughed. "Nah, it wasn't like that."

"Um-mmm." She grabbed her glass of champagne and swigged it. Then she grabbed Flame's hand and put it in hers.

She placed both of their hands on the wooden table. "So tell me, Flame, who has the better body?"

Flame nearly choked on his drink. "What?"

Sasha doubled down. "You heard me."

Flame looked away. "What are you talking 'bout?"

Sasha grinned and cocked her head to the side. Her long brown hair fell softly across her shoulders. "Flame, don't tell me you weren't looking at me when you rescued me. I saw you!"

"I mean . . . I . . . I mean . . ."

"It's all right, dang." Sasha giggled innocently. "You act like it's a crime or something. Anyway, you wanna answer the question?"

"I would, but I can't really say, because I haven't really seen her naked," Flame admitted. He hadn't seen her naked, per se. He had fondled and fiddled all of her naked parts, but he hadn't actually *seen* her naked.

"Yeah, right?" Sasha scoffed and shook her head. "See?"

"See what? Word, I haven't, Sash."

"Well, I'm sure she would love to see you naked," Sasha teased.

"What makes you so sure?"

"I mean . . . I . . . you know, you're an attractive man."

Flame giggled and mocked her. "It's all right, dang. You act like it's a crime or something."

"Ahhh, touché."

They shared a laugh.

For the remainder of the flight the conversation took the same tone: subtle flirting and backpedaling from both of them. Both showing interest, but neither of them wanting to cross that line, the Diamond line.

When they landed at the airport a car was waiting for Sasha, and Qwess was waiting on Flame. 8-Ball took Sasha's bag to the waiting Bentley Mulsanne while Sasha remained with Flame. It seemed as if she was reluctant to leave his side, almost as if she was claiming him as her man.

Sasha hugged Flame and clung to him as if she didn't want to let him go. "Thank you, Flame," she said, sincerity pooling in her eyes. "I needed this. I really did. It's good to know somebody still finds me fun, intelligent, and attractive."

Suddenly, Sasha crossed the code. She leaned over and kissed Flame right on his lips. It wasn't a deep, sexy French number, but it wasn't a stage kiss either. It was a statement kiss, a changing of the guard. The kiss lasted a millisecond but felt like an eternity.

Sasha slid into her car, and Flame found all eyes on him.

Qwess.

Ball.

Amin.

Lisa.

They all looked disgusted, shocked, or disappointed. Maybe a combination of them all.

Flame was confused. Thoroughly confused.

"What. The. Fuck. Was. That. About?" Qwess asked. Flame was speechless. "Yo, my nigga, are you fucking crazy?"

Lisa piped in, stunned. "Flame, this isn't good. You're playing with fire."

"Fire we don't fucking need," Qwess added.

Flame shook his head and walked away. "I don't need any of this shit," he mumbled.

It was as if the universe was conspiring with Flame and Sasha, for the arrangement of the awards show had all of them sitting together. As the top nominees, they were all seated in the front row. Between Flame and Kismet, they had garnered the majority of the nominations for the night's top honors.

Flame was seated beside Kismet's manager and then Sasha was beside her. Qwess was on the other side of Flame, followed by his wife, R&B starlet-actress-model-producer-activist (and closet lesbian) Lisa Ivory. Then came Doe, the VP of Atlantic Beach Productions, and Amin. Diamond was clear on the other side of the auditorium with his crew of midnight marauders.

The night began with a performance by some country group that was nominated for a few awards. Qwess was performing after the following group, so when the Dixie boys finished whining, he left to prepare.

Thirty minutes later Flame was ready to go, rocking thin leather Carolina-blue pants, a matching vest that cut up around his rib cage, and Carolina-blue-and-white shell-toe Adidas. Underneath the vest he wore a wife beater with the Flaming Diamond logo emblazoned in the center.

The announcer introduced Flame, and he took the stage spitting a medley of hits from his rap catalog. He gyrated at the crowd like a ghetto Elvis, spitting his namesake—flames. The crowd hung on to his every word, singing along to his raunchy raps with no shame. Even the thugs were chanting his lyrics and egging him on.

Flame rapped, "All my niggaz over there . . . if you like yo' bitches nasty say, heeellll yeah!"

The crowd echoed, "Heeellll yeah!"

"All my ladies in this bitch . . . say helllll yeah if you like yo' ass licked!"

"Hellll yeahhhhh!"

Flame was in his element, hyping the crowd, asserting his position in the game. He was reminding everyone of who he was and why he was one of the top stars in the game. He was reminding them what a superstar looked like when he was getting busy.

Then suddenly he thumbed his throat and the music screeched to a halt with an explosion. Flame posed in the middle of the stage, dripping sweat, staring right at the camera. Slowly, he shed his vest and bared the hologrammed shirt that sported the Flaming Diamond log. It took a second for the crowd to realize what they were looking at, but when it registered, they went berserk.

The ladies in the house screamed, "We love you, Flame!"

Flame soaked up the adulation. "And I love you back!" He stood in the middle of the stage eyeing the crowd. "Let me show you how much."

Flame gestured to the back, and Anetral sauntered from backstage in thigh-high boots, coochie-cutter shorts, and a ripped Flaming Diamond t-shirt. The music for his ballad came on, and he changed his whole style up in the blink of an eye.

Flame dropped his voice an octave and oozed honey-coated lyrics about real love. At first, the crowd couldn't believe it was actually him. Then they thought he was lip-synching. Flame already expected this, so he made the DJ stop the music and sang a cappella, ad libbing chastising words for the haters and encouraging words to his supporters.

Flame was floating. He felt good. Real good. He saw white faces, black faces, brown faces, all hanging on to his every word, repeating them, reciting them as if they were a part of them . . . Hard knocks who were just echoing his nasty choruses were now crooning his melodic tunes.

Flame ended his performance to a standing ovation and walked backstage on a natural high. He bumped right into Kismet as they were about to take the stage. Kim rushed him and wrapped him in a strong embrace.

"Ohmygod, Flame, I'm so proud of you! You killed it!"

The whole move took him off guard, and he was wondering if Sasha had told her about the kiss on the tarmac. He cut his eyes at Sasha, and she was looking away as if she didn't see Kim had him yoked up. But he knew she saw the whole move.

"Thanks, girl," Flame said nonchalantly and lightly pushed her away. "You up now; show me something. Let me get back to my seat."

Flame returned to his seat and watched as Kismet took the stage with fanfare, all smoke and explosions. When the smoke cleared, all three girls posed onstage in different variations of pink leather. Sasha wore a short skirt that exposed the bottom half of her ass cheeks, while Monica wore tight pants. Kim had on shorts. The bass-heavy music dropped, and they commenced to gyrating and shaking their asses like they were in Atlanta's strip dens.

Then the music switched up to their ballad; the one where they sang about all the nice and freaky things they'd do to their man. That's when shit flipped up and went into the annals of legendary performances.

The women sauntered offstage right into the front row. Monica attacked Doe with her long legs, while Kim made a beeline for Flame, but Sasha intercepted her, forcing Kim to settle for the consolation prize: Qwess.

Kim began winding her hips like she was competing down in Jamaica, all the while humming the chorus's freaky implications. Like a domino, they went down the line, whining and singing, seducing the crowd while they seduced the men. By the time Sasha began winding on Flame's lap, it was a wrap! She placed her pretty ass in his lap like a wicked gift. Her skin was so soft Flame could feel it through his leather pants. He'd received lap dances in strip clubs less provocative, in front of fewer people. Sasha wound on him in front of the whole world while promising to cook him dinner, rub his feet, and even suck his crusty toes. The eye contact made it seem as if she was talking to him.

Flame caught the bug. Seduced by the moment, he forgot that the world was watching. He forgot about being a professional. He even forgot about her treacherous boyfriend lurking in the shadows. Sasha was putting it down so hard, Flame jumped all the way out the window. He reached up and grabbed Sasha's bare ass. He doubted anyone could see it but the people on either side of him. Still, he knew it, and Sasha knew it. Just as fast as his hand melted into her soft flesh, he released it.

Embarrassed, Flame leaned back in his chair and attempted to recover. Sasha, Kim, and Monica wound in unison a little longer then returned to the stage to complete their set.

As soon as they wandered backstage, a slim actress made it to the mic and announced the award for Best New Single.

Flame.

Flame froze. His dick was so hard he could pole vault with it. Surely he couldn't get up now. Qwess patted Flame on his back and stood clapping, as did the rest of the auditorium. Flame couldn't help himself. He loved the spotlight, and his fame was calling out to him. He said fuck it, stood and let the world see what his dad had blessed him with. As he swaggered to the stage to receive his award, his pants were tenting about mid-thigh. The actress passed him the award and shook his hand. Protocol dictated she hug him, but she saw his monster sticking out and wanted no part of it. She stood to the side awkwardly, blushing, while Flame gave his acceptance speech.

"First of all, I'd like to thank the fans for embracing my change. Change is good! I'd like to thank my record label; Doe, Amin, and others for standing behind me. And I'd like to thank . . . the South. We still in this beeeeeiitch!"

Flame ducked backstage to pass off his award and did an interview with reps from Foxy 99, his radio station back in Fayetteville. As he was speaking, he saw Sasha talking to Niya. She and Sasha looked at him and giggled like schoolgirls trapped in a conspiracy. Flame heard Niya screech, "All right, gurl!" Then they high-fived each other.

Flame finished his interview and rushed back to his seat to wait for the results of the other nominations, glad to be the hell up outta there.

Turned out, Kismet swept the rest of the awards. They won a few insignificant awards and gave basic speeches, but when the most important nomination came—Album of the Year—everyone was on pins and needles, awaiting the winner. When the smoke cleared, Kismet emerged victorious again.

The ladies seemed to float to the stage as they took the podium and thanked God like he produced their album or something. Then they left the stage to prepare for their closing set, a rendition of their greatest hits.

Flame took that as his cue to exit stage left to prepare for the after-party. Everybody and their mama was having a party, but Flame was going to the one Diamond was hosting, mostly just to piss Qwess off since he was hosting a shindig also.

Chapter 10

Diamond's party was being thrown in the ballroom at one of L.A.'s finest hotels. From the moment Flame stepped in the door he didn't plan on staying long. It was a typical industry party. Lots of drinks. Hordes of drugs. A bevy of beautiful women. Fake gangstas ice-grilling. Real gangstas smiling. Flame was still riding high from his performance, and everyone bigged him up as he and 8-Ball made their way through the crowd of partygoers to the section where the stars of his caliber were chilling.

8-Ball and Flame hadn't been out since France, and Ball couldn't stop talking about Monica. She had him fucked up!

They found a corner table, sipped champ as if they had just secured the championship, and kicked the bobo. 8-Ball was filling Flame in on the conversations he and Monica had been having over the past weeks when suddenly all the attention shifted toward the entrance. Flame craned his head to see what the commotion was about and saw Kismet strolling into the party.

"Shit, speaking of the devil!" Flame said. "They're

heeeeere . . ." 8-Ball smiled sheepishly while Flame ducked lower in his seat to avoid the ladies.

The stunt Sasha pulled earlier had Flame feeling uncomfortable. He could tell by the curious stares when he came in that people were talking about him. He just knew they were talking about the performance, in his head anyway. He was just making moves and potentially doing big things with Diamond. He wasn't trying to fuck that up. He had been a player long enough to know when a woman was throwing pussy at him, and Sasha may as well have been a pitcher.

Though he'd dreamed about sexing her since the first time he ever saw her, it just wouldn't be good for business. Too much potential backdraft.

Suddenly an idea came to him. He hopped out his seat and found his way to where the ladies had just settled at a table. He grabbed Kim by the arm and took her to a corner near the balcony. He made sure everyone saw him with her as he took her to that corner.

"What are you doing?" Kim asked as she smiled and allowed him to drag her behind him.

"I'm trying to do you," Flame quipped, placing her back against the wall.

They drifted off into their own little alcove. Somewhere they could do them without being noticed.

"We have unfinished business," Flame whispered in her ear over the Chris Brown track rocking the room. He swooped in and kissed her neck.

"What?" Kim giggled. "You jealous that we won."

"Please. Y'all only won a couple awards."

"Yeah, but we won the biggest one."

"Ahh, good one!" Flame said. He wrapped her up and kissed her again. "Cut it out. Let's get back to what you owe me."

"What I owe you?"

"This."

Flame reached under her short skirt, glad she'd changed clothes. She wore no panties.

"Unh-unh, Flame. All these people in here," Kim whispered. "And I'm not about to let you add me to your long list of conquests."

"Cut it out." Flame kissed her and rubbed her kitty.

"Flame, you are crazy!"

"About you right now. Now, come on."

Flame rubbed Kim's shaved pussy, and she moaned inside his ear. She squirmed and fidgeted but she didn't stop him. He rubbed it again, and she drew in a deep breath.

"Flame," she whispered icily.

Flame kissed away her protests and fingered her wetness. In and out. In and out. With two fingers. Kim bucked on his hand and exhaled the smell of breath mints into his nostrils. Flame cupped her tight ass with his other hand and pulled her to him so she could feel his erection.

"Feel that?" he asked. She nodded. "Take it out."

Kim hesitated for a second, then she slid her hand inside his pants and gripped his hard meat with her soft hands. She stroked it a couple times.

"Pull it out," Flame instructed. Kim whipped it out. "Put it in, Kim," Flame whispered, still fingering her. "Don't play wit' it. Let me feel you . . ."

Kim was losing it. She kept swallowing hard, panting as she tried to fight her passion. She was losing the battle, failing miserably. Flame felt her inhibitions leaking out, hot and thick. He felt her resolve breathing hard on his lips.

Flame eased the front of Kim's skirt up to her waist. Right there in the dark room with intoxicated people walking mere feet in front of them, yet oblivious to what was about to go down. Right there with Usher beating the walls down.

Right there in the room while everyone sipped, smoked, sniffed, and popped pills, Kim popped her entertainment cherry and eased Flame's stiffness inside her tight walls.

Flame gasped hard at the suction. Kim was extra tight. It felt like he was plowing through virgin walls.

Kim shrieked and tried to pull back, but there was nowhere to go. Flame gripped her waist and allowed her pleated skirt to fall over their connection. Once her skirt shrouded them he thrust harder. Her panting only enticed him more. Soon she became wetter and he was able to push through her barrier and stroke her like he wanted to.

Flame pushed her up against the wall and drove himself deeper and deeper. Kim wrapped her arms around Flame's neck and met each stroke with a thrust from her hips. When he leaned, she rocked. When he pushed, she pulled him in. Kim wrapped her left leg around the back of Flame's knees and moaned in his ear.

"Flame . . . Flame . . ."

The more Kim moaned his name, the more his mind played tricks on him. Each time Kim said his name he heard Sasha's voice. That turned him on even more.

Flame started hitting Kim harder, oblivious to where they were. Each time she moaned, he heard Sasha's voice.

Then he *really* heard Sasha's voice.

Flame and Kim were snatched back to reality. Flame heard Sasha arguing with someone.

Kim heard it too. "Damn!" Kim muttered. She pushed Flame away from her and clipped their connection. "That's Sasha."

"Sasha?" Flame said. But Kim was already gone.

Kim blew past Flame while he adjusted his clothing. She made it to the fracas just in time to see Sasha dash a glass of champagne into Diamond's face. He calmly licked his lips like LL and smiled. Then security broke the two up.

Flame, with 8-Ball by his side, arrived in time to see Diamond's champagne baptism too. He was stuck between a rock and a hard place. He didn't know if he was the source of the confusion or not. He didn't want to add injury to insult, so he fell back and played spectator like everyone else.

After security cleared things up and Sasha and Diamond were separated, Flame tapped 8-Ball on his arm. "Damn, I feel sorry for ole gurl," he said.

"Shit, I feel sorry for ole boy!" 8-Ball laughed.

"Nah, trust me, I feel sorry for her."

"Why?"

"'Cause first chance he get, he gon' beat her ass!"

Qwess was in VSVIP when Sasha embarrassed Diamond. He didn't see it, of course, because Qwess was on another mission, but he was definitely in the building.

While hosting an official BET awards after-party, Qwess had run into his new friend from Vegas, Liam. Liam claimed that he had come to L.A. because he wanted to talk to Qwess in person. Some things weren't meant to be discussed over the phone, he claimed. However, Liam had to see someone else while in L.A. He shot Qwess the address and asked him to come there as soon as possible. As fortune would have it, the address Liam texted to Qwess was Diamond's party.

Qwess and Hulk arrived at the party while it was in full swing. They ignored the grimy looks from members of Diamond's crew and quickly made their way to Liam in the Very Special Very Important People section.

Qwess found Liam at a table sitting near the edge of the balcony so he could see all the action. With Liam's swarthy skin and tailored suit, he stuck out from the mostly hip-hop and street crowd, but he didn't appear to be uncomfortable at all. Qwess had seen his type before, Jews that hovered over the entertainment industry moving and shifting supposed bosses around like pieces on a chessboard, dangling them around on strings like puppets. People like Liam knew they weren't threatened in these crowds because they controlled the people that set the tone of the streets, athletes and enter-tainers. To touch someone like him would be akin to harming Moses, for he indeed parted the sea to guide people to the promised land of wealth and prosperity. It was people like him that Qwess separated himself from when he went totally inde-pendent. Now, here he was again dining with the devil.

"Liam, what's going on, my brother?" Qwess greeted him over the music."

"Qwess, my friend, take a seat."

Qwess sat beside Liam, and they soaked up the vibe of the party, pausing to point and comment about certain people they recognized.

"Hey, isn't that your boy?" Liam noted, pointing at Flame.

Flame was walking through the crowd chasing Kim with 8-Ball on his heels.

"Yeah, that's him," Qwess said.

"Man, that was a hell of a performance tonight. He's spe-cial, that kid there."

"Yeah, he is. The problem is, he knows it."

"Don't they all."

The men laughed. "Indeed."

As Qwess and Liam watched Flame wade through the crowd, his path led right to Diamond and Sasha.

"Now that guy right there is bad news," Liam said, gestur-ing to Diamond. "I don't know how they let him in the game with all his red gang shit and strong-arming. You would think they learned from the guy on the West Coast," Liam figured. "That girl there is his meal ticket, though. She makes him safe. Without her by his side, he would be gone in a year."

Almost on cue, Sasha splashed her drink in Diamond's face.

"Ohhhhh, shit! Look at that." Qwess laughed, unable to contain his glee at Diamond's misfortune.

"Hey, that's a smart girl right there," Liam joked. "Cool his ass off."

They watched as security intervened and cleared the area. Qwess paid particular attention to Flame. The kiss at the airport was still in his mind, and he wanted to make sure he wasn't about to be a casualty of a domestic. Although he and Flame weren't on great terms, he was still his cash cow and homeboy.

Liam stood. "Hey, let's go up to my suite and discuss some business. This is shutting down soon anyway."

Qwess instructed Hulk to remain behind and keep an eye on Flame while he followed Liam up to his suite.

Inside the suite Qwess and Liam were all alone. Liam poured them more drinks and passed Flame a thick, dark cigar.

"It's a Cuban," Liam remarked.

Qwess walked around admiring the suite while preparing his cigar. In actuality, he was inspecting his surroundings to see who else was inside.

"No one else is here, my friend," Liam said. "You can relax."

Something in Liam's tone made Qwess uneasy. He knew how the upper echelons of the entertainment industry played the game, which is why he retired so many years ago. At the next level, executives used homosexuality as a tool of power. They dangled lucrative opportunities over the heads of artists and low-level execs in exchange for their manhood. Those who bowed down came up. Those who refused were pushed out of the industry with a scandal, most of the time with a sexual assault case from a woman, ironically. Qwess had attended parties where everything was normal, then in an instant things turned . . . different. He witnessed rich and famous men sucking off other men with no shame. He saw men who were the personification of masculinity on television screens all over the world getting pegged by diminutive, dainty men. He recalled one incident in particular that occurred while he was at a party in the Hollywood Hills that a rap mega-producer had thrown. At some point during the night when things had turned different, Qwess stumbled into a room while looking for his coat to leave. He saw the producer in the middle of the floor on his hands and knees. A brolic, convict-looking man was behind him slamming damn near a foot of penis in his rectum while another man stood in front of his face masturbating. The look of ecstasy on the producer's face was etched into Qwess's brain forever. It was then he knew he had to leave the circles of the entertainment industry. It was clear to him, if the devil had a home on earth, it would be in Hollywood. Yet, here he was in Hollywood again.

"Relax? I can never do that," Qwess said.

"Have you ever heard of Streamify, Qwess?"

"Streamify?" He'd heard of the music streaming company that was shaking things up in the industry with their new way of delivering music. "Yeah, I'm familiar. What about them?"

"I can tell you firsthand that Streamify has *them* shaking in their boots. Music streaming is the wave of the future. There are some technical glitches right now, and some problems with the way they do business. They're a European based company, so they don't have the access to resources like we do in the U.S., but they have the right idea. The technology will correct itself, because technology replicates itself every eighteen months. As far as the business . . . they need some help."

Qwess listened intently. He could see where Liam was going with this. Streamify was shaking up the game in the wake of the Rapster scandal that saw millions of songs pirated for free and artists not getting paid. However, the Rapster scandal magnified the problem with streaming music; it was too easy to pirate music. For the fans, it was a great thing, but it created a terrible business model. Qwess told him as much.

"Right! Because they're not doing it right!" Liam slid a folder across the table for Qwess. "Look at these numbers."

Qwess perused the contents of the folder. He saw staggering numbers. Millions of people were streaming music every day from all over the world.

"Imagine if they had their business in order?" Liam asked. "With the right technology to secure the rights of the artists and the right business model, streaming can create the next billionaire. I'm telling you!"

Qwess nodded. "So, what are you saying, you want us to invest in Streamify? Take it over?"

Liam smiled and shook his head. "You're still not hearing me." He stood, walked to the window, and peered out into the mountains in the distance. "I'm saying let's start the company to rival Streamify. Let's learn from their mistakes and correct their business model. Let's be the pioneers of streaming. With your catalog and pioneering spirit, and my relationships and business sense, we can change the game—and become billionaires in the process. So what do you say?"

"I say, why me?"

Liam smiled again. "I thought you'd never ask."

Chapter 11

About a week after the awards and the Cali fiasco, Flame was chilling in his new Manhattan apartment. He was still marveling at how lavish his shit was. He wasn't balling on Diamond's level yet, but his shit was proper. It boasted hardwood floors through and through. Floor to ceiling windows. Granite countertops. Pretty much the luxury basics. The walls were painted a deep purple and the furniture was gray. But the highlight was his home theater.

Flame had a ten-foot-wide screen specially installed with an HD 4K plasma projector, equipped to play DVDs and unfinished recordings. He loved to watch his performances come to life on the screen via YouTube. When the mood hit him, he would fire up some weed and watch porn too. The actresses' asses looked gargantuan on screen. This was his personal sanctuary where he burned good and kept the bootleggers in business. This was where he was relaunching the rebranding of Flame the businessman.

Flame was laid up watching *American Gangster*, blowing pine, scratching his nuts, when his cell rang with a 936 area code. The number was foreign to him. The only person he knew from Houston that would have his number was Kim, and he hadn't talked to her in a week.

He answered the call. "Flame?"

"Hey, gurl. What up?" He immediately noticed her voice sounded distressed.

"Can you come pick me up?"

"From H. Town?!"

"No, silly. I'm here, in New York."

"Oh. Uh . . . where are you?"

She told him her location.

"Uh . . . sure. Sure, I'll come get you. Be there in about forty-five minutes."

"Cool."

An hour and a half later Sasha and Flame cruised from her hotel in his Ferrari in dead silence. The roaring twelve-cylinder whine was their sound bed as he flicked the paddle shifters. He kept telling himself to keep things simple, don't give her any more fuel to get caught up, but he couldn't keep his eyes away from her thick thighs and soft red skin.

She was watching him too, studying his face, eyeing the bulge in his pants. Her eyes flitted back and forth from the vibrant city whizzing by them to Flame. All the while she still never uttered a word.

They made it to his apartment safe and sound, and Flame got the niceties out of the way (food and drink). Then they retreated to the theater room to finish watching *American Gangster*.

As Denzel laid his calculated dominance on the old New York, she snuggled up under Flame and made small talk while they sipped red wine from the same bottle. She was a great conversationalist and she eventually convinced Flame to open up to her about himself. He told her all about his humble upbringing on the streets of Fayettenam, North Carolina. He shared untold stories about his junkie mother and absent father. With defiant pride he proclaimed to her that Bunce Road had always been his daddy and the county jail was his momma.

She patted his hand as he talked and posed a weird question. "You ever shot somebody?"

Slowly he nodded. "Yeah, one time, but it was by accident," he admitted. "Well, not by accident like that. I mean, I definitely had the gun and we were definitely trying to do him some harm. We were just trying to rob him, though, and he bucked the jack. Feel me?"

She was confused. "Buck the jack?"

"Yeah. That's when you robbing somebody and they don't want to give their shit up—that's bucking the jack," he explained.

"Ohhhh."

"Yeah, so this dude was kinda bucking on me. So, when I went to, like, point at him to tell him to hurry up, the gun went off."

"Ohhh, I see. Did you kill him?"

Flame shook his head. "Hell nah. Got him in the knee, but I scared me more than I scared him."

They both chuckled, and she didn't appear to judge him. She just nodded her understanding.

Then it was her turn to run down her bio. She told him more about her upbringing with her family. Their strength is what she recalled most. And the loving way her daddy treated her mother. That is, until it was revealed he had a mistress.

Flame sipped in silence as she laid down her burdens. It was a job pretending he wasn't familiar with the story already. A few times her voice cracked, but she repaired it with more drink. Realizing she had grown uncomfortable, he changed the subject.

"What did you want to be when you was growing up?" Flame asked. "Always wanted to be an entertainer?"

She laughed. A good, hearty laugh. The kind that crumbled the gut. She even spilled a little wine on her shirt.

"What?" Flame wondered, laughing himself. "What did I say?"

She raised her palm. "Wait a minute. It's just . . . hold on." She laughed again. "Well, sort of."

"Sort of? What's so funny about that?"

"See . . . nah, you wouldn't understand."

"What?" Flame playfully wrapped her in his arms. "You gotta tell me, gurl."

She giggled. "Okay, okay."

"All right."

"Well, when I was growing up . . . I wanted to be an exotic dancer," she revealed.

Flame sucked his teeth. "Oh, that ain't nothing. What, like, a belly dancer or something? One of them Vegas girls?"

"No, silly. A stripper."

"A stripper?!"

"Yeah!"

"Why on earth would you want to be an exotic dancer—I mean, stripper?"

"Because! When I was younger they always seemed so powerful to me," she explained. "I mean, to have a man's undivided attention, to make him *pay* to look at you. What could be more powerful than that?"

Flame conceded that he could see her point.

"Sometimes . . . when I'm on stage . . . and I'm dancing . . . I imagine that I'm a stripper."

"Aww, hell nah, that ain't the same!"

"Why not?!"

"'Cause you're only half naked on stage," he joked.

"Shut up." She smacked him upside his head.

"I'm just playing, but for real, though, why didn't you ever do it? Lord knows you got the body for it."

She blushed. "Because I was shy."

"Shy?"

"Yeah! I didn't think I'd have what it takes. Those girls work hard, you hear me. And of course, it would have embarrassed my family."

Flame lit another blunt while she sipped her wine and continued to talk about the glory she would have had being a stripper. He blew smoke rings and watched them waft to the high ceiling. They were both feeling good, buzzed but not inebriated enough to lose all their inhibitions.

"I also didn't know how I'd look. Thought I'd look crazy," she continued.

At those words, an idea popped into Flame's head while she was talking.

"I got an idea," Flame said. "I believe you only live once, and you shouldn't die with regrets," he claimed.

She sucked her teeth. "What are you talking about? There is no way I could go out there and be a stripper now."

Flame smiled. "You're right. Maybe out there you can't, but in here, it's all about fulfilling your dreams. So, I got a way you can fulfill your dreams and see how you look."

"What are you talking 'bout?"

"Unh-unh, don't get scared now."

Flame jumped from the chair and went to his AV closet. He fumbled around until he found what he was looking for.

"Flame, what are you doing with that camera?"

He ignored her pleas and set the camera up on a tripod in front of the table, facing the seats. He fiddled with a few wires on the projector and camera, and in seconds . . .

Voilà!

On his ten-foot screen her face appeared vibrant and strong. "Flame, what are you doing . . ."

"We dream chasers in here, so we chasing our dreams." He patted the table. "Come on, this your stage right here. Come on," he beckoned and pointed to the screen. "You can dance and see how you look on the screen right there. Two birds with one stone."

She blushed. "I don't know about this."

"Girl, please. It ain't like I ain't neva seen it."

She smirked, leaned her head to the side in contemplation, and he knew he had her then.

Flame disappeared from the room. Seconds later, Sade's "Ordinary Love" pumped through the whole apartment. His expensive surround sound system made it seem as if Sade herself was in the room.

"Ooh, that's my song!" she cooed and started whining her hips on the couch. His homework had paid off. He'd read somewhere that Sade was her favorite artist.

"I know. Now hop yo' ass up on that stage and let's see you move, gurl."

She stared at Flame for an eternity, boring her hazel eyes into him for a second, then smiled. "Okay."

Flame took a seat on the chair and watched her climb up on the table, sweeping his weed bowl and glass figurine off with one swoop of her heels. Slowly, she began writhing her body to the beat. She wound her hips and poked her beautiful ass out toward him while fixing her eyes directly into the camera. In this way, he was able to enjoy her from all angles.

As the beat intensified, so did her movements. Flame pulled out a wad of cash from his Crown Holder jeans and skimmed bills onto the table, making it rain tens, twenties, fifties, and hundreds, and just as if they were in a real strip joint, she rewarded the currency parade by removing her top.

A nude-colored bra held her firm titties in place like a cande-labra. Her hard, red nipples pierced the soft fabric and peeked out like a curious child.

Flame rewarded her with more bills.

She swung her long hair around and faced him, but on the huge screen was a G shot of her famous ass. She bent over to show the camera what she was working with. Raised up. Squatted, bust it wide open. Brought it back. Bust it open again then turned around to face the camera. She gripped her titties in both hands and rubbed her nipples. She was infatu-ated by how beautiful she appeared on the screen. It was as if the light was hitting her just right, giving her a seductive glow. She couldn't believe how good she looked. Gone were the parts of her body she felt self-conscious about. Present was her presence.

Flame encouraged her, chanting like Uncle Luke. "Take it off! Take it off!"

She bit her bottom lip, threw her head back, and closed her eyes. Then she flung the bra at his head. It landed and temporarily blocked his view. When he removed it, his eyes zoomed in on her melons plastered across the wide screen. Melons was the only way to describe them because they were round and plump like soft cantaloupes. Her nipples were as hard and red as cold cherries.

Flame stood and rained more money on her.

The music switched up to the "Art of Noise." The driving hard bass beat only intensified things. Flame's heart thumped between his legs on pace with the beat.

Thump thump . . . thump . . . Thump. Thump.

His playful smile was gone. It had jumped out the window with Sade. Lust returned. Lust invaded his face like a deep fog.

On the stage, Sasha faced him with her hands on her hips, boldly baring her beautiful body. Her breasts rose and fell as her chest heaved. Her wide hips threatened to burst through her skintight jeans, so Flame encouraged her some more.

He motioned toward her pants with the stack of money in his hand. "Take 'em off."

Sasha smiled and responded by sliding her tight jeans down her wide hips, bending all the way down to her toes as she pulled her jeans with her. On the screen, her nude-colored thong bisected an ass so pretty it should have been in a museum somewhere. The farther she bent down, the more her perfect femininity peeked at the camera. She was so wet her panties were turning a different color.

Flame noticed her secretion, and his dick throbbed like a heartbeat on speed. He wanted to crawl inside her and beat the warning label off that pussy! Right now!

Sasha's jeans got caught on her heels and she dropped her soft ass on the table while she tugged them off, granting Flame a full view of her center. Her lower lips spilled from the sides of the thin fabric of her panties. The panties could barely contain her plump jewel.

She stood back up on the table in nothing but her underwear and heels. She posed for Flame, gave the camera a pose then slowly started winding just like she did in her video, giving peep shots of her glistening wet cat. Each time she opened her legs for him he got a whiff of her scent. Not too sweet. Not too sour. Just strong and unrelenting just like a real woman was supposed to be.

She teased him, sliding her finger around the edges of her pussy lips through her panties then sniffing it. She slowly placed one finger in her mouth and licked it like a lollipop. Then she took that same finger and traced the edges of her lower lips, circling and swirling. With her other hand she peeled her panties to the side just enough for him to catch a glimpse of her neatly trimmed vagina. She eyed him as he eyed her. He was mesmerized, a slave to her rhythm. She felt powerful, omnipotent. She wasn't just a woman. She was a goddess. A seductress. A raging lioness, and she had subdued her prey right where she wanted him.

Sasha extended her finger toward Flame like she was on stage pulling him from the crowd. She turned that finger over and beckoned him to her.

Flame stood and walked over to Sasha. He stood right in her face with his erection nearly poking her eye out and looked down at her as she looked up at him.

After all the teasing and evading, they were finally here, and it appeared they had reached the point of no return. Normally, Flame would have been dick-deep in Sasha by now, but he felt conflicted. Everything about this moment was so wrong, yet everything about it was so right. Their chemistry was on a zillion, and it wasn't their inebriation. They'd always had chemistry, but he tried to deny it. Yet fate kept putting them together. Fate kept forcing his hand, so he had to play the cards he was dealt and think about himself. Fuck everyone else.

Flame stared at himself on the screen. On the wall, with Sasha's back to him and him standing over her at eye level, it appeared she was giving him head. The vision, though not real, was real enough to take him over the edge of decision.

Flame looked down at Sasha and whispered, "He can never find out."

Sasha gazed into his eyes and licked her lips. "He won't."

Sasha unzipped Flame's jeans and pulled them down slowly. She saw his member hanging down his thigh through his boxer briefs, and she groaned. "Ummm . . ."

Sasha reached into Flame's boxers and pulled out his long, thick dick, which had seen more action than Afghanistan. She gripped it and stroked it, then she put it in her mouth.

She put it in her muthafucking mouth.

Sasha sucked Flame like a pro, caving her cheeks in, giving him lots of spit and hand action. She even attempted to deep throat him, but at ten inches, that was just wishful thinking on her part. She used to be scared of the dick, now she was throwing lips to the shit, handling it like a real bitch. She was so good at it that Flame stopped her.

While R. Kelly crooned his song, "Throw This Money on You," Flame pulled Sasha up from the table, and she followed him to the chair. He sat down and Sasha straddled him. Flame smacked her on her ass, prodding her to stand.

Sasha stood over Flame, her chest heaving, arousal gliding down her leg. She planted her feet into the seat with her heels on each side of Flame. Her beautiful gift was right above his head, leaking . . . steaming . . . begging . . . pleading to be pleased.

Flame raised his head, looked into Sasha's hazel eyes. He pulled her panties to the side and attacked her pussy like he was breaking a fast.

Sasha released a moan that echoed throughout the apartment. She moaned so loud, she could be heard over the surround sound enveloping the room. It was as if her moans escaped from heaven, like the angels were singing Flame's praises.

Flame opened her up with his fingers and plunged two digits deep into her center while he suckled on her engorged love button. She tasted like cinnamon, and her flavorful juices lathered Flame's face like he was drinking from a mythical fountain.

Sasha gripped Flame's head and cried out, "Fuck me, Flame. Please! Fuck me!" She panted, grinding her hot pussy into his face, riding his lips like a cowgirl.

Flame ripped off his shirt and jeans. An instant later, he had Sasha pinned to the table tattooing his own rhythm deep inside her walls as he clutched her waist and held on for dear life. He drove deep like he was digging for gold, pounding like a human jackhammer. He was going to beat it until the red light started beeping, warning him that it was too much. This is something he had fantasized about since he first saw her in a magazine years ago, a young dream materialized. Only Sasha was proving to be better than anything he could have imagined. Out of the thousands of women he had bedded, none could compare to her.

Flame looked up at the wall and saw the action in 4K. Sasha's face showed pure pleasure, magnified to ten feet. Her damp hair was stuck to her sweaty forehead, and her head dangled dangerously from the table upside down. Her face was suspended in a mixture of pain and pleasure as Flame stabbed her center with ten inches of unbridled lust. And the camera captured it all.

Flame spared a mischievous smirk toward the camera, and it quickly melted as he felt his nut rapidly approaching.

Flame pulled out, his tool sticky and wet.

Sasha gasped and rubbed a flood of sweat from her forehead. "Whaaa . . . what are you doing?"

Flame ignored her pleas as he moved and sat on the table right in front of the camera with his legs splayed open. His dick jutted up from between his legs like a lighthouse. On the wall it looked like mammoth meat.

Flame guided Sasha onto his shaft, reverse-cowgirl style. She slowly lowered herself on him, inch by inch, expelling air through her teeth as she slowly eased her way down. When he fully lodged himself inside, she squealed like a cat getting punished, like he was too much for her. But she didn't stop until he was firmly lodged inside of her. Then she started rocking back and forth like she was trying to scratch an itch. Flame peeked over her shoulder at the wall and watched her clit swell right before his eyes, like a flower blooming from a bud. He especially got a kick out of seeing himself stretch her to capacity. Thick veins bulged through his skin, crisscrossing like a roadmap.

Sasha bucked hard like she was riding a bull, and her breath quickened. Flame reached around and played with her hard nipples, tweaked them like he was changing channels.

Sasha moaned louder and bucked harder.

Flame thumbed her clit, rolled it between his thumb and forefinger.

She moaned even louder.

He stuffed his wet fingers inside her mouth. Sasha moaned and sucked her juices until his fingers were clean. As she sucked his fingers he played with her clit with his other hand. She leaned and rocked on him harder and harder.

Then . . .

Her body shook violently as she lost control, moaning a variation of Flame's name. She came hard and loud in a flood of release, squirting all on Flame's hardwood floors. He watched her orgasm on the wall in HD. Her fluid was so thick and creamy he could have placed a cup down there and sold it at Mickey D's. He felt her vaginal walls clench and release on him repeatedly until they seized up and held him in a nice grip.

He could no longer hold back.

Flame erupted so hard it was a wonder his seed didn't shoot out through her mouth. He gripped her small waist and thrust his babies deep inside her, exploding like a fire hydrant. The sheer force shook them both as if they were enduring an earthquake. Sasha squeezed him with her inner muscles, milking him like a cow until every drop was inside her.

Miraculously, with no X pills or blue diamonds, after his eruption, Flame remained harder than a missile. He pulled Sasha from his lap and situated her so their bodies were sideways to the camera. Then he ran up in her like he had dreamed about so many times: doggy style.

For the next hour, Flame and Sasha fucked, sucked, and fucked some more in every position imaginable. His trusty camera captured every stroke and angle of the sexcapade. Most of the time, they watched simultaneously. That is, when their eyes weren't glued shut from sheer pleasure.

Sasha turned out to be better than Flame ever imagined. Her sex was so hot it could start its own fire on the sun, and her head game made Superhead seem like Mother Teresa. She even licked his back door like it was ice cream. Flame couldn't get enough!

From his theater, they took it to his bedroom, where they got it on until the break of dawn.

Then they slept.

Flame and Sasha slept through *Good Morning America*. They slept through *Maury* and *Good Day New York*.

Around the midday news she padded to the kitchen to fix them some water.

Then they slept some more.

Flame woke up to Wendy on the television cackling about something. Every centimeter of his body was sore. His abs were on fire. He felt like he'd performed ten thousand crunches nonstop.

Sasha awoke right after him, and she lay on his chest playing with the light hair on his stomach, breathing peacefully.

Then their peace was interrupted by Wendy.

"Ooooooh, and guess who got smacked up at an AMA after-party? Sasha Beaufont!" A train sound effect roared like a locomotive was about to careen through the wall.

"Yes! Say Diamond put the pimp hand down, y'all! And while this was going on, her sister was getting smacked up by Flame; but the good kind of smacking. Um-hmm, right on the wall in front of everybody! Sounds like my kind of party, y'all. Break-ups and make-ups . . ."

Before Wendy could finish snitching, Flame tried to formulate his alibi in his head. No way was he about to fuck this up!

Fortunately, Sasha bailed him out. "I hate Wendy," she whispered. "Always spreading gossip. And I didn't get smacked up. I smacked him!"

She never asked about Kim, and Flame never volunteered more info either.

They listened in silence as that media wrecking ball crashed through the walls of more celebrities' façades; drifting between the land of the living and dead. Then out of nowhere Sasha spoke.

"Diamond is using you, Flame."

Flame wasn't sure he heard her correctly until she repeated herself.

"What'chu mean, using me?"

"Do you know where Diamond is right now?" Sasha posed.

"Yeah, he's in Europe meeting with distributors so we can push our product over there," Flame replied confidently. Diamond had hit him up right before he left.

Sasha shook her head slowly and closed her eyes. "No he's not," she whispered. "That's what he wants you to believe. Flame, Diamond is using you to get back at your boss, Qwess. He never had plans on being fair with you," she explained.

Flame's ego wouldn't let him believe that. He felt his clothing line was too fine not to be pursued by Diamond. Diamond had blown his head up with all the attention he was putting on the brand. He thought that Diamond saw he was about to smash the clothing game and wanted in.

He foolishly said as much to Sasha, and she laughed lightly.

"If Diamond wanted your designs he would've muscled them out of you with paperwork. Believe me, I've seen it before," she assured him.

But Flame was adamant in his denial. Too headstrong. He insisted she was speaking madness. He knew that if anyone knew Diamond's plans it would be her, but he still didn't believe her.

"Flame, you don't know the half," Sasha insisted. "Diamond is connected worldwide. The entertainment industry is just how he cleans his money up."

Sasha's word held too much conviction to be invalid. Qwess had taught Flame long ago how a man, no matter how powerful, always shares his secrets with the one he shares his bed with. So Flame checked his ego and submitted to her intel.

"What do you mean?" He asked. "He still selling dope?"

"Drugs?" Sasha scoffed. "Hell, no! This is how Diamond got rich . . ."

Sasha informed Flame that the source of Diamond's power was his namesake. Diamonds. Diamond owned diamond mines in Sierra Leone, South Africa, and Democratic Republic of the Congo. He had slaves toiling in them like it was the nineteenth century. Like some twisted form of retaliation for slavery, this nigga actually abducted his enemies and exported them to work in his mines. Since he owned the mines, some of them the most productive in the world, he was able to put his own price on the rocks. He, in turn, passed the exponential discounts on to some of the most influential people in the world. Not America alone. The world! These people controlled stock markets with the twitch of a finger. Started wars with a simple phone call. Decided who was going to live or die with a hidden finger sign.

Flame asked Sasha what these people would need with Diamond. Surely they could operate without him?

She explained that Diamond forged alliances with the local tribal leaders where his mines were located, then supplied them with whatever they needed—in the world. In turn, these tribal leaders ensured no one got near the mines except Diamond's people. The diamonds were so important to these men because they enabled them to travel with their wealth throughout the world without detection or attention.

For instance, it was difficult to travel from one place to another with, say, a hundred thousand dollars in any currency. The sheer size of the paper would raise suspicion, not to mention declaration concerns with various government agencies when entering different countries. On the flip side, a pocket full of stones could easily exceed a hundred thousand dollars in any country in any currency. More important, they went undetected and undeclared.

Diamond received these people's courtship as they constantly attempted to undercut the next man for better deals on the rocks when they were still just rocks. Since all of the men were affiliated with the entertainment industry in some capacity, that was often their bargaining tool. Diamond took care of them with the stones, and they took care of him within the industry, distributing his records and cutting other favorable deals.

By the time Sasha eased her conscience, Flame was filled with more confusion and questions than before. A man—A BLACK MAN—owning slaves in this day and age was blasphemous! However, more pressing to Flame was why Sasha was revealing all of this to him. He asked her.

"Because you're a good person," she stated simply. "And I don't want you to get caught up in Diamond's mess, his chess games and politics."

"And what about you?" Flame asked. After all, she was sharing his bed with him, which made her guilty by association. "If he's so bad, why are you with him still?"

Sasha sighed loudly. "Me and Diamond's relationship is complicated. I mean, I love him, but . . ."

Flame blocked her out after she declared her love for him. He felt she was the typical woman. Declaring her love for another nigga while lying in his bed. Like she hadn't just had her drawers full of his dick.

"It started out as a marriage of convenience," Sasha explained. "You know, guy from the streets links up with the good girl. Our fans cross over to each other's music out of curiosity of the other. Like, *What is it about this woman that makes the biggest hardcore rapper in the world want her?* And vice versa. You know . . ."

Indeed he did know. He saw it all before. When Qwess married Lisa Ivory, both of their sales doubled, seemingly overnight. Amin called it the bandwagon approach, celebrity-style.

"That's how it started. Well, that and he reminded me of how my father used to be. Now . . . it's too late. I'm locked in."

Flame could hear the sorrow in her voice. He kinda felt sorry for the girl. So talented. Beautiful. So smart. Yet she was trapped, or so she thought.

"Yo, you could always leave him," Flame suggested, knowing the futility of his statement. Even he knew it wasn't that easy.

"What? And end up in a diamond mine?!" She shook her head, tossing her hair everywhere. "I don't think so. I got a good life. I'd rather continue to enjoy it." She chuckled.

Flame had to admire the girl. Amidst drab circumstances she still found her humor.

They kicked around a few ideas of escape until the sun disappeared behind the buildings outside Flame's window. He thought about going a few rounds again. Lord knows, he wanted more of that heroin disguised as a vagina between her legs.

Unfortunately, someone knocked on his door. He had a doorman that was paid good money to alert him before permitting anyone up to his apartment. He hadn't, which meant only one thing . . .

"Damn nigga! Fuck you been? I been calling you all night!" 8-Ball lumbered his hefty frame past Flame right into his apartment. "Gotdamn nigga! Smell like pure pussy up in here. Crack a window or something. Let a nigga breathe. Damn. Who you got up here anyway?"

8-Ball stuffed his face with grapes and chugged from Flame's milk jug like he had purchased it.

"Where you coming from?" Flame asked, evading his question.

"Yoooo, nigga," 8-Ball said as he jumped up and plopped all 375 pounds on Flame's granite countertop. "I been wit' ole girl Monica. Aww, man, bitch is a freak, dawg. Hell, I'm a freak. We been fucking all week, J. We just got back from Miami. She down in Texas now. I been beating it up all fucking week!" He humped the counter, simulating how he did Monica. Then he stuck his tongue out and flicked the air with it.

"Yo, I stuck my tongue so far up her ass I can tell you what she had for lunch. I think I'm in love, dawg. Love. Word!"

Flame was multitasking hard. He was listening to 8-Ball while praying that Sasha didn't come out of the bedroom. The last thing he wanted was for 8-Ball to know she was there.

8-Ball asked him again, "Who you got up in here anyway?" He tilted his head, curious. "Smell like potpourri and pussy all up in here, nigga, so don't think yo' ass slick. You been fuckin' all night. That's why you ain't answer yo' phone. So, you done got one of these mouthy New York bitches, huh?"

Flame grinned sheepishly, content to keep his secret; until his secret revealed herself.

Sasha peeked her head around the corner and said, "Flame, can I see you a second?" Even though only her head was exposed, her hair was disheveled enough to draw the conclusion to how it was messed up.

"Ohhh, shit!!!" 8-Ball exploded. "What. The. Fuck?

Dawg . . . aww, damn . . ." 8-Ball dropped his head in disbelief and kept whispering, "Damn."

Flame dropped his head in embarrassment too. "Sure, Sash, I'll be right there."

Sasha smiled prettily and threw a dainty wave at 8-Ball. "Heeey, Ball," she cooed.

"What up, Sasha," Ball replied, then as an afterthought, "Uh, how long you been standing there?"

Sasha smirked. "Long enough to know my girl is eating well when she's with you."

8-Ball covered his mouth and erupted in laughter.

Flame met Sasha in the hallway. She was wearing one of his Flaming Diamond tees. Her fat pussy lips peeked from beneath the bottom of the shirt. Flame reached down and palmed it. "What's good?"

"Uh, I'ma get ready to go," Sasha said.

"What?" Flame kissed her passionately and palmed her soft ass with one hand, kneaded it like dough. "I thought we were gonna . . . you know?"

She palmed his naked chest and returned his kiss. She spoke between kisses, punctuating every word with a peck. "I want to . . . but . . . you have . . . company. Besides, you tried to kill me last night. Look."

She pulled up the shirt and showed him her swollen twat.

"I don't think I ever had her beat like that," Sasha claimed. "You wore a girl out."

What could he say? That's why they called him Flame the Furrier.

Flame jerked his thumb toward his kitchen. "Yo, let me get rid of him and we can jump in my Jacuzzi and I can massage it for you, maybe suck on it 'til it feel better," he suggested.

Sasha closed her yes. "Hmm . . . as good as that sounds, I have to get going. I can't stay missing for too long."

Sadness washed over Flame's face. "I understand," he conceded.

"Look, I had a good time, Flame. An amazing time! I don't regret coming over here at all." She closed her eyes like she was reliving every stroke. "Maybe we can do it again sometime."

"Definitely."

Shit, Flame was ready to gut her again right where they stood, Ball be damned, but he wasn't going to press his luck.

"I'll call an Uber," Sasha suggested before it was too late.

"An Uber? Nonsense. Nah, take one of my cars. I'll get it from you later. You can take the Bentley since it's tinted. The key's on the wall by the door."

Flame and Sasha kissed a few more times before he rejoined 8-Ball in the kitchen while she dressed to leave. A few minutes later Sasha walked past them wearing a pair of Flame's basketball shorts that fit her like knickerbockers, a Flaming Diamond tee, and one of Flame's Yankee fitted hats pulled low over her eyes. One of Flame's LV backpacks was slung loosely over her right shoulder. She looked nothing like the superstar that she was. She looked just like what she was at that moment: a woman who had just gotten her back blown out by the other man.

"My Uber should be downstairs by the time I get down," Sasha said. She waved her hand. "Bye, Ball. Flame, I'll call you later."

As soon as Sasha disappeared through the door, 8-Ball tore into Flame.

"Fuck is wrong wit'chu, J?! This is bad for business, man. Sasha?! Sasha?!" He shook his head so hard it was a wonder it didn't roll around like in *The Exorcist*.

"Yo, it ain't like that, dawg! I ain't push up on her, she came on to me," Flame proclaimed. But he could tell 8-Ball didn't believe him. His philandering history testified against him. "I'm telling you," he persisted. "Matter of fact, come on."

Flame was going to show him the tape. The tape made it obvious that Sasha was the instigator. If Flame was being totally honest, a part of him wanted 8-Ball to see him punishing Sasha, if only for his own benefit. Ball was there the first time he ever saw Sasha and said he was gonna fuck her one day. 8-Ball didn't believe he could.

"Watch, nigga, you'll see," Flame guaranteed, making a beeline to the camera that was still on the tripod. He snatched open the back where the tape was and screamed.

"What's wrong wit'chu, nigga?" 8-Ball asked. "What's up?"

The tape was gone.

Chapter 12

Fayetteville, North Carolina

Qwess walked into his conference room on edge. All of his heavy hitters were on deck: Amin, Doe, Lisa Ivory, and his father, Khalid. Prince, King Reece's son, was in the room also, even though he wasn't sitting at the table. Qwess had pressing business matters to discuss with his inner circle.

Since his last meeting with Liam, his whole life had been turned upside down. Just as Liam had promised, the industry was shutting him out. Distributors were returning his albums and refusing his calls. His media sources were refusing to allow him or his artists to come through. Even ABP's videos were being pulled. Niya had a new album that was due to be released, as well as Flame's new R&B album that they were planning to drop in the fourth quarter. ABP had already spent more than $5 million promoting and advertising Niya's new project, with another $2 million ready to be pumped into the music economy gearing up for the release in a couple of weeks. Since going fully independent, ABP financed everything, and thus they felt every penny of that $7 million and were looking forward to their return on their investment.

"Good afternoon, everyone. I'm glad that you all could make it," Qwess greeted. "We have some pressing business matters to discuss. As you know, I told all of you that they're shutting us out. I called you all here to show you what that looks like in real time and for us to come up with a solution moving forward. Amin?"

Amin stood and put some figures on the screen on the wall. "This is where we were last year at this time. This is where we are now—before the shutout."

According to the screen ABP had lost $10 million. Because of the scandal surrounding Niya's release, her last album hadn't done as expected. Then, Qwess retiring put a bigger dent in their coffers than expected. Add the other challenges of going fully independent, and they were in the red.

Doe spoke, "Aye, ain't no way we in the red that much. I mean, I know we ain't winning that much, but shit, we ain't losing this bad, are we?"

"Numbers don't lie," Amin insisted.

"You know I believe in transparency, so I'm not gonna front, we fucked up right now. I don't know how many more losses we can take," Qwess said.

In truth, everyone in the room had grown accustomed to living the life of the rich.

Qwess and Lisa maintained homes and offices in Atlanta and North Carolina, they had properties in the Caribbean, California, and New York. They owned a private jet, and Qwess's car fetish had his auto collection at over twenty-five automobiles, most of them exotics.

Doe and Niya's lifestyle wasn't quite as outlandish as Qwess's, but the grounds upkeep on his North Carolina home was nearly a million a year alone, and he also had a lavish home in Atlanta. His wife was accustomed to being the princess of R&B, so she still spent as if she was at the top of the charts. Even though she hadn't made money in years, she had developed a shoe fetish, and Christian Louboutin was her favorite. After she stayed with Doe after his affair, spoiling her was part of his makeup plan.

Amin was the most frugal of their team, and his monthly expenses were over $100,000. Add the fact that he played Santa at Jumu'ah every Friday, sponsoring the expenses for the Islamic school, and his numbers quickly tallied up for the year as well.

For acting as house counsel, Qwess had been paying his father handsomely to the tune of a million dollars every year. He spent most of his money traveling and spoiling his wife. Still, it was a lifestyle he was accustomed to.

The short of it was that no one could afford to lose any more money.

"Shit, we can't take any more losses at all," Khalid said.

"I know," Qwess said. "You know I'm always thinking ahead, so I got something planned to bring us out the red and take us all the way into the black."

This bold statement garnered everyone's attention. They were all ears.

Qwess slapped a small cube-shaped Bluetooth speaker in the middle of the table. "This is the future."

Everyone's eyes fell on the cube while Qwess toyed with his phone. A few seconds later, an unreleased track from Qwess bled from the tiny speaker. They all listened to the song in silence, nodding their heads as they thought the answer was evident.

Doe broke the silence first. "So, you're coming out of retirement? It's about damn time. That'll get us out the red for sure."

The others in the room agreed with Doe. They all piped in with their comments, issuing high-fives to each other, excited that the problem would be solved soon.

Then Qwess burst their bubble.

"I'm not coming out of retirement!" Qwess yelled above the cacophony of side conversations.

"What?"

"I'm not coming out of retirement," Qwess repeated. "That's not what I'm talking about. I'm talking about this."

Qwess pointed to Amin, and he cued up a video on the screen. On the video, a colorful graphic showed current streaming numbers. Another graphic showed where streaming numbers were projected to go in the next few years. The numbers were astronomical. And that was just the music. With new streaming movie companies emerging, the possibilities were limitless.

"And these are modest estimates," Qwess added. "That's the future for us."

Lisa picked up the speaker and examined it. "I mean, what? You talking like this is the wheel, like it's going to change the world or something."

"Baby, we gonna come off like drug dealers in the crack era," Qwess assured her.

Khalid picked up the speaker and examined it as well. "What I want to know is how did you figure this out, son."

Qwess relayed the story of Liam to them. He briefly told them about how Liam approached him with a warning of what was to come and offered him a way out.

"Okay, so this Liam guy . . . how you know he's legit? He could be working for those same people and really trying to clean you out," Khalid reasoned. "How much of an investment would this cost us to start this up?"

"Hmm . . . about thirty to fifty million up front," Qwess

estimated. "But we could make that money back in under six months—or less."

"But how can we trust these Jews, bro?" Doe asked. "They more slippery than an eel in oil. This nigga could be trying to use our money to start *his* shit."

"True."

"True."

"True."

Qwess raised a hand. "I thought about that. And to be honest, I don't see how he could play us."

"My thing is," Khalid said, "why would this Jew boy go against his own people for you, us, a bunch of *niggers*? I been in the joint with them Jews, and they always put themselves first."

"I asked him the same thing," Qwess informed them. "But he said something that made sense to me. He said, 'Sometimes the visionary is the last person to see his vision come to life.'"

"Okay . . . and what the fuck is that supposed to mean?" Doe asked.

"It means his people not down with this streaming shit," Khalid answered.

"You're right. They actually trying to prevent it," Qwess agreed.

"Because it would take the power from their hands," Amin said. He rubbed his unkempt goatee. "I mean, think about it, everyone knows the Jews run the entertainment industry. They do so because they only allow their people, or people they've endorsed, to make it to the next level. They control radio, television, movies . . . they run it all. So, they can make or break an artist or company by moving a hand. They can refuse to distribute, play their music on radio, pull their videos. I mean, shit, look how they got us in a trick bag right now."

"Yep, and streaming is the great equalizer because it puts power in the hands of the people," Qwess explained. "Look at how YouTube is changing the game."

"Okay, but how can we monetize this streaming thing?" Doe asked.

"The new rules are still being rewritten, but basically technology is the key. Either we can utilize the technology that is already there, or we can design our own and patent it so whoever comes after us will have to pay us for it."

The more Qwess spoke, the more the others warmed up to the idea. Everyone except Khalid.

"I still can't figure out why this Jew boy will side with you over his own people," he said.

Khalid had played the streets at the highest level in his day. He had done business with Jamaicans, Dominicans, Colombians, Mexicans, Turks, and Russians, Every nationality he had dealt with was willing to go against their own, but not the Jews. They stuck together like Superglue.

"Pop, what's one thing Jews love more than their people?" Qwess asked. "Money! And with this type of money, he could circle back around and build a whole new nation!"

Everyone laughed.

"Seriously, though, I really think Liam wants to be the Christopher Columbus of his circle and show them they were wrong to go against him," Qwess assumed. "Either way, I think this could get us back on top. What you think?"

Everyone seemed to be on board. They took a vote, and Khalid reluctantly agreed.

For Qwess, he saw the streaming deal as a way to reset the balance. Just as Liam had a point to prove, so did Qwess. He wanted to get his wife and Doe's wife back on top. The declines of their careers were directly related to their allegiance to ABP. They were still superstars in their own right. With Flame's new R&B album highly anticipated and a back catalog of never-released tracks from Mysterio aka King Reece,

Qwess had enough ammo to mount a hostile takeover of the music industry. If he could pull this deal off and execute the numbers he projected, he could make ABP the biggest independent label in the history of the music business.

The only obstacle in his way was the lawsuit hanging over his head that threatened to bankrupt him.

Chapter 13

Qwess couldn't believe what Malik Shabazz was telling him. He looked at the papers again and shook his head. He passed the papers to his father, and Khalid took a look at them too.

"Yeah, this is bad," Khalid agreed.

"You told me that everyone in your crew was solid," Malik Shabazz said. "That's not what this paper says."

Qwess shook his head. Someone in his crew was telling something about the assault at AMG's offices in Charlotte. AMG had filed for a summary judgment, which meant they felt as if they had substantial evidence that would guarantee a win at trial. A summary judgment would save everyone the time and the embarrassment of a trial.

"Mr. Shabazz, if they had all the evidence that they claim, why not just go for criminal charges then?" Qwess asked. "They trying to call my bluff, man. This ain't nothing but a shakedown!"

"Not really," Malik Shabazz said.

"How you figure?"

"The burden of proof in a civil suit is less than for criminal charges," Malik Shabazz and Khalid said in unison.

Malik Shabazz raised his finger. "But if they can secure a victory on this, then criminal charges may follow."

Qwess smacked Malik Shabazz's marble conference table. "Fuck!" He stuffed his face into his hands. "This can't be happening, man. This is bullshit."

"Calm down, son. There's gotta be something we can do."

"Oh, it is. You can offer a settlement, but it must be sizeable, I'm sure," Malik Shabazz predicted.

Qwess was disgusted. "Settlement offer? I'm not paying you a thousand dollars an hour to tell me to settle."

"No but you are paying me to win, and sometimes a win looks different than what we expect it to." Malik Shabazz shrugged. "Hey, losing ten mil may be easier than losing seventy-five mil."

"Look, I'm not losing shit! Now, you need to fix this, man." Qwess leaned over the table, got in Shabazz's face and snarled, "Fix this shit, fast too!"

Shabazz was unfazed by Qwess's scare tactics. Shabazz had just successfully defended Justus Moore at trial on multiple bodies. Justus Moore was one of the most terrifying men Shabazz had ever encountered. He was a straight sociopath—cool and smooth as an ice cube, smarter than Einstein, but more deadly than Hitler. If Shabazz could deal with him, then surely some rapper wasn't going to ruffle his feathers.

"My brother, I can understand your frustration, but *we* must direct it in the right direction. We're on the same team here."

"He's right, son. Calm down."

"Now, if we can figure out who this CI number one is that they're referring to, then maybe we can make an offer to him or her and make this all go away," Shabazz suggested.

"Apparently, that's the only thing they have that ties this to you. Everything else is pure speculation."

Qwess calmed down a bit. "Yeah, but how can we find that out?"

"That's the million-dollar question," Malik Shabazz said.

"Yeah, and I will find an answer, believe that!" Qwess promised as he stood to leave.

All he could think about was the money he was losing by the day with all the blackballing. He felt like Sonic the Hedgehog running through the maze of life. Every time he gathered his coins, an obstacle came by and knocked the coins out of his pocket.

Outside in the parking lot, Khalid stopped his son before he hopped in his Aston Martin. "Son, that man isn't lying to you. If that confidential informant testifies against you in that case, everything we built will go down. Don't ever put your legacy in the hands of your trust for another man. Think about what they did to me at trial."

Qwess recalled the parade of former comrades testifying against his father in his federal trial. Guys his father had fed, lived for, and killed for had stabbed him in the chest in court. They didn't even have the decency to stab him in the back with a secret statement. They came to open court and pointed him out and handed him an elbow.

"I'm not telling you to get dirty, but I am telling you whatever you have to do to win, you have to do it. Understand what I'm saying?"

Qwess heard his father loud and clear. Billions were riding on the lips of one person, and he was going to find out who it was one way or another.

Bone stood on the second level of Club Flesh overseeing the strip club while it was in full swing. Tits and ass were on full display, hustlers were making it rain, and the DJ was spinning nasty jams.

Club Flesh had been one of the jewels in King Reece's empire. He had built it up to not only be Fayetteville's premiere strip club, but it was the hottest strip club in the Carolinas. Women came from all over to be featured and get some of that money. Upon King Reece's demise, Bone had made sure to keep it going.

See, the strip club was essential to any drug crew. The strippers were the female version of a dope boy. They were in tune with the streets, for the streets regularly pulled up. Veteran strippers could observe the crowd on any given night and tell who were the get-money niggas. They could also tell who the up-and-coming hustlers were too. Because a lot of the strippers maintained coke habits, they could also tell when good coke came into the city. Most importantly to the Crescent Crew, the strippers could rein enterprising hustlers into the ranks of the Crew.

In fact, King Reece had pulled one of his main chicks from the stage and made her his second wife. To this day, the girls still talked about Vanilla, mostly about her mysterious disappearance just before King Reece's death. Some said that she was buried underneath his mausoleum, his love for her so great that he wanted her to join him in the afterlife.

Bone didn't plan on wifing any chick from the club, but he definitely had his way with a few of them from time to time. One of them was his main floor girl, a Latina named Tatiana.

Bone stared at Tatiana as she flitted across the floor on tall heels, her bronzed ass jiggling around her thong. Bone watched as she asked a Mexican man if he wanted a lap dance. Bone had instructed her to pull the man's card because he had been sitting down all night without buying anything. He had been watching everything that moved all night. With an ongoing war against the Mexican cartel, everyone with tan skin was suspect to Bone.

Bone's phone buzzed, and he saw a text from Qwess: *Open the back door.*

Bone smiled. He didn't even know his OG was in town. He bopped downstairs and opened the back door. He saw Qwess's car—a low-key black Dodge Challenger—idling in the alleyway. When Qwess saw Bone, he opened the door and got out with his hoodie pulled over his head and his hands in his pockets. Bone whipped his Desert Eagle out and covered the alleyway while Qwess came in the building.

Qwess kept his hoodie on because he didn't want to be seen, but a sack chaser could sniff out a rich man, and Qwess reeked of money. By the time he made it upstairs to Bone's office and closed the door, all eyes were on him.

"*As salaam alaykum akh!*" Bone greeted. "What brings you down to mingle among the common folk, OG?"

Qwess ripped his hoodie off his head. "Shit, same ole, same ole."

"Oh, yeah?"

Qwess sighed and shook his head. "Yeah, that problem just won't go away."

Qwess walked around the office tapping the walls for hollow points. When King Reece was alive, this office was the headquarters for the Crescent Crew. He knew that Reece had this office reinforced with Dynamat to prevent eavesdropping and bugging. This office was probably the safest room in the city for a criminal.

Bone leaned on his desk and crossed his arms. "Yeah, but you told me not to take care of it."

"Nah, I told you not to do that. If you would've done that it would've brought the wrath down on us." Qwess shook his head vehemently. "Nah, they're too big."

Bone didn't see the problem. To the Crescent Crew, no one was off limits. They killed police, judges, attorneys . . . the only people that were off limits were kids.

"Off limits?" Bone questioned.

"Not like that," Qwess clarified. "Anybody can get it, but it's chess, not checkers. Always remember that." Qwess tapped his forehead.

"I had to take the li'l homie out back in Charlotte," Bone informed him. "He didn't follow through with the move, and he knew too much. I feel kinda bad for 'em now since that move wasn't the right one."

"Yeah, well, you might want to save those tears for later because shit is about to get worse."

Bone cocked his skeletal head to the side. "What you talking about, OG?"

Qwess had mulled over his decision the entire ride over to the club. His heart was heavy with grief, but he had no choice. He thought about what Reece would do in this situation, what Reece would say if he knew what he was contemplating. Qwess had thought of a million scenarios to not make the decision, but it kept coming back one way only. Too much was at stake. Too many lives depended on it. He was on the brink of making history.

Qwess leveled with Bone. "You ever thought about leaving the game? You ever thought about doing something else?"

"Sheeeit, and do what? Be a regular mofo? I can't rap. Box. Shoot ball. None of that shit. But I can sell the hell out some motherfucking dope. I feel like this what Allah put me here to do."

Qwess shook his head. He knew where Bone's head was at. He had been there before himself, trapped by the allure of the game. At one point, he couldn't see past the game himself. Then, his career took off, and he couldn't see the game the same again.

"Okay, let me ask you this: if you could do anything in the world or be anything in the world, what would it be?" Qwess queried.

Bone stroked the thin hairs on his chin for a moment, really giving some though to the question. In the end he was still lost for words. "I don't know, OG. The game's been too good to me for me to even dream about anything else. I mean, I just turned thirty-three, and I've been playing with millions since I was in my late twenties." He shrugged. "I never gave it much thought."

"Do you think you could've done it all if you weren't a part of the Crescent Crew?"

Bone palmed his chest with pride. "I *am* the Crescent Crew, OG. I know you and the King built this shit and I will always give you your proper respect, because without your sacrifices, I couldn't have become the man I am." Bone dropped his head, then raised it with pride. "But I rebuilt this brand with blood, sweat, and tears. Them Mexican mother-fuckers would have taken over this city if I didn't run them out of town. It's a few more left, but they won't be around long."

Qwess listened to Bone proclaim his allegiance and wondered just how deep his loyalty ran.

"I see you, Young OG, you doing your thing, man. I can't front, every time I call on you, you answer."

"As I always will."

"Yeah, about that . . ."

Bone smiled, showing all of his gold and diamond teeth. "Spit it out, OG. You ain't come all the way down here in this dirty den to bullshit me. Speak your mind."

"Yo, about how many brothers would you say still with us from that time the stunt got pulled in Charlotte?" Qwess asked.

Bone thought for a second. He mumbled names to himself as he ticked off numbers on his hand. When he started count-ing on his second hand, Qwess shook his head. Allah said to kill *one* Muslim unjustly is equivalent to murdering all of mankind. Qwess hadn't exactly been on his *deen* since adopt-ing a Hollywood lifestyle, but he felt Islam still lived in his heart. What he was contemplating now made him question not only his Islam but his humanity. But desperate times called for desperate measures, and he refused to be denied.

"About fifteen now," Bone finally answered. "Why, what's up?"

Qwess stared at Bone and confessed his conclusion. "Yo, one of them niggas is sour, Akhi. I don't know who, so you know what you have to do, right?"

Bone closed his eyes and shook his head. These were his brothers, comrades, brothers in arms. He had been with some of them when their children were born. Attended weddings. He was some of their children's godfather. Above all that, he was their big homie. They trusted him to lead them to the promised land. Now *his* big homie was asking him to do the unthinkable, it seemed.

"It's time to purge the line," Qwess ordered. He couldn't believe he was saying that. It felt so surreal that he didn't even hear his own words. He just felt them leave his mouth. "We don't know who is sour, so every one of them that could possibly know about this has to go." Qwess shrugged. "It's the only way."

"How do we know it was one of them?" Bone challenged. "What if your intel is suspect?"

Qwess had thought about that himself, but the information was too accurate. "Brother, I wish it was, but the information is too accurate. Someone is talking, and this isn't going anywhere. It's holding a lot of things up. You can imagine how I'm feeling right now, but it's the only way."

Bone dropped his head in defeat. He was being asked to eliminate the crux of his whole line. What would that move do to the loyalty he had engendered over the years? What would that do to his money? Who would he appoint to control those territories? The men in question were more than mere soldiers; they were bosses with legions of men under them. What of those men? How would they react to their

captains being murdered? Bone respected Qwess to the ut-
most, but he was second-guessing his call.

Maybe I should pay Samson a visit, he thought.

Just as quickly as the thought surfaced, he dismissed it.
They were under strict orders not to go see Samson. He was
incarcerated under an alias that had nothing to do with the
Crescent Crew. The real Samson had the murder of a federal
police officer over his head, and any visits from the Crescent
Crew would raise suspicion.

Qwess saw Bone questioning his decision. "Here is what
you're missing, little brother," Qwess said. "If your line is
sour, I'm not the only one in jeopardy; *you* are! Now, I know
you don't have the death penalty in your plans, do you? That
Amadou Diallo move can put you in the afterlife with a needle in your arm."

Qwess was referring to the infamous murder that earned
Bone a slot in the Crescent Crew. He had shot a cop forty-
one times in retaliation for the cops killing Jersey Ali.

Bone had to admit Qwess had a point.

Qwess saw him softening up a bit, so he drove his point
home. "Yeah, I'm never going to make a decision like that for
just my own benefit. This is Crew business," he claimed.

Bone nodded, only half convinced. "Yeah, Crew business," he muttered in defeat.

Qwess patted Bone on the back and walked to the door.
"This needs to happen ASAP before any more of our line get
contaminated," he said. "I know you don't like it, but this an
OG call."

Bone opened the door for Qwess to leave. Standing outside the office and all around the stairs were members of the
Crescent Crew. They'd heard he was in the building and
quickly got in position to protect him with their lives, if
need be.

As Qwess carefully descended the stairs on his red bot-
toms, members of the Crew saluted him with tremendous re-

spect. One of the members Qwess recognized as one of the first fruits of the Crescent Crew. He stopped to give him a hug and a pound.

"*As salaamu alaykum!*" Qwess greeted over the loud music. "How you been, brother?"

The man's smile nearly wet his ears as he returned the greeting. He couldn't believe Qwess had come down to the trenches to kick it with the fam. This only elevated his status in his eyes. He couldn't wait to tell the other members of his set that he had kicked it with Qwess. This made his night, his year even.

Little did he know, Qwess had just sentenced him to death.

Chapter 14

Over the next few months, things heated up for the Crescent Crew. The Mexican cartel stepped up their assault in a last-ditch effort to save face. So while Bone was devising a plan that would tear a chunk of his heart from his chest, he also had to defend his territory.

One Friday, the Mexicans abducted Muhammad coming from the masjid and demanded a ransom of $100,000 for his return. Unknown to them, Muhammad was on Bone's list of men that had to go anyway, so Bone decided to use Muhammad's abduction as a chance to flex his muscle.

He arranged for a meeting to make the exchange of Muhammad for the $100,000. They decided to make the exchange in a warehouse parking lot in Raeford after midnight. Bone gathered a few of his newest recruits and took them with him to handle business.

When Bone's driver pulled the Durango into the parking lot, the Mexican faction was already waiting on them. Bone instructed his driver to pull around the building to make sure they weren't about to be ambushed. Once he was sure the coast was clear, he had the Durango pull up across from the Mexican's Suburban and keep the lights on.

Bone's young guns exited the truck first with their AR-15s in hand. Meanwhile, two Mexicans were already out of their truck with AK-47s in their hands.

"Where is Mo?" one of the young guns asked, but the Mexicans feigned as if they didn't understand English.

Bone stepped out of the truck vested up and yelled across the parking lot. *"¿Donde está mi hermano?"*

One of the men opened the door and snatched Muhammad from the backseat. He was bound at the hands and gagged with a bandana.

"¿Donde está el dinero?" one of the Mexicans yelled. The fact that these men couldn't speak English told him that they weren't operating in the area. Their new leader probably had them shipped in from Mexico just for wet work.

Bone tossed the duffel bag stuffed with cash on the ground between them. "Now let my brother go! *¡Dame mi hermano ahora mismo!"*

One of the Mexicans stepped up to get the bag full of cash. As soon as his hands touched the bag, Bone let his Desert Eagle spit.

BOOM!

The shot caught him in the top of the head and blew him over on his back, where he lay twitching and gurgling his own blood.

The other Mexican quickly grabbed Muhammad up in a yoke and put the gun to his head. *"No se mueve!"*

No one expected Bone to jeopardize Muhammad's life with such a reckless move. Now everyone was confused and looked to him for answers.

Bone snatched one of the AR's away from his young soldier and pointed it right at the Mexican.

"No se mueve!" the man repeated. All he could think about

was the $100,000 on the ground just a few feet in front of him. He was so close to that money he could smell it. That bag would make him a millionaire in Mexico. He could do so much for his family. He would be the don of his village. He could see the beautiful señoritas lapping at him like a hungry dog. If only he could make it out of there with that bag.

But there would be no fantasies carried out this day.

Bone aimed the AR-15 at the center of Muhammad's chest and pulled the trigger. Muhammad went limp in the Mexican's arms. It was the break Bone needed.

He fired three more rounds—two to the chest and one to the head—and the Mexican crumpled to the ground, dead.

Bone walked over to both fallen men with his young soldiers in tow. Muhammad was still alive and was wheezing through the gag desperately trying to capture his breath while clutching his chest.

Bone passed the AR-15 to his youngster. He pointed to Muhammad. "This nigga here is snitching!" Bone lied. "Ain't no rats gonna be in my line," he said.

Muhammad heard the aspersion Bone cast against him and nearly gagged as he tried to clear the smut from his name.

"What you gonna do?" Bone asked. "Let this nigga know what we do to snitches. Show this nigga Crew business."

Before the first young soldier could raise his weapon, his brother came up from behind him and fired a three-round burst right in Muhammad's head.

"Good job," Bone commended. He smacked the first soldier in the back of the head. "And you, don't you ever hesitate on me when I tell you to pull the trigger. Next time you'll be laying down there with them. Understand?"

The man nodded. His comrade ice grilled him and left no question that he would pull the trigger on him if he didn't move fast enough next time.

Bone climbed in the back of the Durango with bittersweet feelings. He hated to do Muhammad like that with no proof.

Unfortunately, the proof he needed would only be revealed *after* he was indicted. Although he wasn't completely sure that Qwess's remedy was the correct answer, he did agree with Qwess that none of them could take that chance. In the streets, the *other* Golden Rule applied: Do unto others *before* they could do unto you.

And it appeared that Bone had found some worthy allies to carry out his master plan with.

Chapter 15

New York City
New Year's Eve

Flame hadn't heard from Sasha Beaufont since the episode at his spot. It was obvious she had swiped the video. The only question was why.

Neither Sasha nor Kim was returning his calls, and Diamond was still out of the country. Sasha had done a number on Flame, and he was going through withdrawal without her. He craved her sex, her presence, her scent, her passion. He was straight up missing her. How she disappeared on him had only heightened his arousal, so he reverted back to his old ways.

Flame was knocking down everything that wasn't nailed down as he tried to ease the fire Sasha had set loose in his loins. He was recklessly knocking off women after his parties and even banged a few he knew were under age. Nothing worked, though. He wanted Sasha.

Flame stalked Sasha's social media pages like he was a pa-

parazzo waiting to break a story, but other than the same old re-cycled professional photos, he couldn't catch a glimpse of her.

Fortunately, the time came when he had no spare time to worry about Sasha because he had to prepare for the New Year's celebration. He had scored the headline rap perfor-mance for ABC. It was a real good look. National exposure on the most watched show of the year was sure to bring in his New Year on a high note. All at once time, he could touch audiences from South Carolina to Singapore, from Fayette-nam to the Philippines and everywhere in between. This was huge for a Southern artist on a truly independent label.

After his performance he was scheduled to host a party along with Qwess and the rest of ABP at NY Live, the hottest new club just around the corner from Times Square. They were dubbing it the Billionaire Ball because it was rumored that the people Qwess invited as his special guests were all multiple millionaires one hundred times over. Their net worth combined would easily exceed one billion dollars. Qwess was pulling out all the stops to make his party the talk for the rest of the year. He even hinted that he was coming out of retire-ment to perform with Flame. Their grudges aside, Flame was excited because he and Qwess performing together would be huge for the culture. Flame felt Qwess had a lot to celebrate since he had been fleecing his artists all year. Now he wanted to rub his success in everyone's face.

Flame woke up with an eerie feeling that morning, but he just dismissed it as stage fright for the big event that night. More than 10 million people were estimated to be watching him at midnight.

8-Ball shadowed Flame as he ran around the city taking care of last-minute details. 8-Ball was still salty at Flame for fucking Sasha. He swore that something bad would happen behind it, but so far nothing had transpired. Flame just dismissed 8-Ball's mood as jealousy. He knew the big guy had a huge crush on Sasha. Hell, who didn't?

By the time night fell, Flame was ready for the night to be over! He was exhausted from the media frenzy and the traffic. Even though he was being chauffeured around in a customized Mercedes sprinter van, they still were hung up in traffic for most of the day.

It was cold as fuck outside, and Flame had to stay out in it to rehearse. His mink battled the cold a little, but it did nothing for the cold glares the other haters in the industry were throwing his way. Artists he'd had respect for were keeping their distance. Female artists he'd almost fucked weren't even acknowledging him.

Fuck 'em all, Flame thought. This was his night.

At about 11:30 p.m. other performers took the stage in front of hundreds of thousands of drunk revelers and New York's finest, hyping them out. Flame watched a few of the performances from his perch high above the stage while he and 8-Ball blazed some of that good-good to get his head right for his performance.

Flame inhaled deeply and reflected on the past year. The game had been good to him. His performance money was rolling in, and his single was topping the charts. Even his last royalty check had been decent. His clothing line was on par to do numbers next year, and he couldn't forget his biggest coup: he had fucked both Kim Rawls *and* Sasha Beaufont. He was living the dream of 85 percent of the men in the world. He thought about running that number up and trying to fuck the third member too, but she was too skinny to be his type. Plus, he was really feeling Sasha.

At ten minutes to midnight a handler from ABC found Flame and escorted him and 8-Ball down to the performance area and set them up backstage.

With two minutes to midnight, they passed Flame a mic and began his countdown. He was supposed to take the stage right as the ball dropped. Flame dapped Ball up, shed his floor-length mink, and adjusted his leather Flaming Diamond flight suit and waited for the countdown.

TEN!

A handler turned his mic on . . .

EIGHT!

Flame adjusted his diamond ABP necklace . . .

SIX!

He bowed his head, breathed deeply to calm down . . .

FOUR!

He peeked through the curtain at the packed house . . .

TWO!

Happy New Year!!!

Flame took the stage and blazed flames.

Qwess had been looking for Flame everywhere. When he saw him performing on one of the televisions in Times Square, he breathed a sigh of relief. He still had time to get to him.

Qwess's phone was going off incessantly with the same messages. He scrolled over to Twitter, and sure enough he saw it again. It was trending. Qwess shook his head. He couldn't believe this shit!

As he rode in the Maybach with Hulk, he felt the weight of his .40 cal resting beneath his sport coat and felt a little bit of comfort. Ever since Bone started making his move against the crew, Qwess started carrying the strap again. Bone was very reluctant to follow his orders that night, so even though Qwess heard one of the members had been killed, he couldn't be sure it was because of the orders he issued. History is littered with the bodies of those who took the double cross for granted. Qwess wasn't about to go down in history like them.

Qwess knew he had to deal with that later. He had more pressing matters to attend to now. He had to protect his future investment.

Tennessee / North Carolina Border

Bone's heart was heavy as he took the long, windy road up to the cabin in the mountains. He had managed to successfully gather all the First Fruits of the Crescent Crew together in one place. He lied and told them that he was throwing a celebration for the original Crew members as a reward for staying true to the game.

Of course, they were excited to show up and bond with their old comrades. Among themselves, they always felt as if they were a cut above the new members. They had put in substantial work compared to the others and carried the bricks that had built the foundation. It felt good for them to be singled out for their hard work.

Bone rounded the bend and saw the luxury vehicles strewn about the grounds of the cabin. They actually drove these hot-ass cars to a freaking New Year's rendezvous with the biggest drug dealers in the Southeast. He shook his head. *These niggas can't stay low-key to save their fucking lives.*

Bone circled the grounds to make sure everyone was inside. Through the open windows of the cabin he could see them shooting pool, smoking cigars and blunts, and playing cards. He slowed the Durango down enough for him to get a head count. Sure enough, they were all there.

Bone pulled the Durango around to the front of the cabin about fifty yards away from the building. He slammed the truck into park and doused the lights.

He spoke to his passengers in the truck. "You two niggas have been loyal from the first day I pulled you in from the cold, sucking up all the game I kicked down. I've been giving you the game like it was given to me," Bone said. "Now this is the other part of the game. The mo' money, mo' problems part of the game. The betrayals and coups and shit. You have to watch them niggas that's close to you and make sure they do what they supposed to do, 'cause sometimes them the niggas that be thinking about smoking you."

As Bone weaved his verbal web of deceit, it wasn't lost on him that he was testifying against himself. He was about to do the same thing he was warning the youngsters about. Then again, was he? Since the day Qwess had planted that fatal seed in his mind, his suspicions had grown into a full-fledged tree of doubt. That tree of doubt had grown to a forest of convictions. That's how the human mind works: it only takes one string being pulled to unravel a perfect bundle of loyalty. Bone was now convinced he had to act, because inaction could seal his fate and his whole Crew.

Bone pointed to the cabin. "All them niggas in there was plotting to overthrow me and take over the Crew for themselves. A couple of them was working with them folks to case me up too. Then, they wanted to divide the empire with their Georgia folks," Bone said, continuing to put the battery pack in his young soldiers' backs.

"Wait, so they not even from Carolina?" Maleek said.

"Nah. Georgia. Little town outside of Atlanta."

Maleek scoffed, "Go figure."

"You know, when we built the crew, we created it as a haven for hustlers where we all got rich and supported each other. Dig, if we all rich then nobody would be broke because we all would be each other's crutches. But these niggas don't want to be a part of the family no more. Notice I said, 'niggas,' because brothers of mine would never be so foul."

With each word, Bone was sinking the dagger in them

and him. He didn't have ironclad proof of their larceny. He was going on another man's word. It was as if he was about to kill all of mankind on account of another man's word.

As Bone spoke, he pulled up the YouTube video on the burner phone again. He watched the video while he watched his watch. It was 11:55 p.m. Five more minutes to show time.

Maleek was incensed; he was ready to set it. Impatient, he kept clicking his firearm in his lap.

Bone put the parking lights on and made one more circuit around the cabin to make sure everyone was still inside. Once again, he did a head count as he slowly circled the cabin. Once again, he tallied fourteen men.

Bone pulled the Durango around to the front of the cabin, nearly all the way down the hill this time. He was about seventy-five yards away now. He opened the back door and popped open the long green case in the seat. A spanking brand-new AT-4 stared back at him. One of the benefits of running the city where the world's biggest army base was located was that weapons of all types were just within arm's reach. Even soldiers weren't immune to the drug epidemic, and for drugs they would regularly raid their own armories. Bone had paid nearly a quarter brick of coke for this anti-tank weapon. He never guessed in a million years that it would be used in fratricide.

Bone pulled the weapon out and read the words on the top. Just as it promised on YouTube, the instructions were right there on the top.

THIS SIDE FACING BACK.

Bone flipped the cover up that hid the red button and peeked his head inside the truck. "Yo, y'all take cover," he advised.

Bone peered through the sights at the front door in the distance and prepared to fire his shot. He swallowed the lump in his throat that was his conscience trying to come get him, and placed his index finger on the red button. He peeked behind himself and in his head, just as the man had coached on YouTube, he yelled, "Back-blast area clear!"

As Bone put pressure on the button, the front door of the cabin opened, and a man walked out onto the porch. Bone couldn't see who it was, but he did recognize the red cherry at the end of a cigar. He hesitated—only for a second—then he pushed the button.

Whoosh!!!

The missile launched into the night leaving a bright red trail of flames streaking behind it. It crashed into the front window of the cabin, then the building erupted into a huge ball of flames.

Bone tossed the useless weapon in the backseat and fled the scene in the Durango with his new young guns. Fireworks burst high in the air all around him from revelers as they celebrated a happy New Year.

The moment Flame's shelltoes crossed the threshold of NY Live, all eyes were on him. He felt it. He had an extra bounce in his step because the way he tore shit up when the ball dropped, he knew the industry would be talking about him. Ball was at his side as they steered through the crowd. Local muscle led the way, bullying Flame a path like he was the heavyweight champ coming to the ring.

NY Live had three VIP areas on three different levels. Each level told your level of celebrity. If you were fortunate to warrant entry to the third level VIP section, you literally looked down on the haters letting them know you were shitting on them.

As Flame's light entourage breezed past the first two levels, he spotted some up-and-comers enjoying the celebration. Couple down-south underground titans. Flame saluted them, and Gem-star the Golden Child raised his glass back at him while Lil' Rue looked at him in awe. Venom, the female radio personality, shot him the finger. They had history. Flame had pumped and dumped her.

He kept it moving.

The first person he spotted when he made it to the third level was his label mate, Saigon. She frowned at him like he had the cooties, but he ignored her too. He kept it moving and snagged a table in the corner. A gold bottle was waiting on his table just like all the others. Flame settled down and cracked the bottle open. He poured himself and 8-Ball a drink and observed the VIP more closely.

Flame felt a weird energy in the room. People who were famous in their own right were sneaking photos of him with their phones. People who had hit him up and begged him to get at them when the time was right were now acting distant, as if he was a phantom. The VIP was filled with ABP supporters, but strangely, no one was putting respect on his name. In fact, they were treating him like an outcast.

What the fuck?

The crowd began to shift, and Flame saw Qwess bolting up the stairs two at a time. His face was chopped and screwed, and he was looking right in Flame's direction. They locked eyes as he took giant steps to Flame's table. As soon as he arrived Flame offered him a bottle. It was a New Year. No need to drag the same hostility into it. Or so he thought.

Qwess curled his lip up at Flame. "What are you, a fuckin' idiot, Joey?!" he barked.

Flame was taken aback. "What's wrong wit'chu, dawg! Nigga trying to offer you a peace treaty an' shit and you being disrespectful."

"Disrespectful? Are you stupid? Are you fuckin' high and stupid?!" Qwess smacked his forehead in disbelief.

Flame raised up in his seat. "What the fuck is wrong with you, dawg? What is your problem?"

"You my fucking problem, stupid!"

"Yo, I ain't gonna be too many more stupids and idiots."

At Flame's side, 8-Ball tensed up.

Qwess shook his head. "What have you done, Joey?"

"What?" Flame was confused. He had just set the stage on fire in front of the world and Qwess was trying to tear him down?

"Do you not know what is going on?" Qwess asked. "Everybody in the fuckin' world talking about you!"

Flame was really confused now. "Isn't that what we want? What are you talking about?!"

"What am I—tell ya what . . ." Qwess whipped out his phone, hit a few keys, and passed it to Flame. "Look at this shit, nigga."

Flame's breath caught in his throat. His breath got short and his heart started beating like sasquatch feet. Right there on Qwess's phone was a video of him laying wood to Sasha from the back, both of them smiling and grimacing at the camera.

"W-where did you get this?" Flame stuttered.

Surely, Sasha didn't send the tape to Qwess! What the fuck?!!

"Where did *I* get it? Nigga, everybody got it, fool! It's all over the net."

"The net?"

"The Internet. Twitter, Instagram, YouTube. Even Pornhub got it."

Flame zoned out. Qwess was still talking, but all Flame saw was his lips moving. Shock had set in, and his mind was reeling a thousand miles an hour. It felt like the room was spinning.

Suddenly, someone pushed Qwess aside. Flame raised his head at the exact moment Kim splashed her glass of champagne in his face.

"You dirty bastard!" Kim squealed. "You gon' get yours,

nigga!" She threw her glass at him but he ducked. "You and Sasha both. Soon as I catch her I'ma fuck her up too!"

Kim grabbed the whole bottle off the table and tried to hurl it at him, but Ball finally stopped her assault and carried her out of VIP over his shoulder.

Qwess pointed at the door. "That big nigga out there trying to get in here and tear your ass from limb to limb right now."

Flame shook his head in denial. "Nah, he not even in the country."

"Nigga, that motherfucker is outside right now. You listen to that bitch if you want to. I'm telling you he is looking for you." Qwess sighed. "It ain't wise for you to be up in here right now. You need to roll 'til I can smooth this shit over."

"Fuck him!" Flame spat. "I ain't running from nobody. Fayettenam don't breed cowards."

Qwess Ric Flair–chopped Flame in his chest. "This ain't no fucking pissing contest or a fucking album. That nigga is a killer! Now you fucked up by fucking his bitch."

"That nigga need to check his broad; don't check me."

Qwess had had enough. He turned to Hulk. "Yo, get this li'l nigga up out of here before he fuck up my money."

Hulk moved to lift Flame up, but he surrendered. "Aiight, aiight, I'll roll out, but you don't have to be all up on me and shit."

Qwess jabbed his finger at Flame and barked, "You fucked up, Joey! Now go so I can fix this shit."

Flame shucked Hulk's heavy arm from his shoulder and stood to leave.

"I got a car waiting for you in the back alley," Qwess said, looking around for Diamond. It was only a matter of time before he made it inside.

Flame waited on 8-Ball to return so he could go with him, just in case Diamond was waiting for him somewhere in the city.

But Qwess stopped him. "Nah, don't spoil this man fun 'cause you fucked up. Go your tough ass on outside. Chill out, Ball. Sit down. We partying tonight."

Flame walked down the stairs leading to the back door by the bathrooms by himself. His heart was thumping like African drums. Currents of anxiety zipped through his veins, causing him to shake, and his head was on a swivel. Every time something moved he paused and threw his hands up in defense. He swallowed his fear and closed his eyes. As soon as he closed them, he saw the image of himself wailing on Sasha from behind on the Internet. And that was just a snippet. If Diamond had seen any of that, Flame knew he had to get the hell out of Dodge before Diamond saw him.

Flame cracked the back door open and saw the Town Car waiting for him about thirty yards away. He stepped out into the cool night air and walked briskly to the car.

He didn't see it until it was too late. Tucked into the dark alley perpendicular to the Town Car, about three feet away, a two-toned Rolls-Royce Phantom. The New York license plate on the front of the car read *Diamante*.

It was Diamond.

Flame sped up and tried to make it to the Town Car before Diamond could spot him, but when he got closer to the Lincoln, Diamond's large frame materialized.

Fayettenam don't breed cowards.

Flame repeated the mantra to himself for courage and kept stepping until he was arm's length from the Lincoln. As soon as he reached to open the door, he heard Diamond moan something.

"Flame, you break my heart."

The next thing Flame felt was a sharp pain in his gut. He doubled over, clutching his stomach, and felt a warm liquid spill onto his hand, leaking, hot and heavy.

He was bleeding.

Before he could gather his senses, another blow crashed into the side of his head. He tried to stand tall and return a blow of his own. In his head the idea sounded good, but he never received a chance to carry it out because punishing licks rained on him from all sides. He felt the side of his face burst into flaming hot pain before another blow to his stomach buckled him to the ground on one knee.

As soon as Flame's knee hit the ground, Diamond scooped him up and held him high over his head. He spun Flame around for all his niggas to see, then power slammed him on his back onto the cold hard concrete like he was a pro wrestler.

Flame blacked out instantly.

But Diamond refused to allow him not to experience this beating of the century.

Diamond pulled his foot back high in the air and punted Flame's face like he was playing for the Giants. The kick woke Flame up, only for him to drift out of consciousness again.

Diamond's goons kicked Flame awake again with their wingtips. As soon as Diamond saw Flame's eye open, he smashed his beef-and-broccoli Timberland boot into it again and again

"Slick muthafucka!" Diamond spat. "You wanna fuck my bitch, nigga? I'ma beat your ass to death out here!"

So many kicks rained on Flame that he lost feeling. A few more kicks and he didn't even care anymore. He didn't even attempt to block the blows as they came at him now. He gave up his fetal position and allowed Diamond and his goon squad to have their way.

Diamond stooped down and gripped Flame's disfigured face in his meaty hand. Blood poured onto Diamond's pinky ring from the open gash on Flame's cheek.

"Look at me, Flame. I did this to you, motherfucker! Me! Diamond!" Diamond smacked him. Blood flew into the air.

"I fucking told you not to cross me, nigga. You gonna try to play *me*?"

Diamond was determined to teach Flame a hard lesson. He raised his boot high and brought it down right on Flame's dick.

Diamond reached down and grabbed Flame by the collar. "Get yo' ass up!"

He bent Flame over in front of him and stuffed his head between his legs. He flipped Flame up high and power bombed him into the pavement.

Flame heard something crack, and his legs went numb. Through trips in and out of consciousness, he saw the sky spinning, followed by the concrete, just before pain exploded behind his eyes.

"Pop the trunk!" Diamond ordered. He hoisted Flame over his shoulder.

Flame drifted in and out of consciousness as the earth continued to spin. Blood poured from his face and mouth, and he had long stopped fighting.

Suddenly, Flame heard Sasha scream, and he perked up. Through blurred vision he saw her exit the back of the Phantom in tattered clothing and run toward him. Through blurred vision, he saw Diamond smack blood from Sasha's mouth. She crumpled to the ground and didn't move an inch. Flame thought for sure he would see her in the afterlife from that blow.

"Sash," Flame mumbled through the blood pooling in his mouth.

"This nigga," Diamond mumbled. He held Flame over the open trunk and tried to slam him through the floor of the Phantom.

As soon as Flame's back hit the inside of the trunk, a burst of adrenaline washed over him. He knew if he allowed Diamond to close that trunk he would never see daylight again.

He raised his head to climb out, but Diamond kicked him in the face. Flame tumbled back inside, but not before he saw Qwess bust through the back door with a big pistol in his hand, calling for him.

Diamond slammed the trunk. Darkness surrounded Flame. Then he heard shots . . .

Chapter 16

Bright and early on New Year's Day, Bone called a special meeting at the strip club to discuss plans moving forward. He had just returned from the mountains and came straight to the club with his young guns in tow.

Maleek had driven them back from the mountains, and as he piloted his mentor, he just didn't know how much danger he was in. While he was preoccupied with smoking and listening to Jeezy, Bone was wrestling with the decision of whether to leave all the loose ends in Tennessee. He wasn't proud of what he had done, and his conscience was shredding him up. It wasn't that he was feeling bad about the act of murder—Bone had enough bodies under his belt to be classified as a serial killer. These bodies were different. These were more than just his comrades; these were his *brothers*.

Even in the streets, there was honor among thieves. Although these brothers did everything against Islam in pursuit of their wealth—supplying drugs, killing adversaries, and ruling with an iron fist—and enjoying the spoils of their labor, they considered their lives more sacred. Something about accepting that *kalima shahada* made them feel as if they were more purified than the other savages in the streets. With their declaration certain obligatory rights were extended to each other. Primary among those rights was the right of a brother to feel safe when in another brother's presence or company. Bone had violated that sacred right fourteen times, and regardless of the circumstances, it was still tearing him apart. Maleek was new to the Crescent Crew and thus the only link that could refute the story Bone planned to weave. He figured if he killed Maleek and the other new member, he could rebuild his whole family with a clean slate.

However, Maleek had also proven himself worthy of being down to put in work. With the right tutelage he could possibly be as deadly and beneficial to the new crew as Bone had been when he came up in the ranks.

Bone was confused as he waited for everyone to arrive from their respective locations.

"Aye, that shit was wild, like some TV shit, homie!" Lito said to Maleek, reenacting how the building had exploded. He hadn't stopped talking about the incident since it occurred. "That motherfucker said, 'Whoosh' and the whole shit blew."

As Lito kept reliving the mission, Bone stared at him in disgust, but he was so busy being an actor he missed the looks.

But Maleek didn't. He was gangsta to the core and knew that loose lips sank ships.

Finally, Bone had had enough. "Yo, my nigga, do you ever shut the fuck up! Gotdamn! You talking 'bout murders like it's a fucking soap opera."

Lito shrugged and looked around. "I mean, only people in here right now is who were there. It ain't like no one else in here."

He had a point, but he didn't get the point. Bad boys moved in silence . . . and violence.

"Yo, homie, I feel you," Maleek said. "That shit was lit, though." He laughed. "But check it, walk with me out here

and help me bring this shit out the car before these other niggas get here."

"Huh? What shit?"

"Nigga, bring your ass on and see."

Maleek walked out toward the back door to where his
Tahoe was parked. Lito reluctantly followed behind him.

While they were gone, Bone skipped upstairs to the office
to get things right for the meeting. He flipped on the television on the wall and couldn't believe his eyes. Video of Flame
performing in Times Square was on the screen. Below the
video was a caption that read, *Rapper Beaten; Fighting for His
Life!*

Additional breaking news ticked across the bottom of the
screen:

> *Rap Mogul Shot at New Year's Party in NYC!*
> *Megastar Sasha Beaufont Missing; Feared Dead!*
> *Rapper Beaten; Fighting for His Life!*

Bone turned the television on full blast and listened to the
report while simultaneously calling Qwess. Of course, he didn't
get an answer, so he was forced to listen to the news:

> *"Music superstar Flame was brutally beaten last night
> after performing in Times Square, and music mogul Tyshawn
> "Diamond" Barker was shot.*
>
> *Sources close to the case say the popular rapper was al-
> legedly involved in a love triangle with R&B superstar Sasha
> Beaufont, after a tape surfaced allegedly showing the rapper
> and the R&B starlet engaging in explicit sex. Sasha Beau-
> font is engaged to music mogul Tyshawn "Diamond"
> Barker.*
>
> *Barker was allegedly a leader of the Bloods street gang in
> New York City, before he left the gang and began a music ca-
> reer. Rapper Flame, who has ties to the infamously violent*

drug cartel the Crescent Crew, is reportedly in a New York area hospital fighting for his life, while Barker's whereabouts are unknown at this time.

Authorities fear this may not only spark a hip-hop beef between the North and the South, like the tumultuous East-West beef of the 1990s that claimed the lives of two of music's biggest stars, but with ties to two of the country's most violent gangs, this may spill out into the streets of America. Please stay tuned for—"

Maleek came into the office just as the reporter was wrapping up. He saw the images of Flame and Sasha on the screen.

"Yo, isn't that the homie, Flame?" Maleek asked.

"Hell yeah," Bone said, shaking his head. He scrolled through social media on his phone for more information. In this era, social media received news before the news.

Sure enough, people on Twitter were showing video of Flame being wheeled out on a stretcher. His entire body was covered beneath a sheet except his face, and the paramedics went to great pains to cover that, but slivers of his bloody face could still be seen on the video.

Bone scrolled down and saw more video of people holding a candlelight vigil in an alleyway. Even in the video, Bone could see bloodstains all over the pavement.

"Fuuuck!!!" Bone screamed. All he kept hearing was the reporter mention the Crescent Crew. On national television, his family's name was being called out. It didn't get more high profile than this.

Bone looked up from his phone at Maleek, who was watching the broadcast. "This is bad, homie. Real bad," Bone said. "We got to see what the fuck is going on. We might have to shoot to NY to hold shit together."

Bone suddenly noticed that only Maleek was in the office. "Aye, where ole buddy at?"

Maleek shrugged. "He outside in the trunk."

"Huh?"

"Yeah, he ain't cut out for this life. All that fucking talking he was doing was going to get us all throwed," Maleek explained. He pulled his pistol out and unscrewed the silencer from the tip of the barrel. "So I took care of it."

Bone nodded and smiled. *Yep, li'l Maleek was going to be all right after all.*

Damn, it was all good just a week ago.

A week ago he was poised to be on top of the world with a billion dollars at his fingertips. His artist was on track to have the number one album in the country, and the label had garnered five Grammy nominations. Couldn't tell him nothing!

His little man had reinvented himself in grand fashion. Even the haters had to love it. Whether they hated it or loved it, the underdog was on top.

It was all good just a week ago.

Now Flame was sitting in a hospital fighting for his life with tubes and shit hanging out of his mouth like an astronaut. All because of a piece of pussy.

Qwess shook his head.

He'd told Flame not to mess with Diamond. He'd warned him the dude was dangerous with a capital D, but he wouldn't listen. You just can't fuck a man's woman, especially a chick as fine and famous as Sasha Beaufont. Even Qwess didn't fuck with Sasha Beaufont after she got with Diamond, and he definitely could have.

But Flame just had to have her.

Now his gravy train was threatening to be derailed. Everything he fought for was being threatened now because of a piece of pussy. ABP was in the process of reinventing itself on Flame's back. Everything was going great, billions of dollars on the table poised to pile in, and now this. He had to find a way to put the pieces back together.

On the screen above Flame's bed was a constant reminder

of what had transpired the previous night. If not for the media coverage, Qwess probably wouldn't have believed it himself.

Qwess's driver had called him and told him that Flame was getting jumped by Diamond and his goons in the alleyway out back. When he rushed out the back door he saw Diamond slamming Flame into the trunk of the Phantom and Sasha lying on the ground. There was no time to act, so Qwess fired his gun right above Diamond's head. Diamond froze. As soon as the shots rang out, Diamond's goons produced their weapons and pointed them at Qwess.

When Diamond saw that it was Qwess, he smirked and walked right in Qwess's direction, but froze when Hulk and 8-Ball burst through the door and put a wall up in front of Qwess. Right there in the back alley, two of the biggest crews in the music business engaged in a grand ole Mexican standoff.

Without uttering a word, Hulk walked right past Diamond and all of his goons with a calm demeanor. As big as Diamond was, Hulk still dwarfed him as he walked by. While Qwess held Diamond at gunpoint, and Diamond's people held Qwess at gunpoint, Hulk carefully scooped Flame from the trunk of the Rolls-Royce and placed him on the ground. Flame was still unconscious and there was so much blood, his face couldn't even be seen. The awkward position that his body was contorted in told everyone that serious damage had been done.

Sirens wailed close by, and they all knew their time was getting short. All of the men weren't exactly legal, and this was not the time or place to resort to mob-style tactics. All that mattered to Qwess at that moment was getting help for Flame.

With fury bleeding from his voice, Qwess said, "Get your bitch and get the fuck out of my sight, nigga. We will deal with this shit later."

Diamond chuckled and replied, "She not my bitch no more; she belong to the game, my nigga. You'll see."

One of Diamond's people scooped Sasha and tossed her into the back seat of the Rolls like a rag doll while Diamond carefully retreated to the car as well.

Diamond stuck his arm out the window and pointed to Flame. "If that li'l nigga not dead," he said, "he gonna wish he was when I catch him again."

Police and paramedics poured into the alley just as Diamond eased the window up. The Rolls-Royce screeched out of the alleyway just before the authorities cordoned off the area.

That was more than twelve hours ago.

Qwess hadn't left Flame's side since the paramedics rushed him to Lenox Hill Hospital in the wee hours of the morning. They finally managed to stabilize him around noon and give an accurate diagnosis that wasn't good.

Flame's brain had hemorrhaged from the head injuries he sustained in the beating and he had to be placed in a medically induced coma. Maybe that was a good thing considering he also sustained a severe back injury and was paralyzed from the waist down. He wouldn't have been able to live with himself if he knew he couldn't walk. Even heavily sedated, every few minutes he would thrash violently, and the nurses would have to rush in the room and issue him another sedative.

Qwess looked down at his li'l homie, friend, and number one meal ticket lying in the bed, and a wave of emotions washed over him. Remorse. Guilt. Doubt.

"Damn, my nigga," Qwess croaked, shaking his head. "I told you not to fuck with that nigga."

He removed his rose gold Cartier frames to wipe his eyes. So much was coming at him from so many angles. Since King Reece died, he felt all alone. He couldn't grasp this music industry shit. It was so fake, yet the ramifications of it could be so real. The gangsta in him was dying to be released and right all the wrongs, but the businessman in him was keeping the gangsta at bay. He had a billion dollars on the table, and it felt like the universe was conspiring to keep him from touching it.

Qwess felt the door open behind him. He thought it was the doctor, but when he turned around, there was a stranger standing there.

Qwess flinched and reached for his piece that was no longer in his waist. "Yo, who the fuck are you?" he demanded.

The man was brown-skinned, about six foot two and weighed in around 220 with a portly belly. A long black beard touched his barrel chest, and the waves spinning in his Caesar nearly rocked Qwess to sleep.

"Relax, Qwess, I mean you no harm," the man said. He wore distressed denim, construction Timbs, and a brown leather bomber with fur accents on the collar and wrists. "I come in peace."

The man looked very familiar to Qwess. He had seen him somewhere before but with his mind clouded with so much, he couldn't recall where he knew him from.

"Yo, how the hell did you get past all the security?" Qwess asked, looking past the man to the closed door. Flame was being treated in a private wing, and Hulk was heading the security detail, which consisted of people from ABP as well as local muscle.

"You don't remember me, do you?"

"Ahh, I don't remember much at all right now. My li'l man is laying here in a coma."

"Yeah, that's what I wanted to talk to you about." The man looked over both shoulders and whispered. "I need some help, yo."

In that instant, Qwess recognized where he knew the man from. "Ohh, shit! You're that rapper that was signed to Diamond! Motherfucker!"

Qwess lunged at the man, but he parried away smoother than Money Mayweather. When he ducked away from Qwess his coat fell open. That's when Qwess saw the badge.

"Yo, what the fuck is going on?" Qwess hissed. "You better tell me something fast."

"Qwess, brother, relax and I'll tell you everything. We have to talk in here where no one can see me because I can't blow my cover."

By now, it was apparent that the man was a cop, and that blew Qwess's mind more than anything he had witnessed the previous night. Qwess recalled seeing the man with Diamond's entourage for the past year. They were hyping him as the next big thing in the music industry, an underground rapper with a notoriously mysterious persona. Now Qwess knew why the mystery.

"You're Mystikal or some shit like that, right?" Qwess asked.

"Yeah, that's my rap name, but my real name is Agent Roberts. I'm an undercover agent with the FBI."

Qwess was flabbergasted. "Get the fuck out of here."

Agent Roberts nodded. "Yep. I've been undercover with DMP for the past year." DMP was Diamond's record and production company, Diamond Mine Productions. "I've been investigating the music industry with a bird's-eye view for the past year."

Qwess whistled, "A real live fucking hip-hop cop," he said.

Agent Roberts shrugged. "Hey, when the government wants to investigate drug cartels, they assign undercover agents as drug dealers or drug buyers. When they want to investigate the hip-hop industry, they assign agents as rappers."

Qwess was speechless. He'd heard about the hip-hop cops, but he'd never seen one up close and personal. Just hearing him speak about how close he'd been inside hip-hop circles made Qwess shudder. What did he hear about Qwess while with Diamond? What had he heard about the Crescent Crew?

"Makes sense," Qwess admitted. "But what brings you here? At this time, no less?"

"First, let me say I'm sorry for what happened last night, and I'm sorry to have to have this conversation over Flame's body."

"Don't say that!"

"I'm sorry, I mean while he's in this condition. But you understand my need to be discreet."

"Let's get to it, man. Because I got people from all over the country on the way here. This place is about to get messy."

"Fair enough. Bottom line, I'm here for two reasons. I want info about last night. I've been on to Diamond and I know what he's been up to, but I could never catch him. However, what you saw last night can put him on ice until I can make what I have on him stick."

"And the second thing?"

"I want to stop this war. I know who you really are and I know how this can go. I want to warn you, Qwess, or should I say, Salim . . . the whole bureau is watching you. We've been watching you for a while. I can tell you there are criminal charges coming down on you from the AMG situation. I can tell you we had someone planted in your Crescent Crew organization—that is until late last night. Qwess, I wish I could tell you that things are going to get easier, but it's not. However, it can be. It's your choice."

Qwess listened intently. He wanted to hear exactly what he was up against. "What are you saying, Agent Roberts?"

"You know how this thing goes, Qwess." Agent Roberts spread his hands expansively. "You help us, we help you."

"What exactly are you asking me?"

"Help us get Diamond, and we will grant you immunity on everything."

Qwess looked at Agent Roberts, clad in his hip-hop attire and big beard. For at least a year, he had been masquerading in hip-hop circles, perpetrating a fraud as a rapper, gleaning information. He had done a spook that sat by the door reversal on the hip-hop industry. Now, he was before one of the biggest names in the game revealing himself as an agent trying to flip him.

"So, what's it gonna be, yo?"

Before Qwess could answer Hulk peeked his head in the door and interrupted him from answering that fateful question.

"Bro, you okay in here? His five minutes is up," Hulk asked.

"Actually, this guy was just leaving," Qwess said.

"Well?" Agent Roberts asked as he walked toward the open door.

Qwess frowned and motioned at Flame. "Have some respect."

"Does this conversation stay here until we can be in touch again?"

Qwess stared at Agent Roberts. "Again, have some respect."

Agent Roberts left the room.

Chapter 17

Flame remained in a coma for a week, and the whole music industry was in a coma right along with him. He was a star that shined bright in a universe of wannabe stars. He had that "it" factor that birthed stars. As Qwess had told him when he first started in the game: he had to make all the men want to be *like* him and all the women want to be *with* him. Flame had surpassed that edict. He had the whole world reciting his freaky rhymes, and had the whole world digging his lothario persona.

Flame's problem was that fame could blur the lines of consequence. He had soared to unreachable heights on the wings of stardom, heights where his hype made him believe he was untouchable. He had reveled in his status as a ladies' man, fashioned it, courted it, and promoted it. Unfortunately, Flame's persona was his lifeline and possibly his death knell.

In the days that Flame remained in the hospital, more video of him and Sasha emerged online, snippets of their whole affair. On the seventh day that he was in the hospital, the entire thirty-minute video surfaced online. A leading porn company finagled the rights to the video, cleaned up the grainy images, and sold them.

The video made Flame a bigger star than music ever made him. Women salivated over his monster ten-inch dick, and men admired him for giving it all to Sasha in championship fashion like so many of them fantasized of doing. Flame's new single flew off the shelves, and the world was anticipating his new album like dope fiends lusted for their next hit.

Sasha's good-girl image took a huge hit when the whole tape surfaced. Her carefully crafted image the record label had methodically produced over time evaporated quicker than water on the sun. However, the public was divided on what to do with her. Her good Christian followers abandoned her, of course, but the hood really embraced her now. She was the new bad girl, lauded for her ability to remain down to earth among so much stardom. Everyone thought she was too straitlaced to be whining like she did on stage. Seeing her in action changed their perception of her. While the tape alienated her core fans, she gained a whole new fan base. Too bad she couldn't enjoy it.

A week after New Year's still no one had heard from Sasha since she'd been tossed in the backseat of Diamond's Rolls-Royce.

Diamond had resurfaced a couple days after the attack with a new supermodel on his arm. He paraded her around town, taking photos with his heavy arm draped around her, kissing her every time a camera clicked. He was sending the message loud and clear that he was done with Sasha, but the question on everyone's mind was, *where was Sasha?*

Qwess flew into Fayetteville for a day to handle some business that had to be handled in person. Malik Shabazz had summoned him, and that was the one piece of business he was happy to handle.

Immediately after the news of Flame's misfortune, the other leading story was the assassination of fourteen high-ranking members of the Crescent Crew. Because of the brazen nature of the attack, it was being reported that the Mexican cartel was responsible. News outlets were attributing the murders to a drug turf war between the Mexican drug cartels expanding into new territory and the incumbent empire trying to hold on to their power. The use of a rocket launcher in the murders brought the attention of the federal government, and authorities were threatening to activate the National Guard if things grew out of hand. For all the attention the murders drew, Qwess was still optimistic, because the murders confirmed that anyone who could have possibly known about the attack at AMG years ago had been eliminated.

Qwess stepped off the elevator into Malik Shabazz's office with his poker face. He could hardly contain his excitement about getting this much closer to the deal of his life.

"Salim, *as-salaam alayka,* brother," Shabazz greeted Qwess with a smile, but Qwess could see it was forced.

"*Wa alayka salaam,* Brother Shabazz. What you got for me?"

Malik Shabazz sat at his desk and shuffled a stack of papers. He motioned for Qwess to sit down. "Take a seat. We have a lot to discuss."

"Oh, yeah?" Qwess already knew as much. He couldn't wait to hear Shabazz confirm things.

"Oh, yeah." Shabazz slid the stack of papers across the desk to Qwess. "They filed these interrogatories and admissions. We have thirty days to respond."

"What are those?"

Shabazz explained to Qwess that interrogatories were a form of pretrial discovery that plaintiffs used to compel the defense to admit certain facts pertaining to the case under oath, without being in court.

In this case, they were asking Qwess to admit that he

knew Chabo, Gil, and Samson (although Samson was identi-
fied with an alias), that he was a member of the Crescent
Crew at some point, and that he had used drug money to fund
and maintain Atlantic Beach Productions.

"They're crazy!" Qwess exploded. "Who would admit to
that?"

"It gets worse," Shabazz said. He slid another stack of papers across the desk. "They are demanding to see your financials."

"My financials?"

"Yep. They want to see your financial reports for the last
five years. My guess is they're asking this because they want to
see how you benefitted financially from the assault, so they
want to gauge your records before and compare them to after."

This posed a problem for Qwess. He'd had an influx of
capital in the past five years, but it wasn't because of any
money he made from acquiring Niya. Upon King Reece's release, he had invested in ABP to the tune of $20 million.
Qwess utilized a lot of the money in promoting Flame and
Niya's albums at the time. The other money he funneled into
his business accounts in staggered amounts so as not to cause
alarm. A million here, two million there. However, doing
business in the music industry on his level was very expensive,
so the money didn't sit long.

Upon King Reece's death, Qwess was left with the remainder of his fortune. People like King Reece didn't keep
money in traditional banks. In fact, one of their biggest problems was where to keep all the cash the streets brought in. At
his height, King Reece bought houses just to keep his money
in. However, he constantly shuffled the money from place to
place to stay ahead of anyone who would be stupid enough to
steal from him. Qwess was the only person he trusted with his
fortune, and upon his death, Qwess retrieved all the money
from his spots. At the second location, Qwess pulled more

than $350,000 from underground and discovered the money had been ruined by the elements. There was no telling how long the money had been there, and Qwess couldn't afford to take any more chances with the rest of the money. He retrieved all the money from King Reece's spots—nearly $40 million—and funneled it into his accounts in creative ways. Banks would only insure so much money, so Qwess employed creative tactics to essentially launder the money into his accounts.

He purchased hyper cars, like the Pagani Zonda and Huayra, he purchased diamonds and of course real estate—all things that either appreciated or at least held their value. For example, the Pagani Huayra was purchased at $2.7 million. Because there were only so many made, they were ultra-exclusive. This meant, if anyone in the world crashed a Huayra, the remaining Huayras would go up in price. But money had to be utilized as the tool it was, so a large amount of King Reece's illicit funds still found their way into ABP's coffers.

"Brother, we can't allow them to look into my company's financial records," Qwess protested.

Shabazz nodded. "I figured you would say as much. What about these other things? Did you know these other guys? These"—Shabazz referred to the papers—"Chabo and Gil fellas?"

Qwess shrugged. "I mean, I may have saw them in passing a time or two, but they're deceased right now, so what does that matter?"

Shabazz shrugged. "Could be something, could be nothing. Only time will tell."

Qwess noticed Shabazz hadn't said anything about the other witness disappearing. So he pried further. "Are those the only people they're asking about? What about the other witness, the confidential informant?"

Shabazz consulted the papers again. "I . . . don't . . . see anything different," he said, continuing to rifle through the papers.

"Are you sure?"

Shabazz raised his eyebrows with accusation. "Uhh, is there something I should know about?"

"Nah, not at all. I just asked my people about this, and they couldn't think of who it could be."

"Hmm-mmm, and then you just lost a few friends recently as well too, correct?"

Now it was Qwess's turn to raise his eyebrows. "Yeah, yeah, I did."

"I'm sorry to hear that."

"I appreciate the concern, but let's get back to this case. What are we going to do?"

Shabazz shook his head slowly. "I'm not sure right now. I can tell you that I didn't think they were this serious, but they've maxed out these interrogatories—they're going for the jugular, son."

Qwess was in denial. His mind wouldn't allow him to compute what Malik Shabazz was telling him. He figured that maybe the informant being murdered hadn't registered in the case yet.

"Yeah, well, we gotta hit them right back."

Malik Shabazz shook his head slowly. "Son, I don't think you're getting this. We might have to start thinking about a settlement. If you don't respond to these questions, they can file for summary judgment, and you will lose that seventy-five million dollars, possibly more. If you don't offer some information, you will lose this case. I don't know how rich you are, but hell, Puffy would feel a seventy-five-million-dollar loss. I'm thinking if we put a settlement offer out there, we could see where their heads are. Say, offer fourteen million or so to see if they will accept it. This way they won't have to comb through all your shit."

Qwess shook his head. He wasn't trying to feel any of that. He was taking financial losses by the day.

"Salim, there is more than one type of victory," Shabazz schooled. "They're asking for seventy-five million; if you get off with fifteen million, that's a win!"

"Not in my book."

"Are you familiar with a Pyrrhic victory? Because with your attitude, that's what you're looking at."

"Look, I'm not settling for shit. This is soft extortion, and you know it. Now can you win this case, or do I need to get you some help?"

I'm already helping you as much as I can! Qwess wanted to say.

Malik Shabazz raised his head and poked out his chest with pride. "I'm Malik Shabazz, all I do is win."

Qwess offered a genuine smile for the first time since he'd been in the office. "That's what I like to hear. Now show me."

Qwess stood and left the office, leaving Malik Shabazz contemplating how to pull a needle out of a haystack.

Bone offered the Salatul Al-Janazah in the ranks with members of the Ummah inside the masjid on Murchison Road. As he recited the prayer behind the Imam his heart was heavy. This was the eighth and final Janazah he had attended since New Year's, and each funeral service sank him deeper and deeper into despair. To know that he had killed his Muslim brothers in such a brutal fashion that prevented a proper burial tore him to pieces. The explosion had ripped their bodies to shreds, nearly disintegrating them. For the bodies that were found, they were too disfigured to identify. They only knew them by which men didn't come back home.

Bone knew that the Janazah prayer was also for the remaining believers to seek forgiveness for their sins as well, but he didn't feel secure that Allah would forgive him for his sins on this one. In Islam, believers are judged more harshly based on how knowledgeable they are of their faith. Bone was very learned in his *deen*. He read Qur'anic Arabic and he was well versed in Islamic history as well. The younger Muslims in the Crescent Crew often looked up to Bone and considered him their amir, or spiritual leader. So Bone was definitely more knowledgeable than the average. Bone knew that he planned to murder his brethren well before he did it. Yet he didn't show them mercy. Now, here he was praying and seeking Allah's forgiveness. This act made Bone worse than a murderer in Islam; it made him a *munafiq*, or hypocrite.

"*As salaamu alaikum wa rahmatullah*," the Imam chanted, dismissing prayer.

Bone offered a supplementary prayer called a *du'a* then went to the front to put on his Margiela sneakers. As soon as he came out front, he was surrounded by an entourage as if he was the president. Everywhere he moved, a man was on each side of him.

The Crescent Crew was in war mode. Bone had sold the story to his Crew that the Mexicans were responsible for the attack in the mountains, so they were moving extra cautious, taking no chances. After their meeting on New Year's Day when Bone assigned new captains new territory, extra members remained in town to secure their leader and bring smoke to any man in the city that even looked as if he spoke Spanish.

Bone's number one shooter was the young, hungry soldier who knew everything about the latest developments in the Crescent Crew.

Since the night of the explosion, Bone and Maleek had been inseparable. Being Bone's right hand elevated Maleek's status in the eyes of the Crew, and Maleek relished the attention. Bone, on the other hand, kept Maleek around so he could keep an eye on him . . . just in case.

Maleek walked outside the masjid to secure the area and retrieve the car while Bone peeled off hundred-dollar bills to the elders in the community on his way out the door. Maleek pulled the cream Rolls-Royce Ghost to the front, and Bone ducked his tall frame into the back of the Rolls behind Maleek.

"Damn, Akhi, this shit is getting harder and harder," Bone admitted as soon as he settled inside the green leather seats.

"Yeah, I know," Maleek agreed. "This shit fucking with me too, but I understand the call. His wife is taking it really hard, though."

"Shit, his mom too. I have to go by there and take her some more dough," Bone remembered. "Aye, hang a right up here and go on Ramsey. I got to make a stop."

As Maleek piloted the Rolls, Bone turned the music up and allowed the Lyfe Jennings track to help him unwind. His city was on fire, fighting a war that he had started all on a lie, not unlike the Iraq war that so many men from the city had lost their lives in. So far, he was up on the scoreboard, but their mission was to run every Mexican that wasn't cleaning houses out of town. It was hard to tell friend from foe, and he couldn't take any chances, so everyone had to go. Ironically, a lot of regular working Joes were leaving town voluntarily. Now, in the morning when the work trucks rolled through town to pick up day workers, the stops were filled with a sea of black faces instead of brown faces. So, in a warped way, the Crescent Crew was still impacting the community in a positive manner.

"Pull up right here," Bone instructed, pointing to the CVS parking lot. "Pull up beside that black Camaro."

Maleek eased the Rolls into the parking lot beside the black-on-black Camaro. Once the Rolls stopped, Qwess jumped out of his Camaro and hopped in the back with Bone.

"Hey, Maleek, ride up Ramsey by the Walmart," Bone instructed.

Maleek raised the partition separating the front from the back and moved out into traffic.

"You okay?" Qwess asked Bone, shaking his head. "I saw this shit on the national news."

Bone sighed. "I don't know, OG. This shit don't feel right. Those were my brothers."

Qwess looked out the tinted window at the cars passing by. "They were my brothers too, as you are my brother," Qwess assured him. "But I must tell you, as much as it hurts, we made the right decision."

Bone shook his head. "I'm not so sure."

"Trust me, we did."

"What makes you so sure?"

"Because a federal agent came to see me in New York. He told me out his own mouth that the witness against me was killed in that explosion."

"Word?"

"Word!"

Bone allowed himself a small smile. So it wasn't all in vain.

"So, we weren't wrong," Qwess said. He could tell that Bone was still taking things hard. Bone was a stone-cold killer, for sure, but he wasn't a complete savage. His heart was still pure for those on his team, especially the believers. "Bro, this shit never gets easy. When they say it gets lonely at the top, this is what they mean . . . no one to talk to because you don't know who wants your position . . . having to live with regrets. I mean, who can understand the mind state of the man that rose from the trenches to be the biggest nigga in the city."

Bone modestly shied away from the comment, but Qwess had to let him know who he was and what position he played.

"Don't get it twisted, Bone. You are that nigga; you are *him*." Qwess looked him directly in his dark eyes. "It's important that you know that, so you won't ever get lackadaisical and get caught slipping."

Bone took it all in and digested it, but he still had questions. "How you do it, OG? I mean you left all this sheet alone and escaped into the music industry. You didn't slow down one bit."

Qwess shook his head and chuckled. "It wasn't easy at all, Akhi. I took a lot of losses."

"Yeah?"

Yeah . . . like my ex-fiancée, Shauntay. She probably was the love of my life, and all she ever wanted to hear me say is that I loved her. I couldn't do it, though. The game was too deep in my blood back then, but shorty would've done anything for me. She was perfect, bro—smart as hell, cute face, small waist with a big jungle ass. Long hair . . ." Qwess's words trailed off with a whistle. "I've been all over the world, and she is still the finest woman I ever been with."

"Is that the one that . . ."

"Yeah, that's her. She was killed in a case of mistaken identity. You know, I told the story in the movie."

"Yeah, I remember."

"Anyway . . ." Qwess looked out into the gritty Fayettenam streets. "She's the only thing from my past that I can't outlive. I can't shake that part of my past."

"Understandable."

Qwess raised his finger. "But, let me give you this piece of advice that will take you to the next level," he said. "When you out here thuggin', getting it how you live, you will have to go to the depths of hell to get your piece of the pie. Shit gets dirty, so never—ever—look back at the past. Not for validation, answers . . . nothing. Don't go back to the past. And that's the secret to surviving."

Bone digested the jewel and nodded.

"That feeling in your stomach right now, it will pass. Trust me. And when it does, remember how it felt so you won't allow yourself to feel like this again."

Again Bone nodded.

"I wasn't going to tell you because I didn't want you to think that this was why I told you to do what you did, but this move just put us in position to put a billion dollars on the table for the team."

"A billion?"

"A billie, Akhi," Qwess confirmed. "You know I'm always plotting on a way to get the team to the promised land. That's what all this was for in the beginning, and it's still the goal. Now, Reece was stubborn; he was Crescent Crew to the death, and while that's admirable, he died in this shit, and now I'm raising his son. You got how many kids?"

"Four all together; three girls and one boy."

"Right, you have to think about tomorrow," Qwess advised. "Now, even though it wasn't about the money, you will be rewarded for the work you put in to help this go through."

"I appreciate that, OG, but I did that for the Crew. That was Crew business."

Qwess smiled. "And I can dig it, but it's my responsibility to show the Crew a different way to do business."

Qwess felt that as the founder of the Crescent Crew, he was obligated to get them out of the streets. So many years ago, he had secured a deal with a major label to bring his brothers home out of the cold, but Reece wanted to remain true to the game. Qwess only hoped that he could make this move and become the biggest independent record label in the world before Samson returned home to reclaim his throne.

Qwess maintained his allegiance to the family he built, but his methods were different these days. He felt responsible for bringing them to the next level. He knew that for every ounce of blood the Crescent Crew shed, a stain was on his hands as well. He felt if he could redirect that ship to a legit lifestyle, then that would be the true way to honor Reece's legacy.

But he knew that he had to feed his people in order to lead his people. Therefore, it was imperative that he made the streaming deal a reality.

Qwess was back in soldier mode, but this time his mission was survival of the fittest.

Chapter 18

Flame walked across the mountains with a slight limp. He looked up at the sky that was filled with rare, beautiful hues of reds and oranges as far as his eyes could see. The sky appeared high and expansive, but he felt so close to the roof of the bubble. He felt like a giant. As he traversed the valleys, he felt light with not a care in the world, whistling as he walked with no real destination in mind. Every few feet, a pain would explode in his lower back so excruciating that it threatened to buckle him to the ground, but he simply told it to go away, and the pain disappeared.

Flame came upon a thicket about fifty yards ahead of him. He couldn't see the forest for the trees, but something told him he needed to see what was inside the brush. Flame figured he might as well investigate from a higher level of understanding, so he thought about puffing on a huge blunt. Magically, a blunt as thick as a broomstick appeared in his left hand. Flame smiled, wrapped his lips around the blunt, and took a long pull. He was high in seconds and ready to face the thicket of trees.

Flame walked inside the thicket of trees and was surprised to discover that what he thought were trees were actually throngs of people screaming his name. He walked deeper into the brush and saw a stage set up waiting for him. Flame dropped the huge blunt on the forest floor and dashed to the stage.

On stage, he started rapping his heart out, but he couldn't hear a thing. His earpiece was tucked inside his ear, but he still couldn't hear a thing.

Flame thought about how cool it would be if a woman was on stage with him, and immediately a woman appeared on stage dancing in front of him. She was high yellow in complexion with long blond hair draped over her face like curtains. She possessed more curves than a racetrack and she danced on the stage before him in a body-hugging leather pantsuit that left little to the imagination. Flame thought about what the curves looked like beneath the suit and . . . voilà! The suit disappeared, leaving her fully nude body on display as she gyrated on the stage. Flame was noticing a theme here. It appeared that whatever he thought about immediately came to pass.

This is cool, he thought, and began using the power.

With his thoughts, he created a stage set that was a homage to himself. Large photos of him with his shirt off danced as a live mural in the backdrop. Next, he telepathically set two huge speakers up in the corners of the stage. Flame went to work creating a beautiful masterpiece all with his mind. While he rearranged his environment, he watched the beautiful woman captivate him and the crowd with her seductive movements.

He quickly became enthralled with her performance, watching her naked ass jiggle as she twerked. He thought about what it would be like to penetrate those soft cheeks, and as soon as the thought registered, his huge penis appeared in his hands. He walked toward the performer, and when he was within a couple feet of her, she whirled around and showed him her face.

Flame jumped back in a mixture of fear and disgust. The woman's face was grotesquely disfigured, and a mask of blood covered it. She bared her sharp teeth and wailed at Flame. Flame recoiled toward the back of the stage until he heard a noise.

Suddenly, a voice blared his name through the speakers. "FLAME!"

Flame spun around and saw a huge holographic image of Diamond on the screen at the back of the stage. Flame froze and imagined Diamond disappearing. But this time it back-fired. Instead of Diamond disappearing, he came to life and walked out of the screen, towering thirty feet into the air above Flame. As he advanced toward Flame, terror erupted from Flame's lips, but no sound came out.

Flame turned and rushed toward the end of the stage. He ran to the edge of the stage and skidded to a stop when he saw a long drop down into an abyss. He paused and dashed away from the edge, but Diamond was still walking toward him slowly, shaking thunder from the ground with each step. Flame's eyes flitted from Diamond to the edge of the stage. Fear caused him to forget about his superpower. Fear made him forget everything.

Fear made him forget about Sasha until she popped up in his face, wailing his name and reaching out for him with her bloody claws.

"Fllllllaaaaaaaaammmmmee!" Sasha screamed.

Flame turned around and ran toward the edge of the stage. Rather than stop this time, he swan-dived right off the edge of the stage into the abyss down below. He screamed at the top of his lungs until . . .

Flame's eyes flashed open. The first thing he saw were the blinding overhead lights beaming in his face. He gasped for air, but the gadget covering his face made it hard for him to suck any in.

He panicked.

Flame tried to snatch the gadget from his face, but his arms felt restricted. He clenched his fist in an attempt to free his arm, but it didn't work. The mask felt suffocating now. All he wanted to do was breathe, and have the bright light removed so he could see where the hell he was. He writhed in the bed and kicked his legs. Well, in his mind he kicked his legs, but he didn't feel them move. He kicked them again, and again he felt no movement.

Flame really panicked then.

He blew into the mask with all the air in his lungs, trying to move it. When that didn't work, he directed his energy to his left arm. Just like he did in his dream, he thought about his arm moving. Just like it happened in his dream, the arm moved this time, just a little. Flame repeated the actions, and this time the arm heaved high in the air and something clanged to the floor.

Flame tried to do the same thing to his legs, but still nothing happened. He tried it a few more times to no avail. His heart thundered in his chest as more fear set in.

My legs, I can't feel my legs!

Flame realized that he had his voice, and he screamed at what he thought was the top of his lungs. In reality, the scream was no more than a glorified whimper. When nothing happened, he repeated the scream multiple times until he heard machines squealing all around him. Then, in the distant recesses of his ears, he heard footsteps galloping all around him and people talking excitedly. Finally, someone removed the plastic piece from over his mouth.

Flame gulped in a lungful of fresh air.

Flame . . . was out of his coma.

Chapter 19

It was as if Mr. Westside had survived his shooting in Vegas. Or if the Suburban had been bulletproofed. So many years after those tragedies, hip-hop finally received its favor when Flame beat death in New York City.

The industry breathed a collective sigh of relief when news spread about Flame recovering from his coma. People were still visiting the candlelight vigil that had been erected at Times Square when the news broke, so everyone thought it was a hoax. That is, until the earliest photos of Flame in the hospital bed broke the Internet. The images were gruesome . . . raw . . . real. The images were what happened when someone trifled with Tyshawn "Diamond" Barker.

It had been weeks since the incident, and no one had heard from Diamond nor Sasha since the incident. Sasha was officially being reported as a missing persons case, and authorities were exploring bringing charges against Diamond—if they could find him.

While the entertainment industry scrambled to reset itself, it was business as usual for Qwess as he floated high above the clouds in his Gulfstream to New York City along with his team. Before him, on one of the wooden tables, were the prospective expense reports from Liam for the streaming company, along with a partnership agreement. His father had gone over the contract with a fine-toothed comb and assured him that everything was equal. There were no creative loopholes or hidden clauses that allowed for Liam to one-up Qwess. It was an equal split between ABP and Liam's new startup.

The name of their new streaming company was Wave, which was an homage to Qwess's hometown of Atlantic Beach, and it symbolized Liam's home near the Gaza Strip. A Muslim and a Jew teaming up on this level was unheard of, but Qwess and Liam were hoping to create a new wave with Wave.

Reading the actual figures excited Qwess beyond words. He was a visionary, and creating something that would take over the world made his blood pump. Knocking down hurdles was his drug, creating legacies was his mission. So amidst all the chaos surrounding Qwess, as he pored over the reports and sipped champagne, he was in a pocket of peace.

Qwess slid a piece of paper across the table to Amin and Doe. "See this shit, bro?" Qwess said. "We can make over a hundred mil in under twelve months."

"*If* this shit pops off," Amin advised.

"Bro, this is the wave of the future," Qwess insisted.

Doe frowned and ran his fingers through his curly hair. "I don't know, bro. All this shit is fairly new, this technology . . . the streaming . . . it's a huge gamble."

"Yeah, but the rewards go to the risk takers!" Qwess replied, shaking his fist. "Streaming is doing good in Europe. We just have to perfect the technology, and Liam has got that covered."

"Yeah, but what's the ticket for us to get started? The entry number."

Qwess sighed and leaned back in the plush leather chair. "It's gonna wipe us out."

"Wipe us out? What does that mean?" Amin asked.

"It means that we will be all in."

"What's the number, though?" Doe asked.

"Around seventy."

"Seventy, but what about—"

Qwess shot Doe a look that hushed him. He knew what Doe was inquiring about, but everything wasn't for everybody.

"So, yeah, we will be all in, but if it pays off, we will be liquid again in a matter of months. I'm talking allllll the way up."

Everyone silently ruminated on the papers before them. They were in a weird position. Everything they did to take their company to the next level came back to bite them in the ass. The acquisition of Niya was supposed to be their takeover, the feather in the cap of their independence. Instead, it was the acquisition of a beef that pushed them out of the graces of the industry. Setback upon setback tumbled upon their heads, and now their backs were against the wall. They were damned if they did and damned if they didn't. If they didn't go forward with the deal, they would effectively be frozen back to the projects. If they went forward and lost, they would be back to the block. However, if they did the deal, they would be back on top like never before, waving to the haters in their rearview.

Amin broke the silence. "One thing in our favor is Flame," he said. "I hate to sound heartless, but if we can get him back in that studio and get him to pull some music out of this incident . . . we can make hundreds of millions out the gate."

Qwess shot his business manager a scowl, but he had to admit he was right. Flame was still their golden ticket.

"Yeah, well, we'll see about Flame in a few hours. As

much as I hate to admit it, you're right, bro. Everything is still riding on Flame . . ."

From the airport in Teterboro, New Jersey, the ABP squad headed to the hospital to embrace Flame on his return to the land of the living. The hospital was a madhouse! Media from all over the world had camped out outside, hoping to get that coveted sound byte from an A-lister.

The convoy of Maybachs pulled up outside and cameras flashed. As Hulk ushered Qwess out of the car, Qwess pulled the collar of his mink up and pulled the matching mink hat down over his ears. Media thrust mics and smartphones in his general vicinity, but Hulk pushed them out of the way. Still they cackled and fired questions at him, trying to force an interview on him.

"Qwess, what does this loss mean to your ABP roster?"

"Do you plan to seek revenge on Diamond?"

"Did you have Diamond killed? Is that why we can't find him?"

"How do you plan to rebuild your roster now that Flame is gone?"

Qwess was able to ignore all of the questions except the last one. That one rubbed him the wrong way, and he had to respond.

Qwess pushed Hulk aside and gripped the reporter's hand. "Don't you ever disrespect my li'l homie like that ever again. There will be no rebuilding. ABP is here to stay, and Flame is going to bounce back better than ever."

Qwess's answer elicited more questions, but they fell on his back since he was already inside the building.

When 8-Ball led Qwess into the room, what he saw made him question his previous statement.

Flame was fucked up!

Bandages were wrapped around his head, still leaking

blood. The left side of his face was still swollen to the size of a baseball and his left eyeball protruded from its socket. A brace was around his neck, preventing him from moving his head so his one good eye rolled around like a pinball. He had lost at least fifteen pounds over the past few weeks, and his torso appeared emaciated beneath the gown. A sheet covered his lower torso, but it was evident that his legs couldn't move.

As tough as Qwess was, seeing Flame like this crushed him. He pushed past 8-Ball and went to the bedside.

"My nigga . . ." Qwess whispered.

Flame's good eye rolled and settled on Qwess. "D-don't . . . l-let them see me l-l-like this, OG," Flame stuttered. "P-please?"

Qwess sighed and turned around. "Clear the room. Everybody out. Now!"

When the room cleared, Flame and Qwess spoke. "I'm f-fucked up . . ." Flame stammered. His lip and jaw were so swollen that it was hard for him to speak. "They s-s-s-say . . . s-s-s-say . . ." Flame could enunciate what was on his tongue; he just couldn't fathom what had to be said.

Qwess patted Flame's hand. "What up, li'l brother? What they saying? Come on with it."

"They s-s-s-saying I won't ever walk again." As soon as the words passed his lips, he broke down.

Qwess shook his head and tried to calm him down. "Nah, fuck what they're saying, Joey! You gonna walk up out this bitch. Fuck what they talking."

Flame shook his head—as much as he could with his neck wrapped in the brace. "I c-can't even f-feel my dick, man. W-what the fuck am I-I going to d-do now?"

Again, Flame's body rocked with sobs.

A million thoughts ripped through Qwess's head, but his mind settled on the billions slipping through his palms. Here was his meal ticket paralyzed and broken—literally.

The executive in him inwardly chastised his artist for being so reckless. The OG and big homie in him wept for his little brother. All of the disrespect he showed toward him last year was now a small thing in his mind. Here he was fighting for his life, sanity, and his mobility. The petty beef now paled in comparison to reality.

Qwess patted Flame's hand. "We gonna get through this, li'l homie. You'll see."

Qwess was giving Flame encouragement, but he wasn't so sure about this one. He had lofty ambitions for Flame reinvigorating ABP 2.0, but now he wasn't so sure.

Qwess stood by Flame's bedside in silence for a full ten minutes, listening to him sob and break down. Inwardly his heart wept too, for different reasons. At every turn it seemed as if life was trying to break him, but he refused to be denied.

Qwess reflected back to what an old general told him years ago about making decisions in tough times. The general said that when you think you have done everything you can do to solve a problem, and you have implemented every solution possible and still failed . . . think again and come up with a plan, because there is a solution to every problem. This philosophy coincided with Surah 94, Ayat 5 of the Holy Qu'ran. Allah advises the believers that for every difficulty there is relief. In fact, the verse was repeated twice, which meant that was a guarantee. So Qwess knew there was a solution to his dilemma; he just had to think things through.

Qwess stood to allow 8-Ball back in the room. As 8-Ball walked past him, an idea hit Qwess heavier than an anvil. He had an answer all along! He had been sitting on it because he was harvesting all of his eggs in one basket. With his options limited, the other idea shined bright in his head like a star. He began to formulate a Plan B in his mind.

Qwess had a rusty unreleased catalog of music from an artist that had the potential to shake up the game. In the era of trap music where authenticity was king, Qwess had something that could reinvent the genre. He had teased the industry with a snippet on one of his albums in the past, and they ate it up. Maybe if he packaged it properly, with the right promo, it could do the trick. In fact, what better way to rewrite the rules of the game than with a new method of deploying a new type of artist? The stakes were high, but the reward was worth it.

Excited, Qwess walked out of the room to get more info on Flame's condition from the doctors. As soon as he left Flame's hallway, he saw them: a cavalry of federal agents coming right toward him full speed. Their jackets were blue and the letters emblazoned on the chest were bright yellow. Hulk saw them too, and he quickly jumped in front of Qwess to shield him, but Qwess waved him off.

"It's cool, big guy. Let them do their thing. Get Doe and Amin and tell them to get Shabazz ASAP. I was already prepared for this."

The agents beelined toward Qwess with their badges and guns showing. "Mr. Wahid, we have a warrant for your arrest."

Qwess raised his hands and extended them to the agents in surrender. "What for?" he asked. He was already anticipating the arrest from the warning the hip-hop cop gave him, but he wanted to know the exact charges they were trumping on him.

"Pick a charge, fuckhead!" one of the agents barked and pushed Qwess against the wall. He spun him around and put the cuffs on him. "Criminal conspiracy, drug trafficking, money laundering, murder . . . choose one, because they're all yours."

"Murder? I didn't murder no fucking body!" Qwess was so surprised by the mention of a murder charge that he didn't bother to deny the other charges.

"Sure you didn't. Let's go, rich guy."

The agent snatched Qwess from the wall and escorted him out of the building.

Outside, the reporters waiting received a real scoop when they saw Qwess being escorted out in handcuffs. They rushed him, demanding to know what was going on.

Just an hour prior, Qwess had walked in the hospital looking like the million-dollar mogul he was. Now, the music superstar had been reduced to doing the perp walk like a common criminal.

Only in America.

Chapter 20

Doe had been taking the backseat, playing the background. He never had the desire to dance in the spotlight. He was cool with the money; they could keep the fame. He had seen what fame did to Qwess and the ABP roster, and he wanted no part of it. Unable to go to the grocery store without being mobbed. Unable to even attend a movie in public. Unable to do the simple things like walk down a street on a romantic stroll. For all the freedom fame granted, it also came with an invisible cell as well. Not to mention, everyone hurling adoration at you like either confetti or debris. Women throwing themselves at you like softballs. Doe had had a small taste of the limelight and failed miserably when he engaged in a tryst with a video vixen named Dana. For the past few years, he had been mending his indiscretion with his wife, and every day was not a holiday. Doe was content to handle business and spend his days with his wife, Niya, their three-year-old daughter, Princess, and Reece's son, Prince.

But when the feds arrested Qwess, Doe had no choice but to assume the position of the de facto leader of ABP.

Doe quickly arranged for Malik Shabazz to be flown up to New York City from the Carolinas to spring Qwess from the clink. Then, with everything surrounding the label, he felt it was necessary to hold a press conference to project a strong image to the world. He knew the importance of controlling the narrative he wanted presented to the world. His message would be simple. ABP is bruised, not broken. Doe knew that the international community was looking on, and with all eyes on them, he had to set the record straight. He immediately called on his connections in the media and decided to host a press conference right outside the hospital.

A day after Qwess was arrested, bright and early, Doe addressed the media. He stood behind the podium in a burgundy pinstriped suit ready to speak to the world. Amin, to Doe's left, wore a tailored suit. On his right was Lisa Ivory. This was her first public appearance in over a year, so all eyes were on her, which was their strategy. Deflect and conquer.

Their publicist spoke first and iterated what the press conference would be about. Doe watched the crowd and rehearsed his speech. He wasn't one for public speaking so he had had the publicist prepare a basic speech for him at the last minute. He figured from there, he would just play it by ear. He didn't know how ruthless the media could be.

Doe took the mic and began reading from the prepared speech. He was quickly overshadowed by a phalanx of media peppering him with questions.

"Did Qwess get arrested for killing Diamond?"

"Is Flame ever going to rap again?"

"Did Qwess kill Sasha Beaufont?"

"Did Flame relapse back into a coma?"

The questions came at him fast and furiously, quick but soft. Then when someone realized exactly who Doe was, things got intense.

"Did you have a secret love child with video vixen Dana?"

"Are you trying to overthrow Qwess and take the company?"

"Are you and Qwess leaders of the Crescent Crew?"

"Did you put a hit on Flame so you could profit from his death?"

The questions ranged from close to outlandish. Each time Doe attempted to speak he was bombarded with more questions. An amateur on the mic, he was being exposed and embarrassed. It was going so badly that Qwess's wife, Lisa Ivory, nudged him aside and stepped before the microphone. In her vibrant, crystal clear voice she commandeered the press conference.

"Ladies and gentlemen, thank you for coming out to show your support for our family," Lisa began. As she spoke, it was quiet enough to hear a roach crack its toes. "As you all know, we have been taking some hits lately. As our artist, younger brother, and family is lying up there valiantly fighting for his life, this government has launched an attack against my husband, trying to persecute him just because he is a rich, successful African American man. This isn't the first time this has occurred, but just like the last time, we will emerge stronger than ever. Whenever you are the biggest independent record label in the music industry, certain . . . forces may take issue with that, and all of these people are connected. No one has ever done what we've done and no one will ever do it again. After us, there will be no more!"

The media, though they were supposed to be impartial, couldn't contain themselves. Lisa Ivory was once one of the biggest artists in the world. At one point, she was leading the women's liberation movement with her crisp soprano. She was the personification of "girl power," and legions of women followed her lead. Then, she unceremoniously disappeared from the spotlight, leaving her Ivories without a leader. In her absence, a generation of young women had learned about her through her interviews on YouTube. Some of these young women had grown up and entered the media corps. Some of these women were in the crowd and couldn't contain their excitement at seeing her speak in the flesh.

Lisa continued, "Now, we will continue with a few questions, but please be respectful."

This time, they offered more condolences than questions. They wanted Lisa to speak more—and she did.

In the end, their plan had worked too well. Instead of the press conference being Doe's coming out party, it was Lisa's reintroduction to the world that once adored here. For now, she had been able to keep the dragons at bay, but how long could she continue to slay the beast? How long before her husband came home to her?

While Lisa Ivory entertained the peanut gallery, Qwess was learning more about his predicament. The door clanged shut behind him in the attorney conference room on the third floor of the Metropolitan Correctional Center in New York. He saw Malik Shabazz siting at the table and immediately perked up.

"*As salaam alayka!*" Shabazz greeted, trying to lighten the mood.

Qwess massaged his naked wrists where the cuffs had just been cutting into his skin before they removed them. "*Wa alayka salaam*," he returned with a frown. "What's going on?"

Shabazz motioned for Qwess to take a seat. "Sit down."

Qwess leaned against the wall and crossed his arms. "Nah, I've been sitting all night, laying actually, so I prefer to stand. Now what the hell is going on with all these crazy charges?"

Malik Shabazz clasped his hands together and steepled them on the table. "You ever heard of a guy named Tony Hall?"

"Tony Hall?" Qwess chortled. "Man, I know so many people."

"They called him Scar."

Qwess froze.

"Yeah, they *called* him Scar because he's dead, and apparently you ordered the hit," Shabazz said.

Qwess waved at the air. "I didn't order no hit on no damn Scar!"

"That's what they're saying, son. Scar and Dee, two gentlemen who ordered the hit on your fiancée, Shauntay."

Qwess remembered the two old heads who had sent a hit at Reece years ago when he had just signed his record deal. The shooters they sent at Reece mistakenly killed Shauntay in a botched hit because Shauntay was driving Reece's Porsche. Qwess was told that Reece had tortured them both in retaliation, but he was on tour when it occurred.

"Look, I don't know anything about that, but if they are dead, then I'm glad."

"Well, someone is saying different."

"Obviously."

Both men fell silent, contemplating this new info.

"Qwess, the feds wouldn't arrest you unless they had probable cause. For them to bring these type of charges on you, they have to have some serious evidence. They know I represent you and I take pride in gutting them . . . for them to come at you like this . . . someone very close to you is talking about you, son."

Qwess figured that much. He just didn't know who could be dropping these bombs or how recently these statements against him had been made. Hip-hop cop had already warned him that a defector from his camp had been murdered in Bone's attack. Qwess needed to know what was said.

"So, where are they getting the info from?" Qwess asked.

"We won't know until they serve discovery on us. I had to call in some favors to get the info I just told you, but my guess is they're about to put clamps on this case."

"Really? How you figure?"

Malik Shabazz dropped his head and raised his hound dog

eyes. "Well, because they're not giving you a bond hearing until they get you extradited back to North Carolina."

"Extradited? What the fuck?"

"Yeah, they want you to face trial back in N.C."

Qwess was livid. He waved his hands erratically. "Man, I got to get out of here! My biggest artist is laid up in the hospital paralyzed, I got the deal of a lifetime on the table, and I'm already being sued for seventy million dollars!"

Shabazz frowned. "Yeah, and about that, we need to hurry and get these interrogatories returned because if we don't get them back in time, they can file for a summary judgment."

"Well, get me out of here then!"

"Calm down," Shabazz advised. "Now, we can waive extradition and trigger a thirty-day time limit for them to have you back in North Carolina—"

"Thirty days?! Are you fucking serious?"

"Brother, calm down. That may not be a bad thing to have to wait. The longer they take to get you down, the more information we will have to fight with at your bond hearing."

Qwess wasn't trying to hear any of that. He needed to be freed as soon as possible. He was thinking about securing the deal; he never thought for a second about the charges sticking.

He would soon learn just how serious of a predicament he was in.

Bone sat in his Porsche 911 in the Creekwood housing section in Wilmington, North Carolina. Maleek was riding shotgun with a Heckler & Koch MP5K sitting in his lap. Behind the deep tint, they surveyed the block as people scrambled about conducting their daily activities. As people ran to and fro they openly gawked at the shiny, emerald green machine that had captivated their block.

Bone had been parked there for the better part of an hour, and word had already spread that he was in town. Well, *every-*

one didn't know it was him, but they knew that a big-timer was in their neighborhood lounging in a $150,000 sports car.

Bone had driven the hour and a half journey down Highway 87 to surprise his newest lieutenant and see how he was working out in his new position. Thus far, his lieutenant was a no-show.

"Yo, look at these niggas," Maleek said. "'Bout to break they damn neck trying to see who in this pretty motherfucker."

Bone snickered, "Hell yeah, look at 'em."

"Should hop out this pretty motherfucker like, hello!"

Bone chuckled as his skeletal looking head swiveled from side to side taking things in. He didn't miss a beat either. He saw the old head disappear, only to return in the back of a rimmed-up Dodge Charger pointing them out. He saw the old lady yapping on the phone, only to have her son or *whoever* walk up on the porch from the alleyway a few minutes later. He saw the thick-ass hoodrat walk inside the house with a housecoat draped over her shoulder and emerge a few minutes later wearing yellow yoga pants and a tank top with no bra, even though it was forty degrees outside. Even from thirty yards away Bone could see her pussy print bulging from between her thick thighs.

"Gotdamn! Look at that thick motherfucker right there!" Maleek's mouth fell open as he pointed at the thick ghetto diamond in the yellow yoga pants. "You see that?"

Oh, he saw them all right, just like he knew they saw him. That was all part of his plan.

Bone had been doing pop-ups all over the Southeast in the cities where he had installed a new administration. The pop-ups served multiple purposes. For one, he wanted his lieutenants to feel that he was accessible, that he was still a man of the people. Secondly, he wanted them to know that they were accessible too, that he was not too big to come down and pay them a visit, for better or worse. Third, he wanted to remind them of their "why." Why were they putting their life and freedom on the line? So they could ball like him one day. When Bone popped up, he was always riding in something fly, something well above the usual hood fare. Most of the time he never even stepped foot out of the vehicles. He just parlayed on the block making his presence felt.

"Yeah, that li'l mu'fucka thick," Bone admitted. "She look young too. Bet that li'l pussy still got that fire to it."

"Hellllll yeah!" Maleek agreed with excitement. He couldn't take his eyes off her. "You want me to holla at her for you, Big Homie?"

Even though Maleek was imagining fucking sparks from her, he knew rank had its privileges. If his big homie wanted her, he would have to stand down.

"Nah, I ain't fucking with no bitches out here. Them hoes be the one to get your cap twisted back," Bone warned. "But the right bitch can keep you in the game too, though."

Bone thought about the benefit of having a chick dug in inside the city. She would know everything and could feed Maleek all the info without their man on the ground knowing it.

"Aye, go holla at her, though," Bone instructed Maleek.

"Sure?"

"Hell yeah. Nigga, that hood pussy be the best! You better go bag that," Bone prodded, thinking about a master plan.

Maleek smiled at his mentor. That's what he loved about him. He was paid out the ass but still humble enough to encourage him to fuck with a hood bitch.

Maleek looped the strap of the MP5 around his neck and tucked the weapon under his armpit beneath his three-quarter-length suede coat with the fur collar. He peered around the area and closed the coat over the weapon then ruffled his unkempt afro. He stepped out of the Porsche and stood to his full six-foot-three height. His Timberland boot hit the pavement just as the young hottie was walking past the car.

Maleek reached out and tugged the lady's arm. "Whoa, whoa, where you going?"

The young woman looked at Maleek's hand on her arm. "Excuse you?"

Maleek flashed the million-dollar smile on her. "Yeah, excuse me indeed, but I was wondering where you're going?"

"Where am I going?"

"Yeah, you're too cute to be out here walking by yourself. I thought I might offer you some protection."

The young tender recoiled her neck and scoffed at Maleek. "Protection? From who, you?"

"Nah, from these lames out here. I came to let you get swooped up by a boss-ass nigga before these lame niggas bleed all that bullshit on you."

The lady laughed and covered her mouth. "That's a good one."

"Yeah, it's even better because it's true."

"Hmm mmm, I bet." She looked at the Porsche. "That your car?"

"Yeah, that's *one* of 'em. That's my Saturday car."

"Oh, yeah, what kind of car is that?"

Maleek smiled inside. She was really green. "Oh, that? That's just a Porsche 911."

"That's nice."

"Thank you. What's your name anyway?"

"Keisha."

"Okay, Keisha, I'm Maleek."

Maleek and Keisha kicked it for a few minutes, throwing compliments at each other. They were totally engaged when, suddenly, a Black Mercedes S550 rolled around the corner with music blaring out of the cracked window.

Maleek lightly pushed Keisha aside, threw his back against

the Porsche, and tucked his hand in his pocket where he could grip the trigger on the MP-5 through the hole in the coat. The Mercedes pulled closer to the Porsche, and Maleek eased around to the driver's door, creating a shield between Bone and the Benz. The scowl on his face let anybody know he was ready for action.

The Benz door eased open, and Twin hopped out laughing with his hands raised. "Calm down, killa. I come in peace."

Maleek didn't crack a smile. He continued to mean mug Twin as he walked up to him and offered him a pound. Rather than pound him up, Maleek gave him a nod.

Bone eased the window down and tapped Maleek on the back of his leg. "Let him by."

Maleek stepped aside and allowed Twin access to Bone's open window, but he kept his eye on everything around them.

"*As salaam alayka*, brother," Twin greeted. "You coming down here causing a scene in my city."

"Correction—this is *our* city," Bone reminded him.

"No doubt. You showing out, though," Twin said, pointing to the Porsche.

"Yeah, you know how I do. What's good with you, though? Everything good?"

"No doubt."

"You got that situation for me?" Bone asked.

Twin reached in his pocket and instead of pulling out a wad of money, he extracted a burner phone. He passed the phone to Bone.

"Cool," Bone said. "Sit tight for a minute."

Bone put the window up on the Porsche and watched Twin walk back to his Benz. A few seconds later the phone came to life inside his hand.

"*As salaam alayka*, Big Homie!" Bone nearly screamed his excitement into the phone. "Long time no hear from."

"*Wa salaam*, little brother. Long time indeed."

It was Samson. He was calling from a cell phone inside prison.

Bone's main reason for coming down to Wilmington was to retrieve this call. Twin was more than the li'l homie. His sister had a child from Samson, and she and Samson spoke often, but nothing serious over the jailhouse line. Turned out, Samson had been on lockup all this time as a security threat to the institution. Even though they were unable to link him to the Crescent Crew, Samson was a formidable man in his own right. For starters, he was a giant, standing at over six and a half feet and weighing over 300 pounds. As if that wasn't enough, his ties to Mexico made him a man of stature inside. He was fluent in Spanish, and during his exile in Mexico he had put in a lot of work in just a short time. People in the old country could never forget Monstruoso (as he was called in Mexico). He had taken savagery to a new level in a savage country, and his reputation spoke volumes. Inside, on every yard he was transferred to, the Latino inmates quickly bowed down to him, even though he was laying low. Administration quickly got wind of his power, and quickly STG'd him. Since then, he had been doing most of his bid in Supermax, impeding his movements until recently. He had finally managed to bribe a guard to score him a jack. The first thing he did was arrange a call to Bone to address his concerns with what he'd been hearing.

"Man, what's good with you?"

"Shit, another day closer to the world, you know?"

"Fuck, yeah! It's a hell of a world out here waiting for you to claim. I'm holding shit down for you."

"Yeah, well, that's not the word I'm getting," Samson said snidely.

Bone was confused. "Huh?"

"Yeah, I'm hearing shit is fucked up out there. How you let over a dozen brothers get murdered? How you start a war with my family? And what's up with Qwess?"

"Big Homie, I had to avenge the King. I had—"

"I told you he was off limits!"

"Big Homie, even Qwess said he was food."

"Qwess? Qwess? You let a rapping nigga force you to make a move on the streets? A nigga that ain't call no shots in years? Are you serious right now?"

"Big Homie, w-with King Reece gone and you MIA, I didn't know not to listen to him. I was always taught to pay homage to the founders."

"Yeah, and now that nigga 'bout to reward you for your homage."

Again, Bone was confused. "What you mean, Big Homie?"

"You know what they got him charged with up there in New York?"

Bone shook his head even though Samson couldn't see it. "Nah."

"That nigga facing an *elbow* at least, probably the needle."

"Huh? Qwess?"

"Yes, nigga!"

"I thought they hit him with the AMG assault shit, the same thing he being sued for?"

Samson sucked his teeth so loud the phone crackled. "You keep thinking shit, your ass gonna be right there with him."

"Wait, so you saying Qwess snitching?"

"Nah, I'm not saying that at all. Far as I know he solid—for now. But I know a nigga not gonna give a million-dollar lifestyle up for no bullshit. He gonna do everything he can to protect himself. You see me up in this motherfucker, don't you?"

Bone replayed his recent interactions with Qwess. It could be conceived that Qwess was already in survival mode, cutting all ties to his past, ordering the murder of more than a dozen of his brethren—supposedly because they were sour. Who knew if that was even true? Bone had never seen any proof other than Qwess's word.

"I hear you, Big Homie."

"Nah, you better feel me and keep an eye on that nigga. The King left this family to me, and I got big plans for us when I touch down. All I want you to do is hold this car in the road until I can drive it again."

Bone nodded obediently. "Okay, Big Homie."

"Oh, yeah, and that other thing with my people . . . end that shit immediately."

"Big Homie, they murdered over a dozen—"

"It wasn't them!" Samson yelled. Then his voice lowered to just above a whisper. "You know my reach is long. I talked to everybody who is somebody, and they assured me it wasn't them."

Bone swallowed the lump in his throat. What did Samson know?

"How you know they telling the truth? How can you trust them?"

Samson chuckled. "Trust me, they know not to fuck with me. They don't call me Monstruoso for nothing."

"So, if it wasn't them, then who was it?" Bone asked, attempting to get Samson to lead him to what he knew.

"I don't know yet, but I'm going to find out. And when I do, I will let you know so you can introduce them to Crew business."

Bone closed his eyes. The image of him firing the missile into the cabin appeared on his mind's eye as vividly as it was when he was there. In his head, he heard the *whoosh* of the missile as it careened from the tube.

"Yeah, Big Homie, it doesn't make sense. They're the

only ones we were beefing with," Bone said, steering the heat as far away from him as possible.

"Yeah, well, new crews spring up every day and want to be the man. Who knows?"

"Yeah, that's true."

"But if you ask me, it sounds like an inside job. Otherwise, how would they know that all of them were going to be in the same place at the same time?"

Again, Bone damn near swallowed his Adam's apple. "I don't know, Big Homie, but now that you brought it to my attention, I'm going to get to the bottom of it."

"Yeah, between me and you, we'll figure it out. In the meantime, cease fire, my nigga. Cease fire." Samson chuckled. An empty silence sank between them for a second. Then, Samson spoke, "I'm proud of you for bringing the heat to them niggas, though. They need to know the Crescent Crew still a force out there in them streets. They need to know that we didn't get fat and get soft. They need to hear us, and you did that, brother. You put the fear of the God in them muthafuckas. They came crying to me, *'Por favor, por favor, no más! No queremos más!'*" Samson chuckled again. "Muthafuckas was shook—as they should be. But now it's time to get back to the money. So, do whatever you have to do. I'm going to send someone to you from the other side and make it official soon. Just wait for word from me."

Samson ended the call, leaving Bone utterly befuddled. He didn't know who he could trust at this point. Qwess? Samson? His own crew?

Then he was confused as to what Samson knew about the murders at the cabin. What exactly did Samson know? Where was he receiving his info? Did he know Bone was responsible and that Qwess put the battery in his back? Were Qwess and Samson playing him? Testing him? Was he doing too good a job as leader, and Samson felt threatened? Bone didn't know what to think!

Bone gathered himself and morphed back into boss mode before he summoned Twin with a beep of the horn. Twin heaved his hefty frame from the Benz and walked over to the Porsche. Again, Maleek let him pass, and Twin stooped down by the window of the Porsche.

"I appreciate that, brother," Bone said, passing Twin the phone back. "You doing a good job out here. Money flowing like the Nile. Keep up the good work. You making me proud."

"Oh, yeah, I told you I'ma paint this whole city cream and green," Twin promised. "I'm trying to be riding in one of those by the summer."

Bone smiled. The Porsche did the trick. "Aye, man, you stay down and stay loyal, you'll have a fleet of these shits. You should see my Sunday car."

Twin erupted in laughter. "I already know how you do."

Twin stood to leave, and Bone gave Maleek the nod that he was ready to roll.

Before Maleek got in the car, he passed Keisha his phone. She had been standing near the car the whole time observing how he moved. It was clear that she was enthralled with him. She was digging his style, and she definitely wanted in on whatever he had going on. With a smirk, she programmed her number in his phone and gave it back to him.

"I'm going to text you," Keisha said, and walked back up the street.

Maleek watched the yoga pants cut into her soft, jiggly cheeks as she walked away. Her hips were wide like a cobra's head, but she had a gap that allowed him to see clean through her legs. Her waist was smaller than her head, and a long brown weave cascaded down her back.

"Yeah, I'll be fucking her next time we come down," Maleek predicted, as he watched her slide into the house.

★　★　★

The ride back to Fayetteville was a quiet one. Bone was lost in his thoughts, digesting what his big homie had put on his plate. He knew that everything that happened in the dark eventually came to the light. If Samson said he was going to find out what happened at the cabin, then Bone knew he would. He had already proven he still held considerable power. If he fished with enough influence, then Bone knew he would catch the right word. The right word was him, and there were only two people in the world who knew the truth. One of them was riding shotgun, and the other was his other big homie, Qwess.

Samson's call left Bone with more questions than answers. Like, why did Qwess conceal the fact that he'd issued the order to purge their line if he knew the line was spoiled? And what murders were Qwess being charged with? Was it the cabin murders? If so, and if push came to shove, would Qwess hold firm, or would he turn on Bone? Would he sacrifice the Crescent Crew for the music business?

Bone had enough bodies under his belt to be classified as a serial killer. If Qwess turned on him they would bury him beneath the jail in an electric chair with a needle in his arm.

Yeah, Bone's mind was racing at a million miles a minute.

Too many times to count, he looked over at Maleek as he scrolled through social media, and he thought about cutting that loose end, but Maleek was proving to have too much potential. He was always on point and Bone never had to tell him what to do. His type of raw skill and heartlessness couldn't be taught. Even though he wasn't even twenty-one years old yet, he was a throwback hustler. He wasn't trained to go; he was born to go. It would be a shame to clip such a promising future, but the game was the game, and if he had to, Bone would swing for the fences to protect himself.

Suddenly Maleek smacked the leather dashboard and cackled. "Ohhhh, shit! Look at this!" he said, showing Bone the phone. "This the Sasha Beaufont bitch getting dicked down again, yo! Look!"

Bone looked at the phone, and sure enough, there was another video of Sasha getting drilled. This time, it wasn't by Flame, though. This man's skin was too dark to be Flame, and the video was nearly professional quality, unlike the amateur video that nearly got Flame killed.

On the video, the only thing that could be seen is a man's wide back and ashy ass as he pumped what appeared to be a baby leg into Sasha from the back. The cameraman stood over the man's right shoulder and positioned the camera to record his huge penis entering her vagina again and again. The man pulled out and spit on his penis, lubricating it with his saliva. Then, he opened up her soft, red cheeks that made her famous, and laid his erection at the tip of her back door. Slowly, he pushed himself into her back door. Sasha screamed so loud it distorted the small speakers on the phone.

"Yo, that's enough," Bone barked. "I don't want to see that shit."

"Bruh, look at this shit, though!" Maleek scrolled down on his phone, and there were at least three more videos of Sasha getting piped down by different men, each video more humiliating than the last.

Bone shook his head at the wicked display of power by Diamond. It was clear that Sasha wasn't under her own volition in the videos. It appeared that she was drugged, from the way her head rolled around aimlessly. Her movements were lifeless, like she was there in body only. Still, this was Sasha Beaufont, a woman that men had been lusting after all over the world for years. It didn't matter to these dudes that she was getting slutted out like a #ghettogangbang. As long as they were seeing her naked body on display, they were okay with the terms. Diamond knew this. Bone figured Diamond had to humiliate her and destroy her brand for what she had done to him. That was a real street nigga move. Instead of killing her physically for violating him, he opted to kill her and leave her alive to smell the stench of herself. By recording these videos and posting them, Diamond was effectively showing the world that Sasha now belonged to the street. He had used the very tool she used to end them to end her.

The only question was, where was Diamond?

Chapter 21

Flame drifted in and out of consciousness. His days and nights merged seamlessly together. The painkillers they were pumping into his blood had him hallucinating, but they also eased the pain. When he was awake, Flame just stared at the walls and tried to move his legs, but each time his legs refused to comply with what his brain told them to do.

Each time Flame awoke, he saw 8-Ball at his bedside.

His friend hadn't left Flame for one day. He had camped out in the hospital as if he was on a field detail in the military, watching his friend, praying for him and praying with him. Flame's condition had improved slightly, so they moved him to a bigger room where he could receive visitors. Still, Flame was reluctant to see anyone, so 8-Ball acted as a buffer, screening everyone who wanted to come in. Flame's room was like a hotel suite so at night, 8-Ball stretched his large frame over the pullout couch and slept. During the day, he did hundreds of pushups. After his friend's vicious beating, 8-Ball vowed to get in shape and take his job more seriously. A part of him felt that if he had accompanied his friend outside, the results would have been different.

Each day Flame's injuries healed a little more. Well, his physical injuries anyway. The goal was to pull Flame out of the woods far enough so he could be transferred to his home in Atlanta to begin his long road to recovery. There was a full medical team on standby waiting to nurse him back to health.

Flame awoke and rose up in the bed. He looked around the room at all the flower arrangements from various people in the music industry. It seemed that his life hadn't existed before the music industry. There were no heartfelt mementos or gushing soliloquies from people that truly loved him, nothing from family or close friends. Just empty well wishes and cardboard condolences. It had taken tragedy for Flame to realize he had sacrificed his family ties for stardom, and now he regretted it.

"Aye, hand me my phone, man," Flame wheezed to 8-Ball.

This was rare. This was the first time he had asked 8-Ball for his phone. In the nearly seven weeks he had been in the hospital, Flame had not had access to the outside world. It was as if he had been hibernating in a cave. He didn't know what the people were saying about him. He didn't know about the raw footage someone from Diamond's camp had posted online that showed him being power bombed into the pavement. He didn't even know Qwess was locked up, facing a litany of charges.

He hadn't even seen his own face.

"Uhh . . . I don't think that's a good idea, homie," 8-Ball replied.

"What? You don't think I know my face is fucked up? Man, I know that shit! I can feel these fucking bubbles on my cheek. They itching me like a pile of ants biting me. I feel all that shit, nigga . . . I just can't feel my legs." Flame sniffed away the tears. "Just give me my shit, man."

"Yo, Flame—"

"Don't call me that shit no more either! Flame is dead! Okay? He's dead. My name is Joey, all right? Fuck Flame, man!" Flame's body convulsed as if he was about to break down, but he held it in. "Fuck Flame," he hissed.

8-Ball shook his head. "Nah, man, don't say that. Times is just a li'l rough right now, but we'll get through this shit, homie. You'll be killing crowds again soon."

"How, man? I'm a fucking invalid, yo! Mu'fuckas ain't checking for no cripple."

"Yo, this shit just temporary, man. You muthafuckin' Flame—everybody love you."

"No, they love Flame, the nigga that could rock a crowd and back up all the shit he talked. The pretty boy nigga that the bitches love. They don't love me. My name is Joey. Muthafuckas ain't checking for a nigga named Joey, a fucking invalid. Doctors say I'll never walk again."

"Man, fuck them doctors! We believe in God, Joey. With God, all things are possible." 8-Ball had been praying so much while Flame was in the hospital that his knees ached, but the fact that Flame was up and talking made him feel as if his prayers were being answered.

"Man, I ain't with all that church shit, man. I was a god before this shit, a Superman. Now pass me my phone and let me see what I look like as Clark Kent."

8-Ball was believing in God lately, but he knew it would take an act of God to keep Flame together after he saw his face.

Flame waved his hand at 8-Ball. "Come on, man, give me my shit. I might as well see what I look like. I'm ready to get back to the world. Let me see what's been going on while I've been hanging out on this side."

8-Ball dropped his head and shook it. He refused Flame's request for the phone repeatedly, but Flame flipped on him.

"Man, give me my shit, nigga!" Flame roared.

He barked on 8-Ball so loud it pissed him off. 8-Ball walked over to the bed, tossed the iPhone on his chest, and walked to the door.

"Don't say I didn't warn you," 8-Ball said, still shaking his head.

Flame put the code in, and his phone screen lit up. Flame felt like a junkie getting his first fix in months. His phone was more than just a mobile device. It was a gateway to the world, a world where he once reigned atop the entertainment industry.

Flame scanned his apps and quickly located the blue Twitter app icon with the white bird in the middle. Right beside it was the Instagram icon. Below it was the camera app icon.

Flame's finger shook as it hovered over the Twitter icon. One press and he could leave the hospital and see what the world was doing while he was away. If he dropped his finger he could see what the world was saying about him. But he knew the Twittersphere could be vicious, so he chickened out.

He held his finger over the Instagram icon. Instagram was more gentle. People came on the 'Gram to stunt more than take jabs at strangers. And he couldn't forget about the women on Instagram. They were ready, willing, and able to give him some cooperation. It definitely went down in the DM on IG. Flame felt that checking up on some of his women on IG was just what the doctor ordered. He pressed on the IG icon and the phone flashed vibrant in his hands. He was anxious to see what he had been missing, but just when he thought he was in, his Instagram account was requesting he log back in with his email and password.

Flame tried to remember his email and password, but every time he tried to recall it, a black spot appeared in his brain.

"Shit!" Flame hissed.

8-Ball stood by the door with his arms folded across his chest. "What's wrong?"

"I can't remember my email and password for IG."

8-Ball shrugged. "Maybe that is a sign that you shouldn't be on it."

Flame cut his eyes at 8-Ball, but he didn't say a word. While he was still looking at 8-Ball, he pressed the Twitter app icon. At least that's what he thought he pressed. In actuality, he had pressed the camera app icon, and it was on selfie mode.

For the first time in nearly two months, Flame saw the damage that had been done to his face. A long, stitched cut ran down his left jaw, extending from the bottom of his earlobe to the top of his mouth. On his right jaw right beside his mouth was a two-inch horizontal scar that virtually bisected his cheek. His left eye had been placed back into its socket, but it was still swollen, red, and crooked. Scratches were on his forehead, healed, but there nonetheless.

Flame stared at his face in shock. He couldn't believe he was looking at a reflection of himself in the digital mirror. No way was that . . . *creature* him. No way! He slowly lifted his hand and touched his face. When he saw his finger enter the frame on the photo, there was no denying it. The monstrosity on the screen was him.

Flame dropped the phone and screamed.

Qwess sat across the table from his wife and Malik Shabazz. He was in the attorney wing again, so everything said was in confidence. Still, Qwess never trusted the system, so he only said what was needed.

While Shabazz was desperately fighting to get Qwess extradited back to North Carolina most expeditiously, his civil suit wasn't going anywhere.

After Qwess had replied to the interrogatories and admissions admitting that he knew Samson, but not Chabo and Gil, and that he had once been a member of the Crescent Crew, AMG's attorneys filed for a motion for summary judgment against Qwess on the grounds that his being acquainted with one of the known extortionists was enough proof to infer that he had orchestrated the plot and instigated a tortuous interference with AMG's business. Their attorneys had drawn up a beautiful summation, complete with case law supporting their claims. Now Shabazz was here to discuss the worst-case scenarios.

"I don't understand why you had me admit that I was once a member of the Crescent Crew," Qwess said.

"Because it's public record, son. You yourself have admitted it too many times to count in all those publications. It was also mentioned in Reece's court proceedings. I mean, at this point, it's public knowledge. If you had lied about that, that would've automatically impeached your credibility. Once that happens, you are doomed for sure."

Qwess exhaled a stream of stress. "Shit, looks like I'm doomed now."

"No we're not, my king. We just have to figure a way out of this," Lisa assured him, as she rubbed his hand.

"I mean, so what's our defense, Brother Shabazz?" Qwess asked.

"Well, before we get to that, we need to discuss a few things first."

Here it goes, Qwess thought.

"Like what?"

"Well, I hate to have to have this discussion while you're in here but . . . well, the initial retainer fee has run out. You paid me half a million to represent you in the civil suit. And because I know you're good for it, I went ahead and began taking care of things in the new case. However, in order to proceed, we have to square up the first case, then come up with an equitable number for the new case."

"Okay, what are we talking?" Qwess asked.

"Let's see . . ." Shabazz flipped open his file and dragged his finger down an itemized list. "So far . . . I'm owed an extra hundred and fifty thousand dollars on top of the retainer. And if this goes all the way to trial, then I'll just even the balance out at four hundred thousand dollars."

"So that's just under a mil?" Qwess scoffed.

"Brother, these things get expensive. I have my staff to pay, my investigators, my law clerks, the palms I have to grease to gain favor, et cetera et cetera. You've done good for yourself, you're a very popular man, and these people want to take a chunk out your ass. Defending that chunk costs money."

"Damn, I know it takes money, but it seems like these 'people' not the only ones trying to take a chunk out my ass, ya know?"

Malik Shabazz caught the shot, but he didn't respond. He was the best attorney in the country, and if you wanted the best, you had to pay for it.

Malik Shabazz shrugged as if his hands were tied. "Now, since you're retaining me for the civil case, I can cut you some slack on the criminal charges—it won't be that much, but it'll be the best I can do."

"Okay, what we talking?"

"Brother, these are some very serious charges here."

"How much?"

"These type of cases can get tricky; you never know how they turn out."

"Brother! How much?"

Shabazz looked toward the ceiling as if the number could magically appear in the dirty tiles. "Let's start at a half for now, and we'll go from there."

Qwess sighed. "Okay, so right now, we owe you what? Six fifty?"

Malik Shabazz nodded. "Yep."

Qwess mentally tallied up his growing expenses. Again,

Sonic the Hedgehog came to mind. He saw the coins being knocked out of him, but he couldn't let them see him sweat.

Qwess turned to his wife. "Make sure he gets that."

"Sure, my king."

Qwess clapped his hands together. "Okay, now what's next?"

Shabazz opened up another folder and broke the really bad news to Qwess.

Qwess was officially being charged for the murders of Scar and Dee. He was also being charged with criminal conspiracy for the attempted murder of John Meyers. They also hit him with a CCE charge, alleging that he was operating a continuing criminal enterprise named the Crescent Crew. The money laundering charge was just the icing on a big cake. Because Qwess was alleged to be a founder of the Crescent Crew, his charge was enhanced to that of a "super kingpin." This enhancement made him eligible for the death penalty if convicted.

What Qwess thought was just a ruse to make him cough up some funds for stealing away AMG's artist was actually the result of a long-term investigation. Turned out, they had never stopped investigating him through the years, and when an opportunity arose, they took it.

Qwess washed his hands over his face, "Bro, you cannot be serious."

Malik Shabazz frowned. "I wish this was a joke, brother, but unfortunately it's not."

"So you saying he's facing the death penalty?!" Lisa shrieked.

Shabazz nodded solemnly. "Yes, he is."

"Oh, my God! Why? What he do? He's no murderer! My husband is a good man!" Tears gathered in the corners of Lisa's eyes. "Why are they doing this?"

Qwess patted Lisa's hand. "Calm down, baby. They're just fishing. I'm not worried, and you shouldn't be either."

Qwess said those words to calm his wife, but he was actually worried as hell. He had expected them to come but not like this. And why now? He asked Shabazz that very thing.

"Well, they never had anyone willing to corroborate anything until now."

"Still?" Qwess asked.

Qwess thought about the orders he had issued to Bone. Bone had carried out the instructions and supposedly everyone in that cabin was deceased. Did someone live to tell the tale and now they were ready to tell the tale themselves? Or could it be Bone? Bone was the only person alive that could verify he was a founding member of the Crescent Crew. Would Bone turn on him?

"So, did anything change in the last month?" Qwess asked. "Did someone else come forward?"

Shabazz shrugged. "I don't know, son. I won't know until this thing unfolds a bit more. We'll get to the bottom of it, though."

Lisa lost it again. "My king, this can't be happening. You can't get the death penalty! Whatever you have to do, Salim. *Whatever!*"

On cue, the door opened, and in walked Agent Roberts. He rubbed his long beard and smiled. "My brother, Qwess, I heard that you may be ready to reconsider what we discussed before."

Agent Roberts invited himself to the table. He pulled up a chair and spun it around so the back of the chair was touching the table. "So, let's talk."

Chapter 22

Flame overcame the initial shock of his altered face, but the devastation never removed itself from his spirit. He felt as if life as he knew it was over, and if it wasn't for 8-Ball being by his side, he probably would've tried to end it himself. Then again, how could he? He was virtually helpless.

A couple weeks had passed since Flame saw his new face, and his condition had improved slightly. Gone were the neck and back brace, and he was healing enough for him to move around out of bed. 8-Ball decided to push him around the hospital in a wheelchair to give him an opportunity to get some fresh air.

8-Ball rolled the wheelchair close to the bed and carefully helped Flame get settled. He draped a blanket over his legs to keep his mind off the fact that they couldn't move and rolled him out into the hallway.

"Let's go, Joey. Let's go see the world," 8-Ball joked as he spun the wheelchair around like a racecar.

"Chill, man," Flame objected.

8-Ball ignored his pleas and zoomed down the wide corridors. He passed a nurse's station and chunked the deuces up to the staff.

"Hey, is there somewhere we can go outside?" 8-Ball asked a nurse.

"Actually, there is an observation deck right there." She pointed toward the end of the hall. "Just push the button on the wall and it'll open for you."

8-Ball pushed Flame to the door and paused. "You ready to see the world?"

Flame nodded.

8-Ball pushed the button, and the doors opened. He pushed Flame out on the terrace and let him soak in the midday rays.

This was the first time Flame had seen the sun in two months, and the rays felt soothing on his skin. He could see the city all around him, and it felt as if he was looking down on the world. Below them, car horns honked, sirens blared, and tires squealed as the world turned around them. Smells of gyros, Chinese food, and hot dogs wafted up to greet them. It was chilly out, but after being cooped up in the room for months, even the cool air was soothing on his skin. Flame inhaled the cool air and stared at the sun. Looking right into the bright orange orb gave him a sense of peace.

Flame thought about his vision when he was fighting for his life. Inside his vision, it felt like he was omnipotent. He recalled how whatever he thought about materialized. He squeezed his eyes together tighter and visualized himself lifting his legs high in the air. When he opened them, his legs were still stuck to the chair. Flame frowned and whimpered.

"What's wrong, bro?" 8-Ball asked.

"Nothing, man, nothing," Flame said softly. "I'm ready to go back inside now."

8-Ball rolled Flame back inside. He cruised down the long

corridor, entered the VIP hall, and pushed Flame down to his room. As soon as he turned the corner, he saw that Flame had a visitor.

Bone was weighed down with the pressure of being a boss. He had never played the game on this level before. He was barely five years removed from prison, where he had caught a bid for petty peddling compared to the level he currently occupied. Before prison, Bone belonged to a small crew of maybe ten hustlers at best, and he wasn't even the head of that outfit. Now, as acting boss of the Crescent Crew, he held sway (by proxy) over at least ten states, and with the weight they were moving at such low prices, they were expanding territories by the day. But as the old saying goes, mo' money, mo' problems, and Bone was living in the cliché.

Ironically, money was not a problem for Bone at all. The last time he had counted his personal wealth, he was up over $10 million. His biggest money problem was—like so many other kingpins before him—finding somewhere to stash the cash. He had already invested in a few businesses. He owned a few car dealerships in town, a few barbershops, a restaurant, and he had funded a few weave businesses for a few different females. His latest venture was a luxury concierge service that was still in the beginning stages but looked to be promising. Still, no matter how many businesses he dumped money into, the cash from the cocaine and heroin came in quicker.

Bone had long graduated from stashing money at females' homes. In fact, he rarely dealt with females after he blew up. For one, King Reece's debacle with Destiny had him gun-shy about trusting any woman. Two, he hadn't found a woman that could relate to the level he was on, so they wouldn't have much in common. Such were the woes of waking up knowing he was the richest nigga in his city.

The main problem Bone was facing with being at the top of the food chain was the paranoia that came with being "the man." His survival depended upon him winning every day. He had to outwit the authorities, the jack boys, the women, the fiends, and enemies he didn't even know existed. Unfortunately, these were usually members of his own crew. Bone was well versed in the infamous crime legends that came before him and how they met their demise. It was John who had orchestrated the hit on Big Paul. Alpo had set up Rich. Butch sanctioned the execution of Wonderful Wayne. Bone had read about them all during his bid. Never in a million years had he dreamed he would be the man with a target on his back. But it appeared that the trap god was in the blessing business. Or was he?

Since the phone call with his big homie, Samson, Bone's nerves had been frayed. He kept thinking about Qwess being in jail and wondering if he'd turned on him already. Bone couldn't even sleep at night, wondering if the feds were going to kick in his door. He alternated between his five homes in the city each night and still didn't feel secure. He eventually began making the forty-five-minute drive to Raleigh each night and hotel hopping. Each night he fell asleep, he saw visions of the multiple murders he had committed throughout his life of crime. Paranoia will do that; unearth demons that were long buried, and even Bone—the leader of the dangerously ambitious Crescent Crew—wasn't exempt.

Bone was spiraling out of control and knew he had to pull it all together, and there was only one way to do it. He had to go see the trap god.

"Hi, Flame."

Flame thought the drugs had him hallucinating, for surely his eyes deceived him, but when she spoke, he had to admit she was real.

Flame quickly turned his face to hide his scars, but it was too late. She had already seen them.

"Boy, knock it off! I didn't come to see your face; I came to help your soul."

Kim Rawls reached for Flame, and he flinched, waiting for the blow. The last time he had seen her, she had thrown a drink in his face.

Kim laughed, pushed his hand away, and gave him a tight hug. "I should smack you upside the head, but you've suffered enough. Come on and let's go in here. We got a lot to talk about."

Ten minutes later, Flame was settled in his bed and Kim sat beside him in a chair. 8-Ball stood by the door just in case Kim had come with bad intentions.

"How are you holding up, Flame?" Kim asked. She could feel the negative energy leaping off of him, and his head was turned away from her.

"I'm all right," he lied.

"You don't sound like you're all right, but guess what? You will be."

Flame scoffed, "Oh, yeah, how you figure?"

"I want you to look at me when I tell you." Kim reached for his face and wrestled with him until she forced him to look directly at her.

Even with a busted eye Flame could still see her beauty. Her chocolate skin seemed to be radiating, and her luscious scent titillated his senses. Her pretty face made him feel even more self-conscious of his scars.

"What do you want, Kim?" Flame asked with agitation. He tried to wrest her hands away from him.

"Stop it, Flame—"

"My name is Joey."

Kim smiled. "O-kay . . . Joey." She nodded as she tried the name on. "I like that. That's even better. Joey. Yes, we're doing away with the pretenses."

Kim lightly clasped Flame's face inside her manicured fingers. "Joey, I came to tell you that despite what you may be feeling, God loves you, and God's love is pure and true."

She said this with so much conviction that Flame felt the words in his soul. He'd never been religious; he had born witness to the streets and been baptized in the music industry. Yet, when Kim told him those words, he couldn't deny what he felt.

Kim released his face, and Flame lay back in the bed staring at the ceiling.

"Joey, I didn't want to come here. Lord knows I didn't, but some things are bigger than me *and* you," Kim said. "God spoke to me in my dreams and He said that I must come to you, that you are my assignment." Kim reached out and touched Flame's hand. "Yes, you have wronged me and a lot of other people, but I know your soul is pure. He showed me that your soul is pure, and I believe in Him with everything in me so it must be true."

Standing against the wall by the door, 8-Ball nodded his head to Kim's sermon.

Kim continued to speak while Flame continued to stare at the ceiling. "I don't know what your condition is except what I saw on social media, but I am going to be here until you walk out of here."

Flame chuckled. "Your God must be planning to have you here for a long time, because just in case you ain't heard, I'll never walk again."

A knowing smile spread across Kim's face. She pointed to the ceiling. "But God . . ." Her implications were clear.

Something she said caught Flame's attention. "You said you saw something about my condition on social media?"

"Yes."

"What they saying?"

Kim quickly whipped out her phone and swiped away. When she found what she was searching for, she held the phone out for Flame to see, but he quickly turned away.

"What's wrong with you?" Kim asked.

Flame snapped his eyes shut and shook his head vigorously as if he was trying to hide from seeing the boogeyman. "Nothing," he lied.

"Flame—I mean Joey—look at it."

"Nah, I'm good."

"Look at it!"

Flame covered his eyes with his arm. "I said, I'm good."

"Joey, you have to face your fears to get through this. It's the only way. So much has happened since you came in here. You have to see! There's nothing to fear but fear itself."

Flame reluctantly moved his arm away from his eyes. He saw Kim's phone waiting for him. Slowly, he took the phone and closed his eyes. His hand was shaking like a jackhammer was pumping under his skin.

"Go on, look at it," Kim coached.

Flame slowly opened his eyes halfway . . . then he opened them completely and entered the world again.

Bone opened the gate and walked up the long gravel driveway to the marble building. The cool wind blew the fur on his long mink in the wind and pulled the thick cover up over his neck. As he got closer to the building, he saw flowers, CDs, and trinkets strewn around the entrance of the building from those who had come to pay respects and offer a tribute.

When Bone caught word of people coming to the mausoleum to pray, he thought it was comical. An orthodox Muslim, Bone would have never associated partners with his Lord, Allah (S.W.T.). In the Qu'ran, it was this type of thing that had destroyed nations before. People brought calves, camels, and even children to the holy site in Mecca for sacrifice to their Lord. Islam swept through the region and did away with those practices. Yet, here in the modern era, people were reverting back to the practice of worshipping idols. When Bone read about people resorting to such acts in the scriptures, it was foreign to him. Now, in a state of despair, he understood the need for people to believe in something higher than themselves, something that they could relate to.

Bone could never take his concerns to the masjid for guidance. His mind was preoccupied with money, murder, and malice, and he needed clarity from someone who understood. He needed to pray to receive guidance from the boss of all bosses, King Reece.

Bone stood on the marble steps of the mausoleum and offered a two *raka* salaat toward the East. After he salaamed out, he sat in the final position and opened his palm toward the heavens to offer supplication and receive guidance. He inhaled deeply, and the cool air burned his lungs. He forced himself to zone out from the world to hear the distant voice inside his soul. He closed his eyes and the weirdest thing happened.

He heard King Reece talking to him!

"You repping this shit, my nigga! You giving them niggas hell, looking fly, and you staying true to the game. Don't let nobody trick you off the streets, Bone. I groomed you for this shit. You the second coming of me, but don't let them get you. Watch them niggas that's close to you! Watch 'em! Keep making me proud."

No one could tell Bone that what he was hearing wasn't real. He felt King Reece's words in his core. It was what he came for.

Bone continued to breathe deeply, and right there in broad daylight, the God gave him revelation.

Flame scrolled through Kim's Instagram with hesitation. He had allowed her to bring him back to social media gently, and he had been catching up on her life via her page for about ten minutes. It wasn't as bad as he thought it would be. Fortunately, people had stopped associating her name with his since the tape with him and Sasha was released, so there was very little posted associated with them.

"Okay, you ready now?" Kim asked Flame.

"Ready for what?"

"To see your world now."

Flame shook his head. "Nah, I don't know about that."

"Sure you are!" Kim tugged at Flame's hand. "Joey, it's just social media. Look, you have already survived the worst of things. You are healing more and more each day. Whatever you may see on social media is a testament to where you've been. It's all up from here. Right?"

Flame wasn't so sure he was ready. "Uhh . . . I don't know."

Kim grabbed his hand. "Come on, let's pray on it." Flame allowed her to take his hand, and he tucked his chin to his chest while Kim bowed her head.

"Father God, we come to you today in humble submission, Lord God. We ask that you wrap your arms around us and protect us from any pain we may endure. We pray that you offer your wisdom, guidance, and strength as your son Joey bears witness to your mercy. In Jesus name, we pray. Amen."

Flame was slow to repeat after her, but in a voice barely above a whisper he finally said, "Amen."

Kim smiled and clapped. "Yaaay! See, that wasn't so hard now, was it?"

"I guess."

"Okay, so we're protected now. So whatever you see on here is just a testimony since you already passed the test. Okay?"

Flame nodded.

Kim grabbed the phone and hashtagged his name in the search bar on Instagram.

Immediately, a series of pictures flooded the screen. The most recent photos showed him being wheeled around the hospital by 8-Ball. The Gucci throw covered his legs, but his face was easy to see. In one still, someone had blown up his face to show the world just how mangled his jaws looked. It was an earlier picture that showed the bloody staples in his face on one side, and white gauze wrapped around his forehead like a turban.

"Yo, who the fuck took this picture?" Flame barked.

"Ooh, language, language."

"I'm sorry, Kim, but someone in violation. Ball, you see this?"

8-Ball rushed over and saw the photo. It had been taken just a week ago. "Yeah, I know when this was taken. They in violation, and I'm going to handle it."

8-Ball started toward the door, but Kim stopped him.

"Wait! What are you getting upset for? Joey is a star; they're supposed to take pictures of him. People want to know what happened to him," she reminded them. "We should be mad if they're *not* checking for him."

8-Ball caught what she was saying right away, and he knew what she was doing. Flame needed his confidence back. He needed to be reminded just who the hell he was.

8-Ball joined Kim in her plan. "Yeah, Kim, you right. They just paying homage to who Joey is. Let them take all the photos they want."

Kim caught 8-Ball's attention and winked at him.

"So, come on Joey, let's go over to Twitter and see what they're talking about."

Flame tensed up. He wasn't ready for Twitter. Twitter was a savage land where nothing was off limits. Armchair comedians hurled their best routines at the expense of others.

"I'm good."

"No you're not," Kim said. "What are you worried for? We prayed up. Let me show you the power of my God."

Against his judgment, Flame let Kim take him to the

Twittersphere. The first thing he saw was a clip of Diamond trying to power bomb him through the pavement.

Flame tensed up. Closed his eyes. He had a flashback of being hoisted into the air. He heard the wind screaming in his ear as Diamond swung him in the air like a little child. He saw the bright city lights whirling around him before he felt his back crack.

"Ahhh!" Flame yelled and clamped his hands over his ears.

Kim hopped on the bed with Flame and wrapped him in a loving embrace. She cradled his head on her bosom and rocked back and forth with him.

"Shhh . . . it's okay. It's okay, Joey. I'm right here. God got you. His promise is true. Shh . . ."

She gently removed his hands from his ears and placed them in his lap. Then she leaned on his chest and positioned the phone so he could see the screen.

"You ready?" Kim asked. "You have to do this, Joey."

Flame slowly opened his eyes. Kim scrolled down and allowed him to see some of the comments that accompanied the Sasha video:

"This nigga was killing that pussy!"

"That pussy almost got him killed for real."

"Ain't no pussy good enough to get burnt while I'm up in it."

The accompanying memes were even crazier. There was one meme with the wrestler the Undertaker Tombstone pile-driving a man. Someone had superimposed Flame's caricature on the man getting driven into the mat.

Another meme was a picture of Flame's face battered and bruised with the caption, *"When the husband meets the side nigga."*

Reading the consensus on social media made Flame feel horrible. He felt like an idiot for transgressing the bounds. To make it even worse, here was his betrayal laid out in the open, and he was seeing it with the woman he'd betrayed, while she was attempting to help him.

"It's okay, Joey. I've seen it a million times already. I made peace with it," Kim assured him.

"Yeah, but I don't understand it. Why are you here?" Flame asked.

"I told you, God sent me."

Flame shook his head and sighed. "So . . . I have to ask . . ."

"I'm listening, Joey. Go ahead."

"Where is Sasha? Is she alive or did he . . ."

Kim was silent for a second. Then she answered, "She's alive, but she will never be the same again."

Chapter 23

Qwess looked at the calendar on the wall and ticked off day 26 on the countdown to his extradition. They had waived extradition back to North Carolina, so according to Shabazz, the government had just four more days to move him or he would go back before a judge in New York for a bond hearing. His alleged charges occurred in North Carolina, so even though he was in federal custody, the correct federal jurisdiction to hear his case was in the Fourth Circuit. As he waited, his thoughts were everywhere. He had already turned into bid mode, pumping out pushups each time something surfaced in his head. Exercising made his thoughts flow easier.

Qwess dropped to the floor and pounded out a set of diamond pushups while he processed his thoughts.

Every second of every day Qwess thought about Wave, their streaming company. Since being introduced to the idea, he had been consumed with streaming. The paradigm was shifting in business, and the music business wasn't exempt. The power of the Internet democratized business and changed everything. New rules were being written by the day, and just as it had been on the frontier of the Wild West, whoever struck gold first controlled the rules. Streaming was akin to gold for the music industry. With technology replicating itself every eighteen months, digital products would only become more prevalent, then ubiquitous, then pervasive. Whoever controlled the digital space controlled the new narrative.

Qwess sprang chills every time he thought about the possibilities. His photographic memory came in handy while he was inside as he was able to "see" the figures he had studied before being incarcerated. Based on those figures, he was able to envision a huge ROI, or return on investment. The $30–50 million in startup money would be chump change compared to the impact that Wave would have on the culture. He could easily see a billion. He could use Wave to reset the balance in the music industry, pay them back for what they did to the Cold Crush. With Wave, ABP could be the biggest fish in the biggest pond. But he had to be out of prison to make the moves.

Qwess rolled over and snapped off a series of flutter kicks while his mind segued to the next topic.

This time Qwess thought about his cases. They were both tied together by the tongue of the same informant. He was waiting any day for Shabazz to inform him that the witness was unavailable to testify. So far, that word had not come.

Qwess had issued the order to clean his whole line, soldiers who had put their lives at risk for what he founded. Good, strong men whose only fault was surviving a war that defined an era. Their major folly was that they knew too much and were walking around with too much information in their heads, so Qwess had to air it out. At the time he ordered the purge, he felt no qualms about it. It was well understood that in the Crescent Crew it was death before dishonor. This was their oath, their pledge, their ethos. If they were in the Crew, then they knew the Crew didn't raise no rats. Every man knew the consequences of his acts. So if they were snitching, or knew one of their comrades was snitching, then they deserved the death penalty. That was how he rationalized it anyway. However, he wasn't so sure he'd made the right decision now, despite what Agent Roberts alleged.

When Agent Roberts came to visit Qwess that day, he tried to flip him again. He informed Qwess that Diamond had discovered that Agent Roberts was a federal agent, and now he was on the run. Last they heard of Diamond he was in Africa being protected by warlords. Since the video surfaced of him attempting to murder Flame, and the subsequent videos of Sasha being gang-raped, the feds were really after him. The only thing Qwess couldn't figure out was why they thought he knew information to help them in their investigation. Qwess didn't fuck with Diamond at all! He recalled Agent Roberts's smug look when he told him just like that.

"Well, you gonna wish you knew something, Qwess, because if not, you gonna get the needle," he promised.

"Well, I'd rather get the needle before I turned rat," Qwess spat. "A coward dies a thousand deaths; a soldier dies but once."

Although Qwess felt that to his core, as he stared up at the dusty ceiling he had to admit he wasn't up for going to war. Not now. But when was the time ever ripe for war?

Qwess rolled over and pumped out another set of pushups as his mind drifted to the next subject.

He heard that Flame was doing better, and that eased his heart somewhat. If he would've known Diamond was waiting on him, he would've never sent him to the wolves like that. He knew Flame needed to learn a lesson, but the lesson Diamond doled out was too harsh. Qwess felt Diamond was so overprotective of Sasha because he believed he was her first lover. In the media, it had been reported that Sasha gave her virginity to Diamond. However, Qwess knew firsthand that wasn't true. He knew because he and Sasha had shared one steamy night of passion in Atlanta.

Back when Sasha was contemplating leaving the group,

she reached out to Qwess about possibly signing to ABP. They took a meeting at a downtown hotel during lunch. The conversation flowed so well, they continued discussing business over drinks at happy hour at the hotel. Their bartender was very generous with the libations, and it didn't take long for their lips to get loose. It took an even shorter time for Sasha to accost Qwess as he left the bathroom stall in the men's room. She pushed him back into the stall onto the toilet seat and sat on his lap. She wrapped her toned arms around his neck and kissed him passionately, grinding on his erection. Qwess palmed her soft ass as she sat on his lap—'til this day, the softest ass he'd ever felt—and pulled her to him. Like a smooth criminal, he slid his finger inside her panties and traced an outline around her wet lips. Believing the hype he'd read about her in the media, he only planned to tease her with his experience because, surely, Bible-thumping Sasha wasn't going to do the nasty with him. Sheeeeit, Sasha reached down, fumbled with his slacks, and whipped out his dick like it was hers. She pushed her panties to the side and sank her sweet suction cup right on him. She rode Qwess in the stall like a jockey, and when someone walked in the bathroom, she rode him even harder, moaning to the ceiling so there would be no mistaking she was marking her territory. Qwess hoisted her into his arms, pinned her back to the stall door, and gave her long, deep strokes until he climaxed inside of her. After they were done, they walked out of the bathroom and to their cars as if nothing had ever happened.

After that night, Sasha reached out to Qwess a few times, but he was still on his King Solomon shit and wasn't trying to settle down. He was at the height of his power, and Sasha wasn't a superstar yet so she didn't maintain his interest. Qwess went on doing him—during that time, he was taking down two women a day at times—and he didn't see or hear much of Sasha until the following year, when she emerged with a chart-topping song and a new booty and became a sex symbol. Qwess didn't get caught up in all the hype; he wasn't one of those men that needed validation. He was a silent assassin that didn't broadcast his conquests. So, while the world salivated over Sasha, he had that night in Atlanta to reminisce on.

Qwess smiled at the memory. He chuckled at the fact he was reliving the memory. He had subconsciously relapsed into bid mode. In prison, all inmates had were their memories or their imagination to get them through. Qwess shook off his bid-mode mentality since he had no plans of going to prison.

As soon as he got back down South, he was looking forward to getting the hell out of jail and clearing his name.

After nearly three months in the hospital, Flame had finally recovered enough to be released to his own care team back in Atlanta. This was a joyous day for Flame. He had overcome insurmountable odds. With the type of injuries he had sustained, it was a miracle he was alive. He had beat the odds, but it wasn't easy. If it wasn't for *her*, he's not so sure he would've been able to pull through it all.

Kim had been pivotal in Flame's recovery. She swooped in and prayed him back to his sanity, confidence, and health. Flame had never believed in God before, but Kim had him reading the Bible and putting his life in the proper perspective. She helped feed him food. She worked his legs out to keep the stiffness from settling in, raising them for him and massaging his muscles. She even bathed him in bed and moisturized his skin to prevent bedsores from settling in.

Unknown to Flame, when Kim received word that Flame was being released, she arranged his transportation back down South and even added to his care team. She had done what God told her to do, and now Flame was on the way to becoming a new man.

★   ★   ★

Kim rode beside Flame in the back of the Maybach as they traveled to the airport. His feet were propped up on the bottom of the outstretched chair as they rode in silence. Flame watched the city whiz by, and he reminisced about all the things he used to do in New York City. Funny thing was his recollections repulsed him now. He couldn't believe that he had openly engaged in so much hedonism in such a short life span. Flame was about to be thirty years old, and he had lived the life of someone twice his age. Recalling all the times he had exposed himself made him tremble with fear. *If not for God,* he thought.

The Maybach pulled into the hangar in Teterboro, New Jersey, and rolled to a stop just at the wheels of the G550 jet Kim had chartered. 8-Ball retrieved Flame from the car and pushed him from the Maybach to the G550 jet. It was a cool day, and Flame was bundled up tight with a wool Gucci scarf pulled over the lower half of his face, matching the gray Gucci tracksuit he wore. Right at the base of the steps, Flame stopped 8-Ball.

"Hold up, bro," Flame said.

"What's up? You good, bro?"

"Yeah, I want to take a picture to post on my social media."

Kim and 8-Ball looked at each other skeptically. "You sure?"

Flame beamed his smile at them. "Yeah."

Flame whipped out his phone, put the selfie cam on, and angled it high in the air. 8-ball saw him struggling and grabbed the phone.

"I got you."

8-Ball pointed the phone at Flame, and Flame chunked up the deuces with a huge, bright smile. 8-Ball made sure the Maybach and the G550 were in the background, and he snapped away.

To the left of Flame, Kim beamed like a proud parent. She raised her head to the heavens and mouthed, "Thank you, God."

Flame saw her smiling and beckoned him to her. Kim walked over to him, and he snatched her down into his lap. "Make sure you get this pic too, bro," Flame said and kissed Kim square on the lips.

It was the first time he had touched her intimately since the after-party in Los Angeles.

Bone rode shotgun in Maleek's new Range Rover on Highway 87. Bone had given it to him as a reward for his loyalty. Bone had copped the truck at the auction for less than fifteen bands, but the truck retailed for $70,000. To the streets Maleek was rolling like a boss. Maleek hadn't had the truck for a day before he had the vehicle wrapped in the green of the Crescent Crew. The interior seats were cream in color and soft as baby shit. Maleek couldn't stop cheesing as he drove his big homie around.

"Aye, I appreciate you, brother. I really do," Maleek said.

Bone waved his hands. "Ahh, it's nothing. The Prophet Muhammad said, 'Surely, you would not have achieved faith until you want for your brother what you want for yourself.'"

"Indeed." Maleek merged onto Highway 74 and turned the music down. "Aye, I got a question."

"Shoot."

"So, like, we all Muslim and shit, right? But what we doing is super *haram*. So how do you, like, make the shit right with Allah? It don't be fucking with your conscience?"

This was a question that Bone never had answered until recently. He never felt guilty about a murder because those murders enriched his brotherhood. However, the cabin was a different matter altogether.

"For me, it's easy, little brother. I never did anything to a Muslim—not knowingly, anyway. Most of the people out here are *kafir*, so they lives aren't equal to a Muslim. It says in the Qu'ran that one day the believers will have to wage war against the disbelievers. So by us doing what we do, we weakening their army already. Feel me?"

Maleek nodded.

"If I'm being totally honest, though, that cabin shit fuck with me. Even though they were rats and snakes, they still not my teachers," Bone added.

"Yeah, but a rat can kill a snake and a snake can kill a human if you don't keep the grass cut," Maleek reasoned. "So, we did what we had to do."

"Yeah, no doubt."

The men rode the remainder of their journey in silence until they pulled up in the Creekwood community again.

In Creekwood, Maleek hopped out of the truck and walked inside Keisha's spot like he owned it. A few minutes later, the two of them emerged hand in hand. Even though Maleek was technically booed up, he was still on point. As he walked back to his Range, his head swiveled in every direction something moved. This impressed Bone even more with the young lad, because when Bone was his age, he definitely would've been mesmerized seeing Keisha in the tight jeans, Ugg boots, and short bomber coat. Her natural walk was seductive, slinging hips and ass like she was slanging hips and ass.

Maleek opened the back door for Keisha to get in the truck. He helped her inside then hopped in the driver's seat and headed downtown by the Boardwalk.

Maleek pulled into the Hilton on Front Street. He passed Keisha a wad of cash and made her go pay for two rooms. As she was checking in, Bone observed everything.

"Aye, I like her, little brother," Bone said.

"Yeah? Me too. That ass fat!"

"Nah, though, I ain't just talking about that. Fat asses come a dime a dozen when you a boss. You gotta start judging these hoes by a different standard. You need to fuck with bitches that worship the ground you walk on. Fuck what she look like," Bone schooled. "Them pretty bitches be the most disloyal ones because it's ten niggas lined up to take your place. Shit, she can't turn *all* the niggas down. Maybe two or three, here or there, but ten? Nahhhhh!"

Maleek laughed. "I can dig it. So what about her, though? She bad than a muthafucka. Why you say you like her?"

"'Cause she don't know she bad yet. What she, like twenty?"

"Just turned twenty-one."

"Yep, a muthafucka that fine a nigga would've been snatched up and hid her away somewhere. So either she green as hell or she shy as hell. Either way it works for you."

"How so?"

"'Cause she ain't never seen a nigga like you. You see this town? Niggas getting money but they not on no next-level shit. You can take her and turn her all the way up. Have her the shit out here. Then, everybody gonna know you the reason. So what that gonna do for you?"

Maleek chuckled. "Create enemies."

Bone twisted his mouth. "Niggas don't want these problems. On this level niggas don't bring real beef; they congratulate and try to get down with the team."

"Word."

"Yep, and when you lock her in, you can slide back down here and turn the lights on in the whole city on a pull-up."

Maleek liked the sound of that, but there was only one problem. "Wait, what about Twin, though?"

"Ah, I think I'ma move Twin somewhere else. He from here, so he might be more loyal to the city than the Crew. I mean, he performing, but it's obvious to me he more concerned with looking like he the man than actually getting to it."

They saw Keisha round the corner and walk toward the truck. The sun setting at her back created a silhouette of her shapely body. Both men stared in awe at the brilliance of God's creation.

"Yeah, brother, lock her young ass down the right way and she'll jump off the moon for you," Bone coached.

Keisha slid into the backseat and passed two keys to Maleek. "We in rooms 646 and 647," she informed them.

"Cool," Maleek said as he discreetly slid Bone a key.

"Yeah, y'all go ahead in. I'm going to run around the block to the store," Bone said.

Maleek helped Keisha from the truck and followed her inside.

Bone called Maleek's name.

Maleek turned around. "Yo?"

Bone showed all thirty gold teeth. "The moon, my nigga. The moon," he reminded him.

Both men shared a laugh.

As soon as Maleek and Keisha walked into the hotel, Bone went inside and checked into room 734.

The way he was feeling, he didn't trust nobody.

As eagerly as Qwess was looking forward to being given a bond in New York, that would not be the case. The federal marshals came and transferred him like thieves in the night. Because he was considered a high-risk inmate, special precautions were taken to transport him. Two heavily armored vehicles shadowed the black Suburban that held Qwess along with three U.S. marshals that whisked him to the airport. At the airport, a black bag was placed over his head, and he was shackled at the waist until the plane took off.

Three hours later, they landed in Fayetteville, North Carolina, under the cover of darkness, and a silent police escort took Qwess to the Cumberland County jail, where he was only one of four federal inmates.

The next day, Malik Shabazz came to visit him bright and early. He had urgent news.

"Salim, AMG is willing to settle this thing out of court for forty-five million dollars," Shabazz reported with enthusiasm. "But you have forty-eight hours to accept the offer."

This was not what Qwess expected to hear at all. He was looking forward to hearing Shabazz say he'd won the case. Instead, he was coming with an "offer" that required him to carve up his empire.

"Shabazz, what am I not getting that makes them feel as if they have a chance in court?"

"Court can go fifty-fifty. Always. And as you know, trial isn't about right or wrong. It's about who can *prove* their case."

"Right. So what can they prove?"

"They can't prove anything yet."

"Okay then."

"But . . . we can't prove anything either."

"Brother Shabazz, I just gave you a million dollars. I sat patiently in jail for a month while you figured this thing out, and still we don't know who is telling. At some point, the rubber will have to meet the road."

"I agree. They promised me I will have full discovery within the next week.

"Good, so come back to me when you have that discovery. In the meantime, you go tell AMG's attorneys that they can take that settlement offer and suck my dick with it!"

Bone overlooked the ocean from his room on the seventh floor as he waited on a call. The waves crashing against the shore should've soothed his mind, but he was too lost in his thoughts to pay the waves any attention. King Reece's words rang in his ear as if he was in the room with Bone, exhorting him to act. The God King Reece had told him to go hard or go home, rep the Crew like he was doing. He had told him to watch those close to him. Did he mean Qwess was sour?

Bone's contact at the county jail had relayed to him that
Qwess was back in North Carolina being held in PC downtown. So why didn't Qwess reach out to him? Was this con-
firmation that he was ready to go left on the Crew?

Bone's burner phone buzzed to life. He read the text and
returned a text with his new room number. Then he sent the
same text to Maleek. A few minutes later, Maleek tapped on
the door. Bone opened the door for him, and Maleek walked
in with a knowing smirk. Bone nodded, and the lesson was
passed along telepathically. Game recognized game.

"What's up?" Maleek asked.

"Twin on the way up."

"Okay, cool. He good?"

"Yeah, for now he good. Let's see how he act when I
break this news to him."

Someone rapped on the door. Maleek confirmed it was
Twin, then he opened it.

Twin walked in looking like the definition of ostentatious.
He wore a bright yellow silk Versace shirt, yellow slacks, and
black alligator shoes. Around his neck was enough diamond
jewelry to make Mr. T's neck look like a priest's collar. Not
one but two Rolexes jangled on his left wrist, and diamond
pinky rings twinkled on *both* hands. He held two Louis Vuit-
ton duffel bags in each hand. The money inside was so hap-
hazardly wrapped that stacks of it jutted from the sides of the
bag visibly.

Bone looked Twin up and down, unable to hide his disgust. *Who the fuck recruited this clown?* he thought.

"Aye, Big Homie, I got that for you right here," Twin
said before he even closed the door shut.

Bone snapped, "Nigga, what the fuck is wrong with you?"

"Akh, why you talking to me like that?"

In two long steps, Bone was on Twin. He jacked him up

by his Versace shirt and slammed him against the wall. As soon as Twin's back hit the wall, Maleek had his Sig Sauer out and pressed against Twin's forehead.

"How the fuck you come to drop dough off looking like a fucking Miami drug lord? Are you fucking crazy? Mother-fuckers could be watching us right now. We at war with motherfuckers, and our fucking founder is in the feds right now. Do you not know what the fuck is going on?" Bone roared.

Twin raised his hands slowly. "Akhi, I'm sorry. I was just going to the club when we leave here."

"We? Who the fuck is 'we'? I ain't going to no fucking club!"

"Nah, I got my girl in the car," Twin mumbled, embarrassed.

Bone released Twin from the wall and flailed his hands in exasperation. "This nigga trying to get cased up."

"Yo, take them bags back outside with you. Whatever is in there someone will get from you later."

"Huh?"

"Yeah, that's what I'm saying. Hand me that jack and roll out. And don't never embarrass me like this again."

Twin passed Bone the phone, and Bone dismissed him. He shot Maleek the head nod, and Maleek followed him out. No sooner than the door closed, the phone rang. It was Samson.

A few hours after Shabazz left, Qwess received another visit from Doe and Lisa Ivory. By now the whole jail was abuzz with the word that their hometown hero was among them. Because he was in PC no one really saw Qwess, but when word spread that Lisa Ivory was in the building, the jail went berserk. They quickly ushered Lisa and Bone in the attorneys' room and left them alone.

Lisa rushed Qwess and hugged him tight enough to break him. "My king, are you okay? We're worried sick about you."

Qwess kissed her deeply and assured her that he was fine.

"I came as soon as I could," Lisa said.

Doe gave Qwess a pound and a hug. "Man, what is Shabazz talking about?"

Qwess sighed. "Some bullshit."

They sat at the table, and Qwess ran down what Shabazz had told him.

"That's bullshit, bro," Doe said.

"Yeah, I know, but it is what it is now," Qwess said. "You and my dad spoke with Liam, right?"

"Yeah. He's ready."

"So everything is in place?"

"He says so."

"Okay, what's the final number?"

"Fifty."

"And that will cover everything we need to move forward?"

"Yep."

Qwess pondered for a moment. That $50 million would wipe him out, but it was an investment he would see within the year. Qwess knew he needed to decide immediately because timing was of the essence. Liam had relayed to him that someone had recently filed a patent similar to the technology they possessed. Now it was a race to the market. With the $50 million they could be operational inside of a year.

Qwess looked to Doe. He squeezed Lisa's hand, and his eyes blazed with fire as he made an OG call.

"Release the funds to start Wave."

"Can you believe this nigga?" Maleek groused to Bone as they drove back to Fayetteville from Wilmington at the crack of dawn. "Fuck was he thinking coming in there dressed like that?" Maleek shook his head. "When we came outside and he put the money in the truck, his chick was rubbernecking hard as hell."

"Speaking of chicks, I heard you tearing ole girl ass up over there last night," Bone said, smiling.

"Hell, yeah; you said lock it down, so I had to put it down."

"Indeed."

After Bone spoke to Samson, he had switched his room to the first room Keisha had reserved for them. He heard Keisha climbing the walls, screeching like a cat all night. Of course he wouldn't have been able to sleep anyway.

Samson had dropped a load on Bone. He once again scolded Bone as if he was a child, then he ordered Bone to have a sit-down with some big shot coming all the way in from Mexico to call a truce. Supposedly, this man was second-in-command of the Michoacán cartel, and if the truce was accepted, then he would turn the pipeline back on. Then the Crescent Crew could stop getting their heroin from New York. Things would be back to normal. No war, new plug meant more riches.

Samson also told Bone that the word on the block was that Qwess was not to be trusted. Qwess had met with a federal undercover agent twice while he was in jail in New York. No one knew for sure what was said, but inside the bureau they were excited about the prospect of flipping the founder of one of the largest Black crime cartels in the history of the United States. Even though this news was mind-blowing, it was the last thing Samson told Bone that had him spooked.

Samson relayed to Bone that he had been told someone had lured their comrades to the mountains, someone close to them. Samson suspected that it was Qwess, but he couldn't confirm anything yet. However, he assured Bone when they spoke again he would know everything.

Bone was shook. It was only a matter of time before it all fell down. If Qwess was sour, he was fucked. If Samson discovered he killed their comrades, he was fucked. If he screwed up the truce, he was fucked. At every angle he turned, he was fucked.

Bone made up his mind right then: he would be a dick before he became a swallower.

Chapter 24

Flame's Southern home was located in Johns Creek, just outside Buckhead, Atlanta. The 15,000-square-foot, five-bedroom, seven-bath home was centered on six acres of land, equipped with every amenity possible for a young bachelor. There was a full-court basketball space where Flame used to host naked basketball tournaments. There was also a tennis court for the bougie chicks in his rotation. In the back of the property was a track and obstacle course to race his quad runners. In the basement of the home was a shooting range. And of course the huge infinity pool that ran off into the lake on the property. When Flame purchased the property he had added $1.8 million in recreational upgrades. Now, all of that money was wasted, since he was now confined to a wheel-chair.

Flame had been home for a week, and he was still finding it hard to adjust to his new way of life. His physical therapist was scheduled to come over for their first workout session in the pool. The pool would make it easier for him to move around. This session would give a better indicator of if and when he would be able to use his legs again.

Kim had been with Flame every day since he'd been home, right along with 8-Ball. The picture 8-Ball took of Flame and Kim at the hangar had gone viral, and the entertainment world was buzzing like a pack of bees. Some of the sentiments were shady, but for the most part everyone was just glad to see Flame out of the hospital. He or anyone from the label had yet to issue an official statement on his condition or his plans to return to the music world. Given everything Qwess was facing, there was no wonder why.

When Flame heard what was happening with Qwess, he was shocked. He didn't believe one thing they alleged, of course, but he was in no shape to focus on that. He knew Qwess was capable of handling himself. He had to take care of himself too.

Flame sat in his motorized wheelchair on the terrace overlooking the pool. He heard his front doorbell chime through the outdoor speaker. He figured it was either Kim returning from Lennox Mall or his physical therapist.

He continued to peer out over the lawn when he heard footsteps behind him.

Then he heard her voice. "Hi, Flame."

Chills zipped through his body, and he froze.

"I know I'm the last person you want to hear from, but I need to talk to you."

Flame curled his lip. "You got some nerve showing your face here. If I wasn't confined to this chair I would kill you right now."

"I understand," she said. Her voice crackled like a broken speaker. "If I were you I would feel the same way."

"So why are you here?!"

She whimpered like a scared puppy. "Because I have to talk to you."

"I ain't got shit to say to you!"

Sasha Beaufont walked around the deck and stood in front of Flame so he could see her, so he could see the marks of regret she wore too.

Sasha's lower jaw was shaped awkwardly, like she was sucking on an anvil. A long, jagged scar ran down her face, and her hair was shaven, showing the scars where staples had been in her scalp. A hard cast was on her left arm from her wrist to her elbow.

Sasha presented her scars to Flame like a gift. "I'm so sorry, Flame. I never meant for any of this to happen. I'm so sorry." Her eyes swept over his visible injuries and rested on his legs. "Oh, my God! Look at you."

"Yeah, look at me," Flame repeated. "Why, Sash? Why did you do it? Why did you fuck up our lives?"

Sasha looked down at the gray granite tile on the deck floor. For a while she said nothing. Then she broke down. "I did it for love; that's why I did it."

Flame cocked his head, confused. "Love? So you fucked me, stole the tape, and uploaded it to show your love for Diamond? That doesn't make any sense!"

Sasha shook her head. "Not Diamond."

"Who then, 'cause you damn sure don't love me."

"Qwess . . ."

"Qwess? The fuck he got to do with this?"

Sasha cupped her mouth with her good hand. "He's my daughter's father."

"Daughter? Since when do you have kids?"

Sasha nodded vehemently. "It's true. Qwess and I had a one-night stand years ago, here in Atlanta. We had unprotected sex in a restaurant."

"A restaurant? Damn, you just busting it down, Jezebel!"

"We left and went our separate ways. He didn't know

he had impregnated me, and I didn't tell him. I fell back off the scene before I started to show. That's when I met Diamond.

"I couldn't hide my pregnancy for long, and I don't believe in abortion, so when Diamond and I decided we would be together, I confided in him about my pregnancy. By then the paparazzi had already caught wind of our romance. The relationship rumors boosted both of our careers like crazy. Overnight we were on the covers of magazines: Beauty and the Beast. We both had albums on the horizon, and this new publicity put us in a different audience, so we decided it would be best to keep me out the spotlight until after I gave birth. We thought about giving her up for adoption, but when she was born and I took one look at her, I couldn't do it. Of course, Diamond was heated. He thought I didn't do it because I loved Qwess—and he was right. That is why he hates Qwess so much . . . and you."

"Me? I ain't do shit to him."

"Yeah, but Qwess rode your talent to the next level. After he retired, you kept those lights on in that building. Your music was what enabled him to make all those investments and stay on the top of the game."

That statement stoked Flame's ego. It was one thing for him to feel as if he was the shit. It was another thing for someone else to say it.

"So why did you take the tape, Sasha? Why did you post it?"

"To get back at Diamond and to torch my bridge to Qwess."

"What?"

"See, me and Diamond had gotten into it again because I told him he was wrong for using you to get back at Qwess—Qwess hadn't done anything to him for him to want to get back at him! So, yeah, he was mad. Accused me of wanting to sleep with you. I told him, I should. And he said that no one from your camp wanted me because I was 'spoiled goods.' He said, you wouldn't sleep with me because you were afraid of him. So I felt like I had to show him, and the tape would be proof."

"And Qwess? What did he do?" Hearing Sasha confess her sins made Flame feel better in a weird way.

"Qwess snubbed me at the last Gumball 3000. I saw him in Las Vegas, and this was the first time we'd been in the same room since Atlanta. I was feeling all giddy, because as I watched him, he looked just like my daughter. Well, she look like him. She walk like him, move her hands like him . . . She has his ears and his nose. I wanted to tell him about Aminah then, but he acted as if I didn't exist. So, I figured what better way to make him pay for ignoring me than to sleep with you."

Flame shook his head in disgust. All this time he thought he was bagging her; she was bagging him. She had used him and everyone else as a guinea pig, all for what she thought was love.

"So why has no one seen this daughter?" Flame asked.

"You have. The media thinks she is my niece."

Flame recalled the little girl he'd seen Sasha with on Instagram. Come to think of it, she did resemble Qwess!

Hearing Sasha's story saddened Flame, but it didn't absolve her for ruining his life.

"What happened to you that night, after . . ." Flame gulped down the memories. "After he did this to me?"

Sasha closed her eyes and fell silent. Tears cascaded down her cheeks. "Everything," she whispered. "Everything mankind can do to hurt a woman was done to me. He crushed me physically, mentally, emotionally, and, for a time, spiritually."

While she spoke Flame examined her scars and tried to imagine what type of punishment inflicted the marks.

"He turned me into a slave, a whore, a punching bag, a doormat, a Frisbee, and a . . . thing."

"How did you escape?"

Sasha shook her head. "I didn't. He let me go."

"Why would he do that?"

"That's the other reason I came here. Diamond let me go because he wanted me to see Qwess fall from grace."

Flame was confused. "Fall from grace how?"

"Someone from Diamond's old network in New York is supplying the Crescent Crew drugs while they work out a dispute with their old supplier."

"Okay, but Qwess isn't active anymore, so what does that have to do with him?"

"Apparently, someone in Qwess's camp flipped and turned state on him, and Diamond knows all about it. Qwess is being sued for seventy-five million dollars from AMG, and he is being held on kingpin charges all behind this one person."

"Who is it?"

"Diamond knows and his supplier in New York knows, but he isn't telling anyone."

"Wow! So what now?" Flame asked.

"Now she leaves!" Kim said from behind Flame. She had been standing just inside the house listening to everything for the past ten minutes. "She is responsible for all this, and she promised me she wouldn't reach out to you again. Ever."

"I'm sorry, Kim, but he had to know everything!"

"Well, now that he knows, you can get the hell out, Sasha. And don't ever come around here again."

"But—"

"But nothing. Get out!"

Kim pointed to the door. Sasha lowered her head and limped toward the front door.

★   ★   ★

Qwess was roasting with anxiety as he followed the guard through the bowels of the jail. His heart was heavy, but his mind was clear.

Shabazz had paid Qwess a visit earlier in the morning and dropped a bomb in his lap. He now knew the source of all of his troubles.

The guard led Qwess down a long corridor that reeked of old food and suds. Qwess ducked beneath some pots dangling overhead and walked through a metal door. Through the door was another hallway.

The guard stopped at a door in the hall and pointed at it. "He's in there waiting on you. I'll be back to get you in ten minutes."

Qwess opened the door and came face to face with Bone.

"*As-salaam alayka*, OG!" Bone said. He hugged Qwess then kissed him on the forehead—a term of endearment in Islam.

Qwess returned the greeting and peered around the supply closet to ensure they were alone.

"I'm by myself. I came as soon as I got your message. What's up?"

"Maaaaaan, you not gonna believe this shit!" Qwess hissed. "Them niggas trying to take me out, bro. They both signed statements on me. Both of 'em."

"Who?"

"Man, I brought them country niggas up out the woods. I put some dough in their pockets and made 'em men again. And this the thanks I get?"

"Who, OG?" Bone was heated just thinking about the betrayal.

Qwess frowned and shook his head. "They made me kill my brothers, man. I should've known it was them, because

they were the only two people that knew all the intimate details."

"Who, OG? Who the fuck is 'they'?"

Qwess calmed down. He placed both hands on Bone's
shoulders and spat out the names of the snakes that bit him.

Chapter 25

Bone sat at the table in his office at the strip club hours after Qwess had told him the news. From the moment the words tumbled from Qwess's lips it all made sense to Bone. That's why he was trying to plant seeds of doubt in Bone's head, making him think that he was a defecting leader. That's why he kept pulling rank. He was gauging Bone's reaction to see if he was drunk with power—and thus, a threat, or if he would hand over the reins of the Crew without a power struggle. Bone suspected if he showed any hesitation, he would get rid of him also.

Now Bone knew the purpose of the sit-down with the Jefe from Michoacán. He wanted Bone to reopen the pipeline to prove his allegiance so the Crew would be stronger than ever when he came home early. Bone also understood why he had Twin to ride up from the Port to attend the meeting also. Twin was his eyes and ears.

Well, Bone couldn't wait to get the meeting started.

"Yo, is that them out there?" Bone asked Maleek. It was just after seven p.m. on a Monday, the only day the club was closed, and they were all alone as they awaited their party.

"Yeah, I think so."

Maleek trotted downstairs and returned minutes later with Twin and three Mexican men trailing him upstairs. It was clear to see who Jefe was by the way the others deferred to him. Jefe occupied the middle of the line, and while the others' eyes darted anxiously around the club, Jefe was cooler than the other side of the pillow. His huge iced-out belt buckle and gold chain flashed beneath the kaleidoscope of lights whirling around the club.

Bone met the men at the top of the stairs. He issued his salaams to Twin then opened his arms wide to Jefe.

"Jefe! Bienvenido a Los Carolinas!" Bone said. *"Vente, vente."*

Bone helped the men get settled at the table. He poured them liberal amounts of tequila and took his spot at the head of the table opposite Jefe. Bone saw Jefe's beady eyes taking everything in, but he didn't say a word. One of the minions mumbled something to the other, and Bone could've sworn he heard him call him a *mayate*, but he didn't trip. He took it all in stride and got down to business.

"Gentlemen, I appreciate you coming all this way so we can resolve this issue and get back to the money," Bone began, but he noticed as he spoke that the men weren't taking him seriously. He also noted the smug look on Twin's face.

"I would first like to extend my apology for what happened to Chabo; I'm sure he was very valuable to your organization, but he murdered our leader and founder, King Reece."

While Bone was speaking, showing respect, the minion leaned forward and spoke to his partner, *"¿Por qué es este mayate hablando todavía?"*

Now Bone was sure he called him the equivalent of a nigger in Spanish. The respect left the room.

"I see you men like to do things the fast way," Bone said. He stood, poured himself a drink, and leaned against the wall beside Maleek. "So let me cut to the chase."

"No, let me cut to the chase," Jefe interrupted in perfect English. "Monstruoso is a very big man in my country. He is very well respected, so on his word I come all this way to discuss business. He isn't interested in doing business with my family when he is released, but I'm afraid I bring you bad news, my friend."

Bone narrowed his eyes. "What type of news?"

Jefe leaned on the table and pointed at Twin. "I am told that this man is the new leader of your organization. I am told that I am to discuss business with him."

Bone smiled. He saw this move coming a mile away. "So why did you come here then?" he asked.

"Out of respect. We wanted to tell you this face-to-face," Jefe said. "From my understanding, you didn't know?"

Bone chuckled. "Yeah, this is news to me."

Twin piped up. "Basically, we will just be switching roles. You'll be to the Ville what I was to the Port."

"Oh, yeah?"

"Yeah, and with this line right here back open, we will be seeing more money than ever."

Bone nodded. "Ahh ha, I see."

No one expected the transition to be this easy. Bone appeared to be taking things in stride, though. He allowed the words to penetrate his skull in silence. The men at the table began conversing among themselves in Spanish while Twin caught up with the scores on the TV on the wall.

Then the calm broke.

"You must be out your fucking mind!" Bone roared.

One of the minions jumped and yelled back at Bone. "¿Estás loco? ¿Tú no sabes quien es este?"

"Tú no sabes quien soy yo!" Bone returned. "Y tú no sabes quien es Monstruoso. Él es un rato!"

"Hey, hey, speak in English." Twin panicked. "I don't understand that shit!"

Twin may not have understood, but the others in the room heard him clearly.

Bone upped the ante on his claim and smacked a piece of paper on the desk in front of Jefe. "Read it."

It was a detailed statement that Samson had signed against Qwess, detailing him as the active leader and founder of the Crescent Crew.

Jefe scanned the document, and his eyes opened as wide as a tire on a truck. His face went from a symbol of inner peace to a mask of confusion.

Twin caught the change in the energy in the room. "Aye, what's going on?" he asked.

"You just overplayed your hand," Bone replied.

"Huh?"

Bone gave Maleek the nod. Maleek raised the Eagle like Donovan McNabb and lobbed two .45 shells right in the center of Twin's forehead. The impact flipped Twin's body backward over the chair where he came to rest on the floor.

Bone pointed at the minion on the left. "Call me a nigger one more time and you'll be beside him."

Bone redirected his attention to Jefe. "Hopefully, now can we get back to the business arrangement we had before when things were good? Oh, and don't worry, the Crescent Crew exterminate our own rats around here. You'll see."

Sasha Beaufont walked to her silver SLR Mercedes in the parking lot of the mall. After she'd bared her truth to Flame earlier in the afternoon, she felt like a ton had been lifted off her heart. She only had one more deed to do to cleanse her soul totally, and that was to inform Qwess about his daughter, Aminah, and reveal Diamond's plot against him. Maybe when he was released on bond, he could go down to Texas and see her for the first time.

Sasha was so lost in her thoughts that she didn't see the giant creeping up behind her until he was right behind her.

The man called her name, "Sash."

Terror ripped down Sasha's spine as she slowly turned around and came face-to-face with the devil himself.

"Diamond—"

Sasha never saw the blow coming as Diamond brought a slap all the way around from Africa and connected with her jaw.

Sasha crumbled to the dirty, cold ground and lost consciousness . . .

To Be Continued